LIKE *a* MAN

without a

COUNTRY

LIKE *a* MAN

without a

COUNTRY

KIRBY JONAS

Cover design by Birgitta Bright

Howling Wolf Publishing
Pocatello, Idaho

Howling Wolf Publishing
1611 City Creek Road
Pocatello ID 83204

For more information about Kirby's books, check out:

www.kirbyfjonas.com
Facebook, at KirbyJonasauthor

Or email Kirby at: **pocatellocowboy@gmail.com**

Manufactured in the United States of America—*One nation, under God*

Publication date for this edition: February 2019
Jonas, Kirby, 1965—
Like a Man Without a Country / by Kirby Jonas.

ISBN: 978-1-891423-36-9
Library of Congress Control Number: 2019900323

Dedicated to all the veterans of the Vietnam War who returned to a country they no longer recognized

And to the Americans of African descent who were made to feel as if they were something less.

CHAPTER ONE

Thibodaux, La Fourche Parish, Louisiana

♦ *1973* ♦

Tuesday, January 2

Slugger Janx should have hated the color white. His father, Charley, and his mother, Martha May, filled their home with a collection of things that were white, from the refrigerator, to the stove, to the deep freeze, the living room carpet, and even one of their couches—not stark white, but cream. His parents bought vanilla ice cream, and it was a rare day that they bought topping, but even then it was caramel or strawberry.

His childhood and teenage years were filled with white, from white notebook paper, to white shoes, and even white underwear. His whole life he had been told that because his skin was nearly the shade of chocolate cake he would never amount to anything, while his white school mates naturally were destined for glory—more or less. Yes, Slugger Janx had every reason to hate white, but he didn't.

He sure did envy it sometimes, though.

Tall and broad-shouldered, disdained for his color and feared for his temper and his strength, Slugger Janx was known only to his mother and Pastor Williams by his real given name: Bryant.

Slugger sat on a rusty galvanized garbage can in front of a nameless café on Bayou Street, where only the poor people came to eat, mostly poor *black* people. And he hardly had enough money anymore even to eat there. He wished he was back in Vietnam, back at USARVIS, or what he and the guys all called Camp LBJ—literally standing for Long Binh Jail, but by some ironic twist of fate the same initials as a United States president despised and hated by Army grunt and officer alike.

Lyndon Baines Johnson had been no friend to the troops in Vietnam.

It was the second of January, and still pushing eighty degrees. The humid air pressed down on Slugger and smelled sweet, the smell of warm trees and moss and the sluggish waters of the Bayou La Fourche, which glided by just behind the café. But the air coming out of the café wasn't quite so sweet; overpowering the smells of Cajun cooking were the odors of rancid grease and the acrid smoke thereof.

To no surprise of Slugger's, he once more saw the 1965 Mercury Park Lane Marauder turn the corner two blocks away and start down Bayou Road toward him. It was a convertible, and it had everything. Best of all, it wasn't white, although the top would have been, if it was up. This car was light blue and shone in the Louisiana sun like a piece of sky plopped straight out of heaven. Unfortunately, it was filled with white, long-haired hippie freaks, as he and the guys coming back from Nam called them—and they seemed like something that had climbed straight out of hell.

Those hippie freaks hated Slugger Janx's guts. Not because they knew him, but because he was a Negro, and a Vietnam vet.

A baby killer.

Not only was Slugger not surprised to see them, but he had actually hoped they would return. It was the only reason he had come back here today—hoping for another chance. They would come jabbing their fingers in his face, screaming at him. The day before, the young man in the front passenger seat had even spat in his face.

They claimed they were "pacifists," and Slugger was a murderer of babies. He wondered how pacifist they would be today.

All of them were about to find out.

The day before, the six total strangers had taken him by surprise. He had been greeted with the same vile hatred at the airport on his return from Nam two months ago. Foolishly, he had thought that was the end of it. He had served his country! He should have been hailed a returning hero. What was wrong? Why were he and his pals hated so bad here in their own country?

He had been removed from Vietnam because they didn't want him there anymore. He had finished his tour. And he had returned to a United States that didn't want him anymore either.

Slugger Janx felt like a man without a country.

But Slugger was done being pushed. His back was up against the wall. He was on his turf here, and here he would take a stand.

"Hey! It's the nigger again! Baby killer! Baby killer!" Heads jutted out of the Marauder's windows, and the taunting began when the car was still a hundred feet down the road.

Slugger stepped lazily off the garbage can. He flexed his right hand. Today, he was wearing not only the same four pocket fatigue jacket he had been wearing the day before, but his Army pants and boots as well. He was a soldier! He was not going to run.

The Marauder vomited out four long-haired young men and two blond women with Jane Fonda page boy haircuts. He doubted there was one of them over twenty, and they acted thirteen.

They came at him with violent gestures, poking their fingers at him, telling him they didn't want "his kind" in their neighborhood. They were worked up on booze, or something bigger. They were brave. Invincible.

The dark-haired leader wore a many-hued shirt, untucked at

the waist, with an overpowering collar that could jab someone's eye out, and flare-legged jeans. He looked like the type who had to talk loud and bold in hopes that no one would notice his limbs had the circumference of a wooden match.

Marching at his shoulder was a longer-haired blond cohort with a long-sleeved purple shirt and narrow-legged black and white-striped pants that ended in ridiculous looking tan and brown platform shoes. "Mr. Shoes" wasn't going to last five seconds when the action started.

The other four were just as loud as the mob leaders, but they hung back behind them. Maybe somebody in the group actually had enough sense to understand that if a soldier could fight in Vietnam he could fight in America.

Flared Pants got up close to Slugger's face, no more than two feet away, and screamed at the top of his lungs, "HEY, BABY KILLER! I thought I told you we didn't—"

Slugger thought maybe he had intended to say they didn't want him here, but since thanks to Slugger's knee he was now carrying his family jewels somewhere up around his solar plexus, all of a sudden he no longer seemed interested in having a conversation about the pros and cons of going to war in a foreign country.

Without a chance for anyone to do anything but gasp, Slugger turned and drove the heel of his army boot in a sideways kick into Mr. Shoes' knee, making his leg cave in, and making Mr. Shoes go screaming down on his ear, as if the asphalt must have something intriguing to say.

Like a clutch of new chicks, the other four scattered as Slugger stepped close and grabbed Flared Pants by the front of his shirt. Like an old pro trained by the wild and hateful black prisoners he had guarded at Long Binh Jail, Slugger hawked up mucus and returned the same favor Flared Pants had done for him the day before, then screamed in his face: "Look, boy, it's the same color as yores!"

He whirled again as Mr. Shoes was trying to get up on his good knee and kicked him in the side of the face. He wasn't sure, but he thought he heard something crack.

The other four were screaming obscenities at him, yelling for help from any passerby, none of whom seemed to have any inclination to get involved.

Soon, a black Ford pickup appeared and screeched to a stop next to Slugger. A dark-haired man in his mid-thirties with sideburns that would keep a badger warm leaned out the driver's window and said, "Hey, boy, you better get in here 'fore the cops git here!"

The other two men with him yelled their agreement, and Slugger realized they were right. This wasn't going to go well for him if the law showed. He hadn't cared much when he wanted to teach the hippies a lesson, but suddenly he did. He had seen the cages at Camp LBJ. He didn't relish being in a cage here.

He leaped up into the pickup bed, and the pickup spun around and sped away the same direction it had come, out of town. A ways out, they took a farm road too fast, nearly making Slugger fall over the side. They were now heading north, and they bumped along for a few miles over terrible washboard road.

Slugger breathed a big sigh. He wanted to laugh, but he was still too worked up. He had just done what he had set out to do, but now it didn't feel as good as he had thought it would. What he really wanted most of all was to be left alone. He was surprised by but thankful for the kindness of the men in the pickup. Maybe things weren't so bad after all.

They left the last of the farm fields and entered an area where trees loomed thick on either side of the road, hiding secrets deep in their shadows. Here the truck pulled over at the first side trail that jutted off into the trees to the right. There was no longer any sign of civilization, so Slugger was going to have to walk a ways to get back home. But maybe the exercise would do him good.

Maybe it would calm his nerves, and perhaps the heat would be blown over by the time he got back to town. Either way, these white men had done him a favor. The cops sure weren't going to find Slugger Janx today.

He hopped out of the truck bed as the three men in the cab got out and shut their doors.

Sideburns met him by the rear wheel well, as the other two started around to the back of the truck. Slugger was trying to decide if he should simply thank these good old boys or if he dared try to shake their hands. He had shaken plenty of white hands over in Nam, where color didn't really mean anything—at least not to him and his buddies.

"Thanks for the help," said Slugger, not knowing how to address these men, who were, after all, white, and not in his league.

Sideburns didn't feint. He didn't even blink. He punched Slugger hard in the mouth, and when he fell backward it was into waiting arms.

Before he could recover from the blow, he saw Sideburns stepping forward, and a fist sank deep in his stomach, taking all his air and making him gag. He felt the men behind him holding his arms, and he heard them laughing. He smelled strong beer and whisky, and he tasted blood.

Sideburns' fists fell over and over, and Slugger felt his head rocking back and forth. He felt a kick to the groin, and the men who held him let go of his arms, allowing him to fall on his knees.

Sideburns delivered a mind-numbing kick to his chest that knocked him on his back, and he saw the blurry sky whirling around him.

"Them idjits back there might be hippies, an' a bunch o' worthless pricks," Slugger could hear Sideburns growl through the terrible ringing in his ears. "But them's still white folks, boy, an' don't you ever fergit that ag'in. You better learn yore place now yore back in the States. That green coat don't mean squat, an' it shore don't mean you got the right to go fightin' with white folks."

Rollicking laughter filled Slugger's head as one last spiteful kick took him hard in the ribs. The laughter continued but faded in intensity, and soon he heard the pickup doors shut.

The pickup started up, blowing black smoke on Slugger Janx, as it backed out to the road, spun around, and headed back the way they had come.

CHAPTER TWO

At three o'clock in the afternoon of January second, Coal Savage and the Mitchell family finished their seven-hour journey from Salmon at the University of Utah hospital in Salt Lake City.

They would be staying overnight, due to the length of time it would take to drive back to Salmon, and Coal would have liked to bring Virgil along on this trip, but he had gone back to school with the other children that morning, so the father-son outing Coal was planning would have to wait at least until the weekend.

On a good note, after church Sunday Coal had gone to Virgil's room, now that Ray Christian had vacated it and Virgil had his realm back to himself, and he had sat down with him to have a talk. It hadn't gone the way Coal would have liked, but he left his son's room satisfied that at least his boy could see he was trying to make amends. Hopefully after he had some time to think about it, his feelings toward Coal would soften, and they could really talk things out and get something settled. Even if getting things settled meant finding a dog for Virgil to call his own, at this point Coal was willing to bend that far. Virgil had been too good of a son to let him drift away over such a thoughtless mistake.

On a whim, Coal had asked Connie what she thought about bringing Todd's family to their home for some kind of New Year's Eve celebration, which would also be sort of a celebration of Todd's coming out of his coma. Of course Connie, the consummate hostess, was amenable to the idea, and Coal had fetched Jan Mitchell and the boys for a homemade spaghetti dinner, complete with salad and garlic bread. It was likely the best that family had dined in some time, and it filled Coal's heart with emotion to watch them put away spaghetti like there was no tomorrow. Sadly, for them it had probably seemed at times like there really wasn't.

Several times during the evening, Coal had caught one or the other of the Mitchell boys eyeing him, and toward the end of the night, when they were all growing really tired, little Jerry had ventured over and leaned up against his leg, resting one elbow on it. Coal took a chance and lifted Jerry up onto his lap, and the little guy went to sleep there against his chest. For quite a while, Coal was hardly able to swallow past the lump of emotion in his throat.

For some odd reason, it was also during that tender moment when Coal thought of Maura and wished they had invited her for their celebration as well. Maura seemed to be finding herself a new life, starting to go on dates and other things Coal had not foreseen, but he still missed her. Sometimes he felt like his heart was no longer complete, without Maura PlentyWounds' almost constant presence in his life. As much as he hated to put himself emotionally out there, he wished now that he had called her to come over, and he wondered why his mother, who had always seemed so obsessed with Maura, hadn't made that suggestion herself. Maybe she knew something Coal didn't—and he sure was not going to ask. In truth, he was half afraid to find out.

All the fond reminiscences ended when Coal laid eyes on Deputy Todd Mitchell, sitting up in his bed with bandages wrapped like a turban around his head. Emotion closed off his throat. He had had a lot of mixed emotions on the trip down here with Jan

Mitchell and the boys, and he had started to fear how he might react when he saw Todd. Fortunately, he had mulled it over enough to be prepared for this moment. It wouldn't do for an underling to see raw emotion in his supervisor's face.

Coal looked down at this deputy who had become ... it seemed strange to think it ... his friend. He wanted to make a snide or cute quip. He wanted to say *something*. But nothing came, and his throat was too tight to say it if it did. It was not that long ago when he thought he was seeing Todd dead on the floor of the Battertons' house. And soon after that when he thought he would spend the rest of his life as a vegetable, at best. He never dreamed he would once more see the crooked smile that now came over Todd's face.

"I guess you weren't expecting to see me wearing a turban like some guru."

Taken off-guard, Coal stared down at Todd for a few seconds. At last, he felt his face break into a grin. "A guru? What kind of stuff have they been letting you read in here?" He might have expected Todd to say something about looking like a *genie*, but a guru? Considering the popularity of actress Barbara Eden, who had played the leading role in the ever-popular *I Dream of Jeannie* before they ceased production in 1970, that would have made sense. Apparently, Todd was a bit deeper than Coal remembered.

The deputy laughed. He tried to keep eye contact with Coal but found he wasn't able to. "So you came all this way down here just to gawk at me, I guess. The freak show?"

"You know it. Actually, I came all this way down here to kick your lazy rump out of bed. I don't remember approving all this vacation time."

Coal was playing around to hide his emotions. He wouldn't admit that to Todd, and Todd, he knew, would be grateful.

Todd reached up his hand toward Coal, who eagerly took it and held on. The cursed tears that came into his eyes could not be helped, and he thought he should go out and get a pop or something before things got pathetic for both of them. And that darn Todd chose now to refuse to take his eyes off his boss.

"So ... You think you'll come back any time soon and try to carry your load?"

Todd dropped his hand and shrugged. His eyes, like his hand, fell away. "There's a good question."

Coal drew up a chair, blinking the last of the unbidden moisture out of his eyes. He was trying to think of something else to say when Todd broke in on his thoughts.

"I wish you'd brought your guitar down here with you. I need some good music."

Coal blinked. "Now say that again?"

"Your guitar?"

Coal chuckled and shook his head. "Yeah, okay, I heard you, but ... How did you know about my guitar?"

"Funny man," teased Todd. "Apparently you forgot how small that valley is. It's all over town that you're a crack musician with the voice of a mourning dove."

Coal couldn't hold back a laugh, but his mind whirled around in a bit of a daze. "All right. You got me. Where in the world did you hear about me singing? Really."

"They were talking about it in Wally's one day."

Coal's mind hit on a thought. *Maura?* Other than her and Connie, or maybe Jim and Betty, he couldn't think of anyone in recent times who had heard him play and sing.

"Huh. Well, I didn't bring it, so I guess your ears will get a reprieve." He scanned the length of the sheet covering Todd and cleared his throat. "So ... Seriously, when do they say you'll be back on your feet?"

After a long, uncomfortable pause, Todd said, "My legs are still numb—from the knee down. My feet tingle pretty much all the time. They want to have me try to get up with a walker and try to move around, to see if the blood will start flowing down there and help it out. But Doctor Zane says it might be permanent nerve damage. They're still trying to figure things out." Todd sighed and looked down at his hands. "Coal, I—"

Now it was time for the emotion to well up in Todd's eyes. Coal waited in silence.

Todd drew in a deep breath. "Man, Coal. I want to be back out on the road with my hat and gun on, driving through the valley. I want to see Salmon again."

When Todd's face screwed up as if in pain, and his emotions broke down, Coal lurched up out of his chair. "Hey, uh ... I'll give you some time, Todd."

He got out of the room before Todd could regain his composure.

*   *   *

When two doctors went back into Todd's room with a couple of nurses, Coal sat down in the waiting room with Jan Mitchell and her boys. Those little guys made Coal smile. Somehow, even in the rotten, rancid stink of the Mitchell home, Jan had managed to clean the little guys up and comb their blond hair down nice and neat. She had fixed herself up, too, and it was the first time Coal thought he had seen her wearing makeup. It wasn't the best job in the world of applying it, but she had tried. Maybelline would give her high praise for that. She also wore a newer light blue dress with flowers on it of a darker blue shade. It appeared to have recently been ironed. Her shoes were white, and from what Coal had seen it was something new for Jan to look so well coordinated.

Coal was sitting there with three boys who seemed like no other boys in the known world because they were so quiet, when he glanced over surreptitiously and saw Jan Mitchell's chin begin to quiver and her eyes well up with tears. She jerked her head the other way, which was the same direction her boys were sitting next to her, like a row of ducks, from biggest to smallest. Her shoulders began to shake, and Coal reached out emotionally and could feel the ache inside her. By now, he knew her well enough to know she was trying to hide her tears from him and at the same time wishing she could disguise them from her boys. But there was no hiding anything from that sharp six-year-old, Bud.

The little guy slowly reached out a hand and put it on his mom's leg. Of course he couldn't have known it was going to make her have to fight harder than ever trying to hold back her tears. She failed, and with her face squinched up like she was in dire pain, she fought to cry in silence.

Coal took a deep breath. He didn't know exactly what to do, but he knew one thing: Jan Mitchell needed somebody. Almost shaking, he raised his right arm and wrapped it tightly around her shoulders.

The explosion of sobs from Jan took Coal by surprise as she turned to him and leaned into him, putting her right arm up around his neck.

He was helpless. As he saw four-year-old Toby come around in front awkwardly to join his brother in trying to comfort their mother, three-year-old Jerry crossed around in front of them all, and to Coal's shock the one thing in all this raw show of emotion that managed to cloud his eyes with tears was when Jerry reached up and took Coal's left arm in his little hands, and leaned his blond-haired head against him.

Later, when a tall, slender man with curly black hair, wearing a doctor's coat, came into the waiting room, he found Jan Mitchell with one of her older boys on each leg, holding tight to her neck, and little Jerry asleep in Coal's arms.

A warm smile crossed the man's face, and he laced his fingers together in front of him. He started to speak in the accent Coal remembered from the phone call telling him Todd was starting to stir. He couldn't place the accent, but he was sure it must be from somewhere in the northeast.

"I'm Doctor Zane. And of course you have to be Sheriff Savage?" The doctor unfolded his hands and held one out to Coal that had long, slender dark fingers sprinkled with black hair. Coal took it and appreciated its warmth and strength. "And you would be Mrs. Mitchell. So nice to meet you." It was plain that Jan had her hands too full to shake.

The doctor pulled up a chair and sat down in front of them, putting himself on their level. "I want you all to know how pleased we are that Todd is recovering so well. I have to be frank with you in saying we weren't always very confident of seeing this kind of change. But I have to warn you that it might still be a while until he can get up and get around well on his own. We are still trying to figure out why he has such numbness in his feet. Now I have to ask something, and I know this is uncomfortable to talk about. If Mr. Mitchell has to stay with us for another month or so, or at least in a convalescent home, is this something that will present a crippling expense for you?"

The words hit Coal deep in the guts. The county would foot all of Todd's medical bills, but that wasn't going to do anything to alleviate the financial strain on his home from not having any wages.

"His medical bills are covered, Doctor. It happened on duty." Coal didn't address the wage issue. It was something he would have to speak of to Jan in private.

"Good. Good. Well, let me at least give you a little encouragement by telling you that although Todd has numbness in his legs and feet, it isn't complete. He can still feel pressure and painful stimulus. And I know it doesn't sound like much, but that is promising. He really has made great progress, and my hopes continue to be very high for him."

That night, Coal put the Mitchells up in a hotel at the county's expense. Then he sat in his room and numbed his mind watching George Peppard solve a crime on Banacek.

Wednesday, January 3

The next day, Coal busied himself around town stopping in at gun stores, book stores, and wherever else he thought would help him kill some time while Jan and the boys stayed at the hospital visiting with Todd. He came back right after noon with hamburgers to join them in Todd's room for a last feast before parting.

After a tear-filled goodbye, the Mitchells filed out of his room. Coal was left standing there alone.

"I'm going to go into emergency hiring, Todd. I don't have any choice. But I want you to know the second you're back on your feet your job will be waiting for you."

Todd nodded, trying to look calm. "Thanks, Coal. For everything." No one was saying anything about his lost wages.

Coal drew in a deep breath. "I need you to know something else, buddy. I know you're concerned about Jan and the boys. Don't give them another thought. I'll take care of them even if I have to do it out of my own wallet."

He shook Todd's hand and left because Todd could no longer speak, and he didn't need to have Coal seeing any more tears.

As he walked down the hall to where Jan and the boys stood waiting for him, he knew in his guts that he had bitten off way more than his wages could chew, promising Todd that he would take care of his family. He had no idea how he was going to fulfill that promise.

But fulfill it he would, at any cost.

CHAPTER THREE

Thibodaux, Louisiana
Tuesday, January 2, afternoon

Slugger Janx woke up with rain, more like a gentle mist, falling on his battered, broken, blood-crusted face. He had been nicked by a bullet once in the jungles of Vietnam on the side of his thigh, but other than that one small flesh wound, he had come away unscathed. Now, ironically because of serving his country, he lay here hurt worse than any time he could remember in his life.

He sat up feeling like he had gone through the cogs of some massive machinery. Old Sideburns sure did pack one mean punch. And work boots didn't seem to agree with Slugger's body and face, either. The rain whispering down on his hair and running down inside his tee shirt reminded him that when he was lulled to sleep by the fists and boots of his rescuers and new-found white friends, the day had been bright, sunny, and hot. Things seemed to change mighty fast in the universe of Slugger Janx.

There was no wind, so the effect of the low-hanging clouds on the atmosphere must be responsible for bringing the smells of the swamps in from down south, and those musty, dank odors lingered in the soupy mist in the trees. Slugger started to get up, but his right knee screamed at him to go to hell with that idea. He paused in a silly position, with one foot and both hands on the ground, his right leg splayed out behind him while tremors of pain shot up and down it.

But Slugger Janx was a Vietnam soldier. He had felt discomfort and pain before, and this was not going to stop him. Gritting his teeth, he got to his feet and stood there swaying, waiting for a wave of dizziness and the pain in his leg to subside.

After a minute or two that seemed like ten, the dizziness was gone, but if he waited for all his pain to go away he might have to hang out here until the Chicago Cubs won another World Series.

Turning, he looked up the side road they had come down and pushed all thought of the long walk ahead of him from his mind. He had to get home and slither into his bed. He had to get some hot soup in him and some heavy blankets over him. Although he continued to sense that the rain was warm, and even as it fell the day remained muggy and hard to breathe, he was shivering all over as his body rebelled. The sooner he got into bed, the sooner he would recover from this beating of his life.

Dragging his half-numb leg along with him only because he couldn't figure out a way to leave it behind, he struggled along until he got out to the main road. He didn't have a watch, but it felt like a death march of an hour. The rain was now only a warm mist, and the sky a paler gray. The moisture had begun to wring from the pine trees a sweet perfume that filled more than Slugger's olfactory senses: It filled his brain. There had been times when he was a child, out walking with his mother, that he would have found this luring scent to be like a piece of heaven. Maybe it still was, but Slugger Janx's life was quickly rotting into hell.

The first two miles dragged by, and Slugger had to stop and rest several times along his odyssey. Once, he found a stump a ways back in the woods and went into the looming shadows to sit down on it, having to keep his right leg stretched out in front of him because it swore to him it would die before it would bend.

Once more, he started back on the highway, leery of any passing automobile. But maybe even sworn haters of black men and Vietnam baby killers would have mercy on him now, seeing the condition he was in. Or at worst, maybe they would simply laugh and point at him and send taunts his way, but not stop to finish him off. After ten or fifteen cars had passed, and no one had stopped, he guessed that was the best he could hope for.

Just when the day looked to be getting lighter, and he made out a lemony spot in the sky where the sun begged leave to shine, more black clouds started to hunch in from the south, and soon the malevolent sky opened up, and sheets of winter rain bore down on him, soaking his clothing the rest of the way to his bones.

Slogging on through roadside mud that was quickly becoming unbearable, he finally glimpsed a few glittering lights in the gloom ahead and realized that the day's darkness was due to more than the dark clouds: It had taken him hours to walk this far dragging his obstinate leg, and evening was fast spilling over the countryside.

Some two hundred yards from the town limits, the edge of where civilization started for Slugger Janx, he heard a car with a stuttering motor that seemed to be chugging out the last of its life coming up from behind. He winced as the car slowed down, then stopped beside him. He looked over to see the passenger side window rolling down.

"Hey, boy! Boy, you hurt?" The speaker was a silver-haired old black man in a silky white shirt that glistened in the half-light like new milk.

Slugger shook his head, blinking at the water that sluiced into his eyes. He swiped at it with a big hand. "No, Pop, I'm all right."

"All right? Hell you say! Boy, yore lips is so swole I c'n hardly understand you." The man's door opened, and Slugger saw a younger man, almost as dark as he, get out of the other side and hurry around the front of the car as the old man reached him.

"Hey, Jeeb, we gotta get this boy outta the weather. Come on, Son, give me a hand." The old man turned back to Slugger, and Slugger was ingratiated to see the concern in his face. "Come on, boy, what the hell happened to you? We gotta get you in the car and warm you up. Lawd, you shakin' all over, like a dog passin' a peach pit."

The old man took Slugger's arm as the younger one, Jeeb, came around behind him and got the other arm. Slugger fought back momentary alarm. These were his own people. They wouldn't be playing a trick on him like Sideburns and his friends had. He would be safe with Jeeb and the old man.

As the old man opened the back door of the once-green, now rusted out Buick, the headlights of another car approached from the direction of town. Jeeb and the old man ignored it, trying to get Slugger into the car out of the rain as fast as possible, until a siren bleeped, and then a red oscillating light fired up out of the gloaming, lighting up the new-coming automobile like a lazy man's Christmas tree.

Jeeb, the old man, and Slugger froze. Through the glare of the bright headlights of the police car, Slugger sensed, more than saw, two dark-clad figures dismount. They stopped just back from the devastatingly bright headlights so they were two blurry figures that couldn't quite be made out.

"Hey, what we got goin' on here?" asked a white man's voice. "Who you got there?"

The old man replied, "Nobody, sir. Just a kid that's in a bad way an' we gotta git 'im in our warm car."

"A kid? Hey, kid," the voice got sterner, and the passenger of the car started forward. When he came around in front of the headlights, Slugger saw his silhouette against the glare, and his silhouette carried a club.

"Yeah, see if it's him, Billy," Slugger heard the driver say. Billy—a fitting name for someone carrying a police club. Slugger cringed and waited.

The police officer came close, emerging into detail as he closed to within a few feet. He slapped the billy club loosely against the outside of his right thigh, looking Slugger up and down.

"Yep, it's him, all right. He's got the G.I. coat and pants on, and the boots they talked about too. But damn, Harry, somebody's worked this buck over but good."

Harry, the driver of the police car, shut his door, a very muffled sound overpowered by the hard rain. He started forward, and when he reached them he quartered around to the side and rear of the old man.

"You two just git yoreselves back in that there car and drive on," Harry ordered. "Don't even think about lookin' back this way."

The old man had just enough bravery to pat Slugger's arm, trying to comfort him. "Sorry, son." He reached out, making a point not to make eye contact with the officers, and shoved the back door of the car shut. Then he moved back warily to his own door and opened it, climbing in. Jeeb walked all the way around the back of the Buick to stay away from the policemen and got in his side without any comment, as if his silence would keep the officers from seeing him.

Their car sped away down the street, leaving Slugger standing there with one officer in front of him and the other to the side, both wearing their dark blue caps low over their eyes. He was careful not to make eye contact and only stared at the ground, but out of his peripheral vision he could see that the second officer also brandished a billy club.

"Listen, boy," said Officer Billy. "We got six white kids that say you assaulted them for no reason a-tall. What do you have t' say about that?"

"No, sir, it wasn't that way. They come at me and was screaming an' spittin' an—"

An excruciating pain erupted in Slugger's right ribcage, and even as he cringed and slammed his eyes shut, arching to the side, he realized the driver of the police car had jabbed him with his club. He felt a hammer blow to the outside of his left knee, and he went to the ground, first on that knee, and then over on his side as he felt Harry shove him hard with his foot.

Lying on the ground in the hard-falling rain, he buried his face under both his arms. He could hear the officers screaming at him, and Billy kicked him in the ribs. Their inarticulate words weren't registering on him. He had to concentrate. Maybe he wasn't obeying whatever orders they were giving. Maybe if he obeyed they would stop.

"I said get on your face, buck!" one of the officers was yelling. Those were the first clear words he got from them.

He tried to roll over toward Billy, but the officer's foot took him in the chest, and he was forced again onto his back.

This time it was clearly Harry who roared at him again: "What's stoppin' you, nigger? On yore back before I split yore head wide open like a melon!"

The officer's hard boot jamming into his shoulder was helpful in that this time it made his attempt to roll over on his face successful. He lay there against the hard wet pavement as he felt more kicks, mostly from Billy.

Then someone's knee dropped like a boulder into the middle of his back, and he felt his ribs dig into the asphalt as he heard a muffled cry from his own lips. "Shut yore mouth, boy! Yore hands! Yore hands!" the words finally registered.

Numbly, he got his hands behind him, and one of the officers slammed handcuffs on his wrists and bound them down way too tight. "All right, now get up!" Slugger tried. His legs wouldn't obey him. It wasn't his fault.

"I said *get up, nigger!*" He felt a kick from Harry again, and then two, maybe three more from Billy, who didn't seem to want to be left out of the fun.

Somehow, Slugger found strength. He lurched upright, and then he felt both of them grab him by the upper arms, and they swept him off his feet so fast he would have fallen straight down onto his face if they hadn't been supporting him.

They marched for their car, his feet too weak to keep up, and he felt himself thrown much too hard against the hood. The air exploded out his mouth, and he gasped like a fish out of water. He could hear one of the men growling, "Pat him down. Pat him down good." And he almost sensed more than heard that they were telling him to spread his feet. He started to do so, but good, hard kicks to the insides of his feet were really what helped the task be accomplished.

Lying against the hot, steaming hood of the police car, he felt himself being grabbed and groped all over, especially around the area of his belt. He heard one of the officers say something about finding nothing, but the words seemed mumbled and far away. Suddenly, a club struck him across the back and shoulders, then again, and again. Each blow seemed harder than the first, as if both of the officers were wielding the clubs, each man trying to out-do his partner. This time, however, no orders came with the blows. This time they were hitting him for the sheer joy of it.

At last, they grabbed his arms again, jerked him upright, and dragged him toward the rear of the car. As one of them opened the door, they shoved him inside, and he struck his head on the top of the door, making white light flash in his brain. They pushed him the rest of the way into the seat, and somebody picked up his feet and heaved them inside as well. Just before the door slammed shut, he heard one man say with a laugh, "I guess that'll teach 'im his place about beatin' on white kids."

CHAPTER FOUR

Wednesday, January 3

On the morning after Slugger Janx's disappearance, when Martha May Janx found her boy lying in his own urine on the floor of a cell in the jail of LaFourche Parish, she would not have recognized him as her son if they hadn't already told her he was the only one in there. A chubby white jailer with sideburns from hell and a red-dish blond mustache a walrus would envy stood several feet from her with his thumbs jabbed down behind his uniform belt. He wore no gunbelt, assumedly so little old ninety-eight pound Martha May couldn't overcome him and take it away.

Martha May's eyes welled up with tears, and her chin started trembling as she laid eyes on her boy and convinced herself who this blob of battered, once-proud manhood was. Martha May's wrinkled skin was a color somewhere between copper, bronze, and chocolate, washed out by an application of cream. Her husband Charley was responsible for the depth of their son's skin color, and even other black people laughed at him and told Charley if he sat in the dark with his eyes and mouth closed it would take a blood-hound to find him.

The jailer glared at Martha May for only a few seconds before growling in a deep but nasally voice of the Deep South, "You shut your mouth and stop blubbering, woman, or yer goin' out. I got more important things t' do than listen to an old nigger woman caterwaulin'."

Martha May knew enough about her world to bite down on her tongue, slam her eyes shut, and hold back her tears until they gave up and retreated into her soul.

She turned and fixed her eyes on the jailer's collar. "Sir, may I go in with him?"

The jailer stood and relished in torturing her with silence. Finally, he said, "I guess so, but start t' bawlin' again an' I'll just walk off an' leave you in there 'til you rot."

He walked close, and the meek old woman edged far to the side, careful that no part of her body or clothing made contact with him because she could not risk any offense. The door squeaked open, and the man spoke like he was talking to a dog. "You got five minutes, then you go home."

Martha May went in the cell. She intuited the jailer's urge to shove her, but he didn't. She assumed that was not so much out of politeness as it was because he didn't want her to contaminate his hand.

Martha May Janx was some seventy years old, she thought. Seventy, sixty, eighty—it was much the same, in her world. Living the life of a modern day sharecropper made a body old, and remembering one's real age only caused them pain. Her knees clanked and rattled as she sank down to the floor by her boy. She thought the hem of her dress might have gotten some of his urine on it, but it was the least of her worries. She was looking at her shell of a son who suddenly she was not so sure would live through his treatment here if she and Charley couldn't do something about getting him out.

Bryant appeared to be unconscious. She whispered his name, and he didn't move. She wanted to reach out and caress his face, the way she had before he went off on the Greyhound to join the Army, so proud to be going to serve his country. But she looked him over carefully, and she couldn't find one place on his face that wasn't bleeding, or swollen, or both, and her touch would only bring him pain.

"Bryant," she whispered, wishing the jailer would leave ... or die. "Bryant, it's Mama. Can you wake up for me?" She never believed he could. She wondered if he would wake up ever again. But to her utter shock, he started to move his hand, and after fumbling around on the floor for a while he found her knee and gave it a squeeze. His eyes appeared too swollen to open.

"I'm good, Mama. I'm good. You should get outta this place. This ain't no kinda place for a lady." Martha May understood the words from Bryant's swollen and scabbed lips only because his brother, Baby, was mentally retarded, and he talked in much the same manner that Bryant was talking now. She wondered if that was one more way that Baby was a blessing in her life—although people told her and Charley that Baby was no blessing at all, but a curse on them for doing something bad.

"This lady can take whatever they gives her, Son. You hear me now? I can take whatever they gives me. What do you need, Son? What can I bring you?"

"You ain't bringin' him nothin'," the jailer growled from the hallway. "Keep talkin' about illegal stuff an' I'll throw you outta here so hard you'll think you sprouted wings."

The outer door opened, throwing a yellow triangle of light into the cellblock before it shut again and keys rattled outside. The jailer and Martha May turned to see in the doorway a squat, florid-faced man in a gray tweed suit and scuffed shoes. He wore a yellow bowtie that contrasted nicely to the redness in his face, even in the dim-lit cellblock.

"Mornin', Puckett. I help you?" asked the jailer.

It wasn't hot in the room. In fact, it was below the cool side. But the newcomer, Puckett, brought a white handkerchief to his cheeks and dabbed them like a dainty debutante touching a napkin to the corners of her mouth after a bite of quiche.

He let his eyes adjust to the dark of the place as they scanned along the row of metal boxes the prisoners of LaFourche Parish called home. "Mornin' yoreself, Mims," said Puckett through lips so loose-sounding Martha May wondered if they could hold spit. "Help me? Oh, Judge sent me t' look at yore prisoner. That'd be him, I s'pose."

Jailer Mims glanced over at Martha May as if checking to see how visible she was in the half-light. "Well ... Yeah. You can see a nigger woman kneeling by him, can't you?"

Puckett stiffened. Martha May meant to look away any time, but that change in Puckett's demeanor kept her attention. "Now you well know Judge don't like that talk, Mims." Puckett's voice wasn't commanding or even loud, and he didn't even look Mims in the face as he dabbed at overgrown eyebrows with his handkerchief. Martha May thought he must have gotten a thousand dollars' use out of that fifty cent rag.

"Now we c'n both see the ol' man ain't here, is he?" Mims countered.

Puckett's glance at last came up and settled into Mims's face, and there was something hard that Martha May hadn't expected in his wide blue eyes. "I don't like it much either. An' I wonder what Judge would think of bein' called that."

With those words, spoken in a soft tone while eyes as hard as stainless steel stabbed Mims in the face, stubby little Puckett brushed the jailer off like flicking a bug off his shoulder.

He walked past Mims as if he were nothing but an ancient stain on the wall that no one noticed anymore. Stopping at Bryant Janx's cage, he brought both hands up to the bars, giving the bars a close and personal study of disgust before setting his hands on them, the one hand still holding onto his kerchief.

"You Mrs. Janx?"

Martha May stared up at the non-threatening newcomer and felt threatened, because he was white, and she was something else. "I am, yes sir."

Puckett's eyes came down to study her son, lying in a heap of former humanity on the cold concrete floor. "He's a big boy. Soldier, I hear?"

"Yes sir, he was."

"That bein' what prompted his appearance in our fine establishment," added in Puckett. Martha May sensed a tone of sarcasm and distaste in his voice.

"Yes sir, I think. They been callin' 'im a baby killer. I don't think he like it."

Puckett pursed his lips. "No, I don't imagine. I was early in Korea myself, ma'am. So's you know. Soldiers should be treated better. Wasn't their choice to—" He stopped himself and waved the handkerchief around like he was chasing off a fly. "Anyway, no matter. That's the way some folks are now'days. What we gonna do with yore boy, ma'am? What'd they set his bail at?"

"Nobody will tell me, sir. They done told me it uz too high for me t' pay anyhow."

Puckett's florid, round face seemed to pinch together. Without looking to the side to honor Jailer Mims with a glance, he said, "What is this man's bail, Mims?" There was no hiding the disdain in his voice.

"Five thousand dollars."

"Five thousand— Good hell!" Puckett clenched his teeth and turned his head to pierce the jailer with those cold blue eyes. "Good— What kind of justice is that? There's no way this family could pay that."

Mims smiled with tight lips. "Ask the old man—if you love 'im so much. He's yore judge."

Puckett drew a long, deep breath. Martha May saw it only because she was watching him closely. He seemed to be striving to keep himself under control. His next words were significant in that he dropped any pretense of friendliness or respect for Mims.

"Jailer, I suggest you get in here and clean this man up, and while you're at it, clean his cell. With bleach." He reached down and pried a huge silver watch from his pocket and snapped open its lid, peering at it closely. "In one and a half hours it will be dinner time—for me and for Judge. I plan to bring him back down here with me then, and I assume this place will be nice and clean—if you get my drift."

Mims's face hardened. He tried to look tough, but he succeeded like a melting bowl of strawberry ice cream. "Fine. And yer time's up. You too." He speared Martha May with a manly look he couldn't make work for Puckett.

Martha May looked down and scanned her son's face and body for a moment, holding back her tears. She decided a shoulder was the safest thing to touch, and she gave it a squeeze. "I'll come see you again, Bryant. You be strong, Son. You in our prayers."

She stood up as Mims opened the cell door, and she stepped into the hall with her eyes fixed on the floor, just like any well-trained woman her color would do in Thibodaux, Louisiana. And all the while, inside her soul, she hated Jailer Mims with all the vehemence of a lioness and wished she had a knife to drive through his spine.

*   *   *

By the time evening fell, Slugger Janx had been visited by his mother, attorney Lawson Puckett, who said his colleagues knew him fondly as "Law," a Judge Pandra, a doctor, and two janitors who thoroughly cleaned his cage with Clorox and water while he sat on a stool in the one next to it. The jailer then let him back in, with a new set of jail clothes and two fresh-smelling blankets.

Law Puckett came back later, when he was off work for the day, and looked around Slugger's cage. He sniffed the air, processed what his nose had learned for several seconds, then nodded quietly.

"Hello again, Bryant."

"Most call me Slugger."

The corners of Puckett's mouth tipped up. "Slugger? Okay. Slugger it is. Looks like they cleaned things up. I'm sorry I couldn't make it back when Judge came. I had to take care of another matter, away out in the country, and it pressed me from being here."

Slugger nodded. "It's no problem. That judge was nice enough." Because of his fiercely swollen lips, he could hardly understand his own words, even when he already knew what he was going to say. He was surprised when Puckett didn't even blink.

"Judge is a good man. Only thing, I thought I could get him t' lower your bail."

Slugger looked up at him, with a steady, honest gaze he had learned as a G.I., not as a black man in the South. He didn't say anything, just waited.

"But, he wouldn't. Five thousand dollar. That's what he set it at, and that's where it sets, like a statue o' Stonewall Jackson. He says the only way he would lower it is if you had someplace else to go and somebody to get you there—immediately, and safe. Otherwise, you go outside this jail, and soon's somebody knows it, you're dead. Judge won't have it on his conscience. And so ... I have to respect what he says, because Judge is a good man, an' he wants justice much as anybody. He just don't want you dead on account o' him."

Slugger nodded. He hadn't thought about that aspect of his bail. He hated the fact that it made sense, so here he would sit, just like a slave of old. Serving his country as a brave soldier came down to being about as meaningless as the turd of a stink bug on a hot sidewalk.

"How long I gonna be here then?"

Puckett sighed. "Well, son, that's the question, ain't it? I wish I had that answer. Here's another question, because the answer for this one will tell the answer to the other: You got someplace else to go, do you? Or money to get somewhere?"

"Sir, I got nothin'. No check from Uncle Sam, no nothin'. My Mama and Papa, they can barely feed theirselves and my brother. We got nothin', and no way t' get nothin' 'cause the Army said they didn't need me no more an' put me outta work like a used up donkey."

Law Puckett reached inside his tweed coat and fished his handkerchief out. "I'm sorry, son. Real sorry." He chuckled. "If they'd ever pay a public defender a real wage, I'd bail you outta here myself and send you up to Chicago or somewhere. Listen—Slugger, right? I'll see you tomorrow afternoon. Now that I know what they're doin' around here with you, I'll be here every consarned day, too—you can count on that just like the sun comin' up. And thank you for your service of our country, young man."

With that, pudgy little Law Puckett turned and walked to the door, rapping on it with his knuckles, then passing through when someone opened it from the other side.

The cellblock fell into shadow, and Slugger Janx leaned back on his bunk and rested the back of his skull against the hard wall. He found that part of his body was about the only several square inches that didn't hurt.

CHAPTER FIVE

Coal and the Mitchells made it back to Salmon after two hours of driving in the dark, through the most dangerous part of the trip, where thick vegetation on both sides of the road sheltered herds of semi-suicidal deer that seemed to love frolicking back and forth across the highway from an hour before sunset to well after daylight.

He stopped in front of the Mitchell house and got out to open Jan's door, and when the woman looked at him without speaking, then stepped close and embraced him, he felt another surge of emotion. They didn't claim the Lord worked in mysterious ways for nothing.

After Jan, Jerry, who had only been awake for a few minutes, came to wrap his arms around Coal, and Coal scooped him up and held him for a while, squeezing him tight with a memory of the twins, who had been this size what seemed many years ago. As he set the little one down, he was surprised to see Toby standing there waiting for his turn. Toby, as a great big four-years-old, might not appreciate being picked up, but he squeezed Coal every bit as hard as his little brother had. Bud was the only one to stand off a bit, and Coal crouched in front of him and put out a hand. With a shy smile, Bud put his hand in Coal's.

"Just a little harder there, Bud," Coal advised, holding on. "You know, if you want to be big and strong like your dad, people will be judging you by your handshake your whole life."

Bud took the advice well and squeezed harder, and Coal

reached out and clapped him on the shoulder. "Now you're talking! Good grip. Your dad would sure be proud of you. Now you're the man of the house for a little while longer, so you make sure to keep your mom and these boys safe, all right?"

Bud nodded, doing his best to keep eye contact. On an afterthought, Coal looked at Toby and Jerry. "You two boys help him as much as you can, okay? Your mom's got a lot to do now that your dad's staying away for a while."

He drove back down Courthouse Drive and onto Main, his heart full. He would never have wanted Todd or his family to have to go through anything like this, but there certainly had ended up being a silver lining to the thunderheads created by the experience. He had never foreseen growing close to Todd's family, but he knew from here on things were going to be far different between the Savages and the Mitchells.

Coal was home early enough for a grand reunion with his family and the dogs. The dogs finally had to be put out, as they seemed to think Coal had been away for a month, and there would be no way to give his family proper attention until the dogs were set loose to run off some of their energy.

The twins were full of talk about their first day back in school. Katie and Cynthia were only a little more reserved about recounting the day's activities, and little Sissy came over where Coal had sat down on the cowhide couch and stood quietly beside him for a few minutes. He pretended not to notice her for a time, afraid he would scare her off. But when finally she reached out her little hand and rested it on his thigh, he knew her turn had come.

"Hi, Sissy! Wow, it looks like you grew a foot since I left! You're big!"

The shy smile came to the little girl's mouth, and she looked down. But his warm voice and words prompted her to slowly add her other hand to the top of his thigh. Taking a chance, he said, "Can I get a hug?"

It was better than the magic of Christmas when little Sissy put up her arms, and he pulled her into his and held her close. When he was under control enough to open his eyes, they fell on Connie, who had sat down on the La-Z-Boy and was looking at him. He was pretty sure that with her own eyes so full of tears she could not even see him.

The only thing missing was a happy greeting from Virgil. All Coal had gotten out of him was a "Hi, Dad." But no matter. He was going to fix that soon.

"Maura just left a little while ago," said Connie, dabbing at her eyes.

The sound of the name made Coal's heart give an irritating little jump. He wished it wouldn't affect him like that.

"Yeah? What did she want?"

Connie stared at him for a moment. "What did she want? Well, I don't know, Coal. Maybe just to say hi? Can't someone visit without wanting something?"

Moms sure have the power to make their sons, no matter how old they might be, feel foolish. He refused to reply, and he knew that would irk her. He almost hoped it would.

"I guess you don't want to know how she is." Connie had been silent for a minute or so, and a lot of the attention in the room by now was returning to the television. Sissy seemed to be completely content under the shelter of Coal's right arm, and he relished in the feeling. This girl's acceptance had been hard-won.

Coal shrugged his left shoulder. "She's fine, right?" A typical man reply.

Connie made a disgusted grunt and got up to go to the kitchen. Coal could see her puttering around for five minutes or so, but as far as he could tell she was wiping down an already immaculate countertop and then cleaning a refrigerator handle that knowing her was probably not only spotless but free of a single germ.

After a while, he saw her pause, looking out the window toward the barn. She drew a deep breath, came back and sat on the brown chair again.

"You know, it would be nice if you at least called her sometime."

Coal was looking at the television now. He had turned his attention to it in a hurry when he saw his mother coming back with new battle plans in her eyes.

Pretending he had barely heard her, Coal turned to her and stared for a few seconds, irritated that his mother was back at it again. He calmed himself down inside before he spoke, because he was dangerously close to grabbing the tiger's tail, and he knew it. "Sure, I guess I will. But I think she's been pretty busy with Jordan lately."

Connie grunted. "Oh, Coal. That Jordan is a really nice boy. But that's all he is. Maura doesn't have feelings for him."

This made Coal laugh. "Okay, Mom. Okay. I'll call her."

"It's not really that funny," Connie pressed. "What's funny about what I said?"

"Nothing. It's just you that's funny, period. I'll call her. Okay?"

Connie sighed. She held back a smile. "Okay."

It took a long time for Coal finally to get Sissy to bed that night. Now that she had warmed up to him, she didn't want to let go. He wished he could know what was going on inside her head, but he knew it made it harder for her going to bed in that cold, dark bedroom where all three of the girls slept when Katie and Cynthia both wanted to stay up a little longer and had earned that right by getting perfect grades in school.

Coal finally told Sissy he would lie down beside her in her little twin-size bed, and that was how he finally got her to go. As they lay there, with her head using his arm for a pillow, he had an inspiration, and he was a little proud of himself.

"Hey, Sissy? Do you want to know something?"

She looked over at him and nodded.

"I'm never ever going to go away, all right? I will always be here with you and I will always keep you safe, no matter what happens. No one will ever hurt you again."

Sissy didn't reply with words, but after a few more seconds, she snuggled up against him tighter than ever. That was all the response he could need.

After Sissy had gone to sleep, he went to Virgil's room to say goodnight. He took the typical book out from under his sleeping son's nose—an Ernest Haycox Western—and set it on the nightstand, pulling the covers up tight around his neck. With a sigh, he turned off the lamp. There would always be tomorrow.

Thursday, January 4

Coal spent Thursday playing catch up with the affairs of running a jail, along with a few phone calls of simple courtesy, and what some might refer to as "politicking," which was ironic, since the last thing anyone could truly say about Coal was that he was a typical politician.

He touched base once more with Elmer Keith and Rick Cheatum, to thank them for their part in recent events. He called Jim and Betty, just so they would know he was thinking of them, and he even called Judge Sinclair, who seemed surprised, yet genuinely pleased, to hear from him. He also made a phone call to Governor Andrus, to thank him for stepping in in his time of dire need.

Once all of the "politicking" was out of the way, he dialed up Kathy MacAtee. He knew she would be home alone, if she were home at all, for all her girls would be back in school.

Hello? MacAtees.

Coal's heart caught in his throat. "Yeah. Hi, Kathy. It's Coal."

Kathy emitted what Coal would have called a squeal of delight. *Wow! What's wrong, Coal? And by the way, I knew it was you the second I heard you.*

He laughed. "So what do you mean what's wrong?"

Just being a smart aleck. It seems like it takes something big for you to call me. Sorry, bad humor.

She couldn't make the comment go away by playing it off. "Hey, Kathy. I'm really sorry. It's kind of been a week from hell."

You don't have to apologize. I've heard all about it. You doing okay?

"I guess. I made friends with the wrong guy. Again. I can't trust my judgment very much when it comes to people, I guess."

No sound from the other end of the line for a few seconds. Coal realized he had left her an opening, and he hoped she would have the couth not to embarrass them by taking it.

The girls and me would love to see you, hon. Want to come over for supper?

Coal's heart melted a little. He wanted to scream *Yes!* He had missed seeing Kathy, and he really longed for the way she and the fact of being in her home made him feel so close to Larry again. He guessed his family was just going to have to get used to his being involved with a lot of other people. He couldn't always be home.

"I'd like that."

Great! Tomorrow night?

Coal paused and thought. He had to struggle against his typical tendency to say yes too fast. "I'm going to be getting ready for a trip with Virgil. Could we do it next week? Maybe even on Monday?"

Sure. Monday. So ... your favorite?

Coal let out a laugh. "No, Monday isn't my favorite."

Very funny. I meant do you want me to make your favorite food?

"How do you know my favorite?"

Well, I'm not as old as I look, hon. I still have a memory. Thick beef stew, so thick you can cut it with a knife, peach pie, and wheat bread straight out of the oven, right? With tons of butter.

He was still laughing. "Okay, you're pretty good."

And ice cold water.

"You got it right. Seven o'clock all right?"

Seven would be great. But you can come over any time before that if you'd like. You ought to see all the things these girls have King doing!

Coal hung up thinking of Larry, and Rowdy, and the good times he and his buddy had shared. He hoped Kathy wouldn't get the wrong idea with him coming over, but he sure was glad to have her still in the valley. Without her, the Lemhi would never feel the same.

Coal had told Connie he would call Maura. He didn't. Instead, he drove down to McPherson's, hoping she would be at work.

He walked in smelling all the wonderful scents of a Western store, mostly leather and in this day's case some kind of smoky incense—probably pine or cedar. It mingled with a hint of cigarette smoke and coffee.

The owner himself, Florin Beller, greeted him from the counter. "Hi, Coal. Can I help you?"

"Hi, Mr. Beller. You can if you can tell me where I might find Maura. Is she working today?"

"She sure is. She's in the back."

The door bells chimed, and Coal turned. Apparently having the GMC out front wasn't enough of a warning for some people, or else some people didn't care. Jordan Peterson came to a stop a few feet in from the door.

"Hi, Jordan. What's up?"

"Nothin', boss. Just came in to get Maura."

Florin Beller's glance flickered over to Coal, then to Jordan.

"She's in the back, Jordan. She's a popular girl today."

Jordan must have caught his drift, and he met Coal's eyes. "Did you come in to see her? I can give you a minute."

A minute? thought Coal. What was a minute supposed to do? "No, buddy. I'm just going to pick up a shirt and head out. I'm getting tired of the same old wardrobe."

Jordan grinned and looked at Coal's shirt. "Yeah, I've seen that one on you a few times. Well, we've gotta get. See you later."

The big deputy wandered to the back, and Coal could hear him and Maura speaking in low tones. He turned back to Florin Beller. "Well, show me to some double X shirts, would you?"

Beller took him to a rack of shirts that were either plain colors or simple plaids of dark or subdued colors, and Coal started sorting through them, pretending he really cared.

Soon, Jordan and Maura came threading their way up through the clothing racks, and Maura met Coal's eyes. "Hello, Coal."

He looked up pretending to just become aware of her presence in the store. "Hi, Maura. How's it going?"

"Great. I'm on my lunch." She paused, and her glance bounced to Jordan, then back into Coal's eyes. She had something to say, and so did Coal. But there was too little time, and too much pride.

Coal felt like he was back in junior high. "Well, I guess I'll see you later."

"See you later." A cloud fell over Maura's visage, and she turned and walked off with Jordan. He was walking too close to her. Was that because of Maura or because of him? He waited for Jordan's arm to go around her waist. It didn't, but he wondered if it did the moment they passed beyond the big windows.

After leaving McPherson's, Coal had to get Maura and Jordan off his mind, so he set about putting into play a plan he had been thinking of all the way home from Salt Lake City with Jan Mitchell and her three boys. He went around to all the grocery stores in town and gathered up as much donated food as they would part with—

which in some cases was quite a bit—and then stopped at a number of other businesses as well to ask for cash donations. He kept a list of where he had been, as he had intentions of going to every place in town in the next week or two.

Then, with a big smile on his face and a warmth in his heart, he drove up to present all the food, along with two hundred and fifty-five dollars in cash, fifty of it being out of his own pocket, to Jan Mitchell. That family was never going to starve in his town, not while he was still around to draw breath.

CHAPTER SIX

Lawson Puckett liked a fine cigar, and Judge Irving Pandra had a whole box of them, in the same drawer of his dark oak wood desk where he kept his 1911 Colt .45 from his days as a Colonel in the Army of the Pacific, under General MacArthur.

Puckett was happy knowing he was well-liked, even respected, by the man he referred to as "Judge," and Judge quite often gifted him with one, sometimes even two, of those fine cigars whenever he had done something of which Judge approved.

Puckett had the cigar in his mouth, and he pulled a mouthful of smoke in, very carefully, and savored it on his palate. Wine would be coming to his table, in time, and with it a huge helping of the crawfish gumbo he loved so much. Here at the Blue Crawdad, they knew how to treat Law Puckett right.

The cigar smoke puffed out into the room to mingle with the smoke of a hundred cheap cigarettes, ads for which freely littered every magazine known to mankind, except for maybe *Boys' Life*. The smokers of those Marlboros, Camels, Saratogas, and Virginia

Slims, they simply did not know what they were missing. Maybe when they smelled the flavor of this gift from Judge, it would make them believers.

Puckett mulled in silence over the plight of the man sitting in jail: Bryant "Slugger" Janx. He had read all the reports. The report from the anti-war hippies was obvious bunk. It painted them as the sweetest, most wonderful, most God-fearing group of little angels ever to walk the earth. In fact, after reading it, he wasn't sure why God didn't just take them all up to live with him in heaven now and be done with it.

And the police reports, written by William A. Armstrong, and Harry C. Mulligan were about the most wonderfully fabricated fiction Puckett had forced himself to slog through since his last Mike Hammer novel.

Now anyone who read each of those reports, then spoke with Slugger Janx for five minutes, would know where the truth lay. A funny combination of words, that one: "The truth lies." It always made Puckett smile.

Reaching up with his left hand, he absently took his bowtie, wiggling it back and forth. He sucked on the cigar again, a fleeting thought of Judge Pandra's kindness flitting through his mind.

Slugger Janx was going to be in trouble when he went to trial. County prosecutor Jib Slate had already offered them a deal: plead guilty to disorderly conduct. Honestly, considering the color of Slugger Janx's skin, it was the fairest deal he could hope for. And it was even the truth, thought Puckett, thinking back on Slugger's story: No one could deny that he had been disorderly, and he had indeed been the one throwing all of the physical blows.

However, Slugger had proved too stubborn, and he wasn't interested in pleading guilty to anything, disorderly conduct or even spitting on the sidewalk. Puckett had been a little irritated, at first, but then he couldn't blame the young man. Here he had honorably served his country in Vietnam, first as a guard at the terribly filthy and intolerable Long Binh Jail, and then in the jungles of Saigon, during his second and third tours. Three tours of Nam. How many could lay claim to that? Slugger was a good boy, he had served his country well, and he had a right to come home with some expectation of being treated with respect, at least by his own government.

Instead, society at large ignored him, at the very best, and at the very worst spat upon him and taunted him with names like Baby Killer. And his own government, which should have handsomely rewarded him for his service, simply tossed him back out on the street, with no proper medical care, no attempt to reassimilate him into a peaceful world he no longer had a frame of reference to understand, and not even a paycheck he had been promised on boarding the plane in Hanoi would be waiting for him at home.

Slugger's only other choice was to go to court, where attorney Jib Slate was set to lay a number of serious charges to his credit, from battery with a deadly weapon (for it was Slate's argument that Slugger had been trained to kill in Vietnam with his hands and feet) to assault upon police officers and resisting arrest.

Slugger couldn't deny that he had, in his anger, committed battery—although to be fair, the hippies had battered him first, with spit—but trying to claim that it was "battery with a deadly weapon," to Puckett that was a long stretch. Had Slugger wanted to kill one or two of those kids, he could surely have done it. But the other charges Slugger had flat-out denied, and after speaking with him at length, he believed him. In fact, he believed that every single word Slugger had told him was the truth.

The whole problem was, this court would be in southern Louisiana, the year was 1972, and Slugger would be testifying against two pillars of society, Officers William A. Armstrong, and Harry C. Mulligan, and six fun-loving and adorable white kids who would never think of raising a hand against another human being. Shoot, those kids were so sweet they wouldn't be able to crush a tick. In a court of his so-called peers—meaning most likely twelve white men, or maybe eleven and a token black who would fear for his own skin if he made the wrong choice—Slugger Janx would be found guilty, of every charge.

But Slugger was going to fight. Apparently, according to his mother, he had spent his whole life as a fighter, befitting his nickname.

Puckett then thought of Judge again. Judge once had been a defense attorney himself, and Puckett had grown to respect and honor him, and they were friends. Judge would do all he could at sentencing to be lenient with Slugger, but he could only do so much if he wanted to retain his seat in this county. Slugger would be slapped with a guilty charge, he would serve time in the state penitentiary, and he would come out a hard and bitter man, and perhaps then a *real* menace, to the society who had thrown him into a pit of adders.

Law Puckett's wry sense of humor made him pause for a moment to ponder the mystery of why the Bible always picked on adders—never subtracters, dividers, or multipliers. But that was none of his business. He still had a stupid smirk on his face he couldn't erase when the waiter appeared with his gumbo.

Puckett dined alone, as he lived alone. Well, alone but for a little ragged mutt he called Smiley, maybe Chihuahua and probably Shit-something or other. Perhaps that last was not one of the actual breeds in Smiley's mix so much as it was Smiley's way of life.

The gumbo was impeccable, as always, and the wine supreme. Puckett had put out his cigar as he ate and sipped his wine, and when he finished, he leaned back, threw down his napkin, and finished the cigar, down to a little nub, and snuffed it out on his plate.

It was already after ten, and the little café had dwindled down to him and three other people, all of whom sat at a table together in a dark corner—not that there were any *light* corners in the Blue Crawdad.

Standing out of his chair, he unconsciously reached up and straightened his bowtie once more, grabbed down low on the front of his suit coat and gave it three hard downward jerks, to straighten out the wrinkles.

He wove between the round tables toward the front of the place, and as his waiter stepped out, he stopped and beckoned him over. "It was perfect, Marc," he said, holding out his hand. When the waiter took it, he slipped a folded five-dollar bill into his hand, which was more than the price of the meal and wine together, and gave him a wink. Marc said thanks, and Law Puckett went to the front door and pushed through.

The winter night was refreshingly cool. The heavy mugginess of Louisiana's summer and autumn was gone, although that ever-present murky-sweet smell rolling north from the swamps permeated the town's air. Puckett rather liked it, actually. The swamp country had always been his refuge.

He walked out to the parking lot. There were only five cars. He drove a dark green Alpha Romeo Berlina, and the other diners must have come in a dark-colored Chrysler, because Marc, the waiter, drove the little gold Toyota, and the bus boy and cook's cars were parked over by the back door.

He heard a marsh bird cry, off in the distance probably on the Bayou LaFourche. It made him stop and listen, knowing it would come again. It did. He smiled. A hound bayed, not the thrilled bay of the hunt, but the cooped up baying of a dog probably trapped in some dirty back yard, longing to be out in the dark woods. Puckett loved the night. He loved the sounds of Thibodaux after dark.

He had nearly reached his car when he saw the flicker of a cigarette, toward the back of the lot. There in those shadows loomed a separate shadow, darker and taller than those around it, ominous by its stillness. The tip of the cigarette glowed brighter, then dimmed once more.

Puckett got to the back of his car before he saw glitter on the ground by the passenger side. Still conscious of the shadowy figure with the cigarette, he stopped and squinted at the glitter. He puzzled for a moment. It looked like glass—auto glass, to be precise.

Curious, he walked around that side of the car. At the same time he realized his passenger window was broken out, and that the glitter on the ground was indeed caused by its glass, he saw another shadow stir in the front seat of his car—the passenger side. Then he saw another one, this one in back.

The two near-side passenger doors and the rear door on the driver's side clicked and slowly came open, and three dark-clothed figures unfurled to stand tall and unmoving in the dark. He peered closer to see faces, then realized why he couldn't: Each of them was wearing a ski mask, the kind with three holes for the eyes and mouth.

Panic raced up through little Law Puckett, and his knees felt suddenly weak. From the corner of his eye, he could see the man with the cigarette coming his way, moving in what he would call a saunter.

He turned and looked at the front door of the café. It was fifty feet away. And in front of it stood three more dark shadows. Even as he saw them, they started forward.

In a daze, his mind clouded perhaps a little by the wine, Puckett let his eyes scan the parking lot and all the way out to the street. There was no one else in sight. Not even another automobile.

His gaze bounced over all seven of the dark figures that were slowly forming a ring around him, every one of them taller than he was by inches. The last one to arrive was the man with the cigarette. He stopped a ways back, threw down his cigarette, and crushed it on the pavement with the toe of his shoe. It was then that Puckett realized he wasn't wearing a mask, but he was too far away to make out any features of his face. Even as Puckett saw this, the man reached behind his back, then raised his hands and worked a dark ski mask down over his face.

With this done, he walked close, moving with an aching kind of slowness, drawing out what Puckett knew was to come.

The man stopped in front of Puckett, and no one spoke. Five seconds went by. Then Puckett heard himself say, "Who's going to pay for my window?"

Cigarette chuckled. "You've got bigger worries than that, *Law* man."

Puckett didn't recognize the voice. But a visceral part of him did somehow appreciate the play on words with his nickname, in spite of the danger he was in.

"I could ask you to go on a vacation, little man, but you probably wouldn't do it, would you? And if you did, you'd just come back."

Puckett stared. What did they expect him to say?

"You and the judge are the only two men in this whole town pretendin' that nigger over in the jail didn't do somethin' real bad. Why is that?"

"He has to have his day in court," Puckett said softly. "Nobody has found him guilty." He heard his words as if they were being spoken by someone else.

"He's guilty. You know it. You're just lookin' for your little moment of fame. Well, son, we're here t' give you that fame."

Cigarette turned his head slightly to look in the direction of Puckett's left shoulder and gave a nod. Puckett heard his head start to clang, and dizziness came over him. A pain suddenly shot all through him as his knees began to buckle.

Pressure came to his low back. Then to the back of his head. Both places burst into hot centers of pain in the flash of a second, and he realized he was on his knees. Somebody pulled him up. Maybe two somebodies. Cigarette stepped close and stomped down with all his might on Puckett's instep. Puckett heard a voice cry out in pain, and he realized it must be his own.

He was standing again, or at least he was upright. He couldn't feel his own feet. Cigarette struck him in the belly. He did it again, and again. The fourth blow must have found his solar plexus, for Puckett realized no air would come into his lungs.

He was down again, this time on his left side. The world was reeling. Street lights blurred and flashed around in his mind, and then he heard a car's engine start, and he forced his eyes open to see red taillights, and blinding backup lights flared into his face. A car was backing up toward him. He wanted to watch. He tried to scream again.

And then all the world was dark.

CHAPTER SEVEN

Friday, January 5

The next morning, Coal stumbled down the stairs, hardly able to focus his eyes. He had stayed up with the kids as long as Connie would allow them to stay up, then put Sissy to bed with the same ritual as the night before, which took a little of his all-important time, sure, but the feeling of which he cherished. His guts told him that girl had been rescued from a life of certain doom in just enough time that, here at the Savages, she might grow up to lead a normal life. Every time he thought about it, it filled his heart with warmth.

After Sissy was asleep, and the other kids were all down as well, he had sat in front of the fire and played the guitar and sang—which was what he had been doing for an hour before, at the insistence of the twins. He had a large enough repertoire to keep

Connie from inserting any nosy questions between songs.

Now, in the darkness of dawn, he was paying for his late night. Connie was apparently out with the horses, assuming she had risen at her usual hour. He wasn't feeling it, but he also wasn't feeling a desire to get fat, so he went downstairs and did a heavy workout for almost an hour, then came back up to the aroma of bacon and eggs.

The kids still had half an hour of sleep left to go as he showered, dressed, and came in to find six eggs and several strips of bacon on his plate. He sat down to it, still feeling groggy, but at least awake enough to thank Connie. He probably shouldn't have, though, because the sound of his voice seemed to wake a sleeping giant.

"So how did things go at work yesterday, Son?"

"Fine. Lots of paperwork."

"Is it okay if I ask about Ray?"

He looked up, gnawing a piece of nearly cooked bacon in half, and let out a sigh. "Well, I don't know. Fine, I guess. He seems pretty down, but I guess that's what you'd expect."

"Is his brother still in the hospital?"

"Nope. We've got him at the jail now. And I have to tell you, that man is pure evil. If I had somebody come up wanting a tour of the jail, I'd have to tell them to wait 'til he's gone. The whole place feels dark."

Connie shook her head, looking away for a moment to take a waffle out of the iron. Those were for the kids. She knew Coal's love-hate relationship with waffles and pancakes and tried not to tempt him because it didn't take much to make him cave in and ruin his normally dedicated regime.

She started humming a seemingly innocent tune, and Coal cringed. Humming meant his mother's mind was furiously spinning. He turned and looked at the stairs. Did he have time to escape?

"Hey, Coal?"

Nope.

"Yeah?"

"So I don't want to butt into your business, but did you remember to call Maura?"

He wanted to laugh out loud. She didn't want to butt into his business? Since when!

"I didn't call her, but I went down to see her at the store."

"Oh, good! How did it go?"

"Well, I bought a new shirt."

"What?"

"Mom, Jordan walked in less than twenty seconds after me and took her to lunch. That's how my visit went. I stayed and let Florin Beller sell me a new shirt—which, by the way, I think you'd really like—and then I left."

Connie stood and digested the news for a moment, sliding some fried eggs onto a plate and glancing at the clock. Her face said she wanted in the worst way to say something, but for once maybe she really couldn't think of anything.

Coal stood up. "I'll go wake the kids up and send them in."

"Wait. Coal?" He turned. "Don't shut down and give up on her. You trust me, right?"

"Mom. This isn't a question of trust. Some things just aren't meant to be. Leave it alone, all right?"

"But—"

"Just leave it alone."

He turned and went down the hall to knock on Katie and Cynthia's door. After he had them waking up, he went up to the boys' rooms. Connie was smart enough not to follow.

*   *   *

Coal brought in breakfast from the Coffee Shop and took it to the Medina brothers, then was glad to vacate the cell block. He hated the evil feeling back there and truly wished they had had

some big charge waiting for Angel in Vegas so they would extra-
dite him and Lemhi County wouldn't have to deal with him. But
he had a fistful of charges here, including the murder of Drew Run-
nigan, so here he would remain. He was going to cost the county a
lot of money before all was said and done.

The phone rang, and Coal looked at it distractedly. He wondered if he could take up meditation and it would make him hate
the sound of a ringing phone less. As it was, he often felt like drawing his gun and blasting it off the desk.

On the fifth ring, he answered.

Hi, Coal. In his head he swore.

"Hello, Maura." For a while he had been thinking Angel Medina was the last person he would like to talk to. Now he stood
corrected.

How are things? she asked.

Stop it with the damn small talk, woman! What do you want?
Of course he didn't say anything of the kind out loud.

"Oh, all right. Busy as usual." In lawyer-speak, that was called
building a case—a set up in case she had any foolish suggestions.

Do you think you might have some time today?

He took a deep breath and bulled forward, glad for that case he
had started building. "That's a tough one. I have to meet the county
prosecutor over lunch to discuss the case on this Angel Medina and
figure out what the plan is for Ray," he lied. He hadn't even met
the prosecutor yet.

Oh. Well ... What's your schedule like for tonight?

He disgusted himself with the sadistic delight he took in saying, "Virgil and I will be packing up for a trip out of town."

After a pause: *Oh, really?*

"Yeah. I'm trying to decide where to go with him. Probably
Missoula."

That should be fun. Now her voice sounded almost listless. It
certainly lacked its normal sass and spunk. He almost felt bad.

Coal, I'd really like to talk to you.

This was the opening where Coal could stop being stubborn, cave in, and blurt out that he wanted her, he thought he might be in love with her, at least a little bit, and that he couldn't live without her. His mother would be so dang proud of him.

"Is everything okay?" was all he could muster up.

Well, yeah, I guess. Sure.

"Oh. Okay, well, yeah, we can talk sometime. I'll give you a holler whenever things slow down." Which as he was learning, in Lemhi County *sheriff*-speak meant just about never.

After they hung up, he didn't go back to work. He couldn't. Instead, he just sat there staring at the phone. He had sure shown Maura PlentyWounds what his priorities were. Maybe now she would quit bothering him. He stared at the phone some more. What were his priorities again?

At last, with a heavy sigh, he looked up the prosecutor's number and dialed it.

A light, almost nasally voice came on the other end. *Fica.*

"Yeah, is this the prosecutor's office?"

Oh yeah, sorry—Fica. Prosecutor's office. A rollicking laugh followed, as close to a jolly laugh as anything Coal could think of. *I always forget to say that part. Can I help you?*

Coal wasn't sure how to take the man behind this voice and laugh. "This is Sheriff Savage, downstairs. I had a note on the desk to call you—about the Medina case?"

Oh! Well, if you have some time we could talk right now.

"Sure you're not too busy?"

Again, the jolly laugh. *Ha! I'm always too busy. Seriously, come on up, Sheriff. For you, I'll make time.*

Coal downed the last of his coffee, cold as it always was by the last inch. He braved a burst of frigidity to get from his door to the courthouse door and ascended the stairs to the prosecutor's office. Painted on the door in black letters, it said *Prosecutor M. Fica,* something any responsible sheriff who knew his job should have long since had occasion to see—explaining why Coal hadn't.

When he stepped inside the inner office, there was no one sitting behind a desk he assumed belonged to a receptionist—typical business in this town. He knocked on a tinted glass door that bore the legend of *Prosecutor* on a brass plate above it.

"Come on in!"

One step into the office, Coal stopped. Behind a desk nearly buried in stacks of open and unopen books, papers, paper weights, and manila folders, sat a man of massive proportions, not massive like Bigfoot Monahan was massive, or even big like Coal, but ... *big*. At a glance, the man would go close to four hundred pounds. He wore a black and red striped tie that was very loose, despite the massive size of his neck, and askew on the front of his shirt. Thin, short-cropped honey-colored hair was plastered over to one side on top, and his rosy, rotund cheeks created a picture for Coal to match the word "jolly" that came to mind when Prosecutor Fica laughed.

The man was speaking to someone on the phone, so he held up a hand to Coal as if to tell him, "Just a minute." Coal nodded and scanned the room. There were bookshelves full of law books mated without any concept of organization with books on travel, and even a few novels—*Animal Farm* jumped to the forefront because it lay on its side atop a self-important row of black and gold tomes of law. A radio and cassette player sat on an otherwise nearly empty bookcase behind the man's right shoulder, and other shelves were cluttered with all kinds of relics and collectibles, things like whiskey bottles and wine decanters, and trophies which, whether important or not made up for it in sheer volume. Different plaques and certificates in frames decorated the white walls in no particular design, and there were bits of paper cluttering the floor here and there, as if a mouse had been chewing through paperwork and housekeeping had been banned.

In spite of concentrating on all these other important images, Coal couldn't help but hear the prosecutor's side of the phone conversation. He was amazed at the profanity that came out of this fellow's mouth, but for some reason it didn't come across as offensive as it might have.

Finally, Fica hung up the phone and lurched upright, an act he seemed to do with surprising ease, despite his size. He exploded a hand across his cluttered desk. "Hi! Mike Fica. Sorry about all this damn mess," he said with a laugh. "I keep thinking I'll clean it up, and then I keep not doing it." This time the high-pitched laugh was almost a roar.

Coal couldn't help but laugh as well as they shook hands. "Don't worry about it. Sheriff Savage."

"Coal, right?" Coal looked into the man's eyes as they maintained their grip. There was something genuine in this man's gaze he couldn't help but like on the instant.

"Yeah, that's right: Coal."

"You're a hell of a legend in this valley, man! Hey! Sorry, why don't you have a seat?"

Coal looked down at the padded seat of the wooden chair in front of Fica's desk. There was a book sitting there, face up. On the cover, above a smiling image of "Mr. Rogers," it read *Mister Rogers' Songbook.*

Coal returned his eyes to Fica, who realized something was wrong and leaned forward to peer over the desk. "Oh! Sorry. Just throw that up here, would you?"

Trying to hide a smile, Coal picked up the songbook and handed it across to the attorney. *"Mister Rogers' Songbook?"*

Fica gave his laugh again, acting only slightly embarrassed. "I know—funny, huh? Sorry, but I'm a bit of a fan."

Coal shrugged. "Hey, somebody has to be."

After making sure there weren't any more surprises on the chair, Coal plopped down.

"Why don't you tell me what's up, Coal?"

"Well, I thought you called—about the Medina brothers?"

"No, I didn't call. When you said that, I had no idea what you were talking about." Fica giggled.

Coal digested this news for a moment. "Huh. Well, all I know is there was a note on my desk telling me to call you about the Medinas."

"Oh. That was probably my deputy attorney, Bryan Wheat."

"Great. Anyway, I've got a couple of men in my jail you're going to have a chance to meet pretty soon. The Medina brothers? However the note got on my desk, since we're going to end up in court with them, we'd probably better start looking into their case as soon as possible. And I want to apologize for not coming up to introduce myself to you sooner."

"Well, hey now. Don't even think twice about that, bud. I've followed everything you've been going through since you came to town. I don't know how you get it all done. No worry. I knew we'd eventually get together."

So they sat and talked about the Medinas, and now and then Mike Fica took an unofficial moment out simply to talk about life. The biggest thing Coal took away from his visit with the county prosecutor wasn't his impression of the man's uncommon size or his cluttered office. It wasn't even his impression of Fica's disrupted, disheveled, disorganized look or his relaxed use of sailors' language. What he took away from that office was how likeable that man was—something he didn't expect out of a man who prosecuted criminals for a living.

Before Coal's departure, they shook hands again, and Fica said, "We'll be in touch. You might also get a call from Bryan. You'll like him. He might not be quite as ... lively as I am, but he's a good kid—sharp as a whip."

After work that evening, Coal was packing up anything he thought he might need for his trip. He looked in on Virgil to make sure he was doing the same, and although he was, he didn't seem too enthusiastic about it. Coal prayed he could change that before this trip was over. Virgil was proving to be a hard nut to crack.

When he tired of packing his duffel bag, Coal went downstairs to take the dogs out. As he hit the living room floor, he startled Connie, who was on the phone. She turned away from him and lowered her voice.

Figuring she was in the middle of a conversation about him, he stepped past her and called the dogs. The last thing he wanted to know was what match his mother was making tonight.

Saturday, January 6

In the morning, Coal rolled out of bed at six and got his workout in, then showered and ate breakfast with a very sleepy looking Virgil as the other children slept on. He would have liked to tell them all goodbye, but he had done that the night before, and he knew how much they liked their Saturday mornings in bed.

He and Virgil were heading for the front door when the phone rang, and Coal cringed. He paused for a second, out of habit, as Connie hurried across the room and picked it up. Then he nudged Virgil toward the door. Instinct told him to get going.

Virgil had just opened the door when Connie called out: "Coal! Wait." She was holding up a finger to him.

He gave her an impatient look, figuring it was just Maura and that Connie must have convinced her to make this call. "What? Mom, we've got to get on the road."

"But, Coal, it's long distance. I think you should take it." She had her hand over the transmitter.

He stared at her, trying to change gears and wrap his mind around the fact that it wasn't Maura. He turned and looked at Virgil. He had promised him this weekend was just for them. NO. He was not going to mess this up. He shook his head apologetically and made a kissy face at his mom, then stepped outside into a day that felt cold enough to be the inside of a snowman and shut the door.

He and Virgil were going to Montana, and nothing was going to stop them.

CHAPTER EIGHT

The drive over Lost Trail Pass was treacherous. Even with the temperature at around five degrees Fahrenheit, it was trying to snow, and up on the pass it was succeeding. In spite of the slick roads, the surrounding blue forest looked hushed, magical, and with a billion snowflakes twisting and turning their way down out of the bright gray gloom it was a Christmas painting straight off a *Leanin' Tree* card.

Coal stopped as soon as they got into Missoula and paid cash for a room at the Missoula Hotel, and they had dinner a little early, at eleven o'clock. After that, they drove around another Christmas card image, that of downtown until they found a gun store, with a wreath made of a fir bough still hung on the front door, a remnant of the season just past. Coal pulled the pickup over to the curb and stopped. In typical fashion, Virgil looked out at the store front but said nothing. One might have believed him a mannequin, for the vacancy of his expression.

"I'm going to go in here and look around, buddy. You should come in and check it out."

The idea of the gun store had come to Coal in Salt Lake, when he had been wandering around town by himself to give the Mitchells some alone time. He wanted to be here for two reasons: One, so he could get a feel for the Smith and Wesson Model 29 .44 magnum which Elmer Keith had helped design, and of which the old man was so proud, and two, to see what kind of hunting rifle would suit his boy. If Virgil was anything at all like his father had been at fourteen, receiving a rifle of his own would make up for a lot of his father's mistakes.

As Coal suspected, the Model 29 Smith and Wesson felt much the same as his 27, the venerable .357 magnum. He was a little cautious about how the much more powerful kick of the .44 would affect the way the thumb piece, which released the cylinder, would hit his thumb, but after his experience with .357 rounds bouncing off the sharply slanted window of the fastback Charger, in the car chase with the Medina brothers, Coal had set his mind on something more powerful.

As for Virgil, Coal was grateful to see a light come over his face, the same light he knew must have been on his own when Prince bought him his first rifle, a Winchester .30-06. Virgil was a stout enough kid, and this rifle would hopefully be with him for many years to come—possibly his entire life—so Coal steered him toward the ubiquitous ought-six as well. His had never failed him in the worst of conditions, and as an added bonus the owner of such a rifle would never be in a position of being unable to find cartridges for this rifle. They could be had in most any hunting camp.

After looking over the rifles, Virgil surprised him by choosing a Savage, the plainest looking rifle of the lot. The fit of stock to barrel was fine, as well as the fit of the butt plate. But the wood itself was very plain and almost without grain, and the finish was nothing to draw the discerning eye of a boy seeking his very first hunting rifle. Even the finish of the steel was a flat black that appeared to have been spray painted on.

Virgil had chosen the Savage, but Coal had noticed the brightest spark in his eye when he was holding a Remington Model 700

BDL. The difference in price was significant, and unlike the Savage the Remington didn't come already set up with a scope, but that rifle was an instrument of incredible beauty, with a wonderful grain in its stock, the smoothest fit of metal to wood possible, and a beautifully blued barrel and shiny steel action.

After Virgil made his choice of the Savage, which seemed to surprise the salesman as much as it did Coal, Coal told the man they would have to do some thinking about it, and they wandered off to look around the rest of the store.

As they looked at the available optics—shooting scopes, spotting scopes, and binoculars, the boots, wool pants, and all of the other magical things that put stars in the eyes of a boy contemplating his first hunt, Coal searched himself for a way to let his boy save face while at the same time letting him know that he understood why he had chosen the Savage, out of all the rifle brands he could have picked. After all, while Coal would never be able to read a woman's mind, he was pretty good at reading the mind of a boy—*his* boy—in the act of picking out a hunting outfit.

Virgil, never a boy to burden his father with costly things, had chosen the Savage because of its price tag. And that very reason was why Coal was more than willing to spend a little more on him—because he didn't demand it as one who believed he was entitled to the best of everything, and because he deserved it.

Finally, Coal felt ready to approach his son about the rifles. "Virg, let me tell you something. I got a really good pay check when I left the FBI, and I get a decent salary as sheriff. Plus, you know Grandma lets us stay at the house for free, right? She's just happy to have the company."

Virgil looked up at his father, his face a little puzzled. "Sure, Dad. I know." Unlike his father, apparently Virgil wasn't yet accomplished at reading other men's secret meanings.

"All right. Since we both understand that, I want to tell you something. I still feel bad about giving away Burro, but that isn't why I want to do this, okay?"

A faint cloud came over Virgil's eyes at mention of the dog. "Do what?"

"I think you should have that Remington instead of the Savage."

"No, Dad," the boy said instantly. "It's okay, really. I think the Savage is a nice rifle. And it has a scope on it."

Coal smiled. "You know what? You're sure a good kid. Buddy, we're getting you a scope too, all right? And we're getting that Remington. It's not that much more. I promise you it won't break us."

Virgil's eyes flickered. "Are you sure?"

"Sure, I'm sure. You're about the best son a man could ask for. And you're getting pretty close to being a full-grown man. You need a rifle that'll be with you for decades, not something you're going to want to trade off to a pawn shop as soon as you get old enough to get the one you really want."

Virgil looked up at him. Coal could see that he wanted to speak. But he really didn't need to. Coal saw the message all over his face: He had gambled right.

"When you're as old as I am and you're getting ready to go out in the woods on a hunt, you're going to want to look at the rifle you're oiling up and know it's the same one you killed your first deer with. Believe an old man, Son. You'll thank me later."

Virgil was beaming as they went and found the salesman again. Coal had told him to pay careful attention to how business was done, so Virgil followed closely.

"How set are the prices?" Coal asked the man.

The man shrugged. "Fairly set."

"Okay, talk to me. I have a friend with a firearms license back in Salmon—Elmer Keith?"

The man stared, then chuckled. "Elmer Keith? Wait. Are you serious? *The* Elmer Keith?"

"One and the same."

"He lives in Salmon?"

"He does."

"That's amazing. Is he like they say?"

Coal laughed. "Well, I'm not sure what you've heard, but I'd say probably so."

"Wow. That's pretty neat."

"It is. So the reason I brought that up is I would usually buy my guns through him. And I still might, but my boy took a real shine to that Remington 700, and I wanted to see if we could work something out on it."

"Really?" He looked over at Virgil. "I thought you liked the Savage."

"He liked the price," said Coal. "He was trying to save his dad some money."

The clerk looked appraisingly at Virgil. "Wow. Good kid. You don't see that kind of thing much."

Coal agreed. "That's why I want to get him the Remington, if you'll work with me on it."

"Well, I could probably give you a ten percent discount."

"So the truth is I would also like that Model 29 I was looking at, and a holster—a hunter. And maybe four boxes of shells for each, along with a scope and a sling for the rifle. I could get all the extras back in Salmon, of course, and the guns through Elmer, but you've been pretty helpful to us, so it would be nice to have you make a profit today too."

"All right. All right, let me go grab a calculator and see what we can do," said the man. He told another customer he would be with him as soon as he could, then went behind his counter and crunched some numbers on a fat, ugly gray Texas Instruments calculator.

When he finally looked up at Coal, he said, "If you buy all of that here, I can give you a fifteen percent discount on everything.

And please understand, that really is the lowest I can go."

Coal didn't want to make the man feel insulted. And he wanted to be sure his boy got a rifle with nice grain—a rifle he had picked out himself. So he and the clerk shook hands on the deal, and twenty minutes later they left the store, Coal with a brand-new Smith and Wesson .44 magnum in a wooden box under his arm, and his boy floating a couple of feet off the ground even though with all his new paraphernalia he now weighed more than ten pounds more than he had going into the store.

The rest of the trip was wonderful. They ate supper that night at the Hungry Man Cafe, making it possibly the dozenth time his boy had eaten in a restaurant. Virgil still wasn't glib, but he never had been. However, he talked as much to Coal as he ever had, and anyway, it really didn't matter. The look in his eyes let Coal know how his boy really felt.

Sunday, January 7

It wasn't until they were on their way home the next afternoon, with a wonderful prime rib dinner under their belts, that Coal brought up the subject of the dog. It was something they had to get settled.

"I want to talk to you man to man about something, Virg. Okay?"

Virgil nodded. "Sure."

"It's about Burro."

Virgil nodded again. The veil that came over his eyes was nothing compared to what had been there now for many days. "Okay."

"Son, I really wish I had known how much that old dog meant to you. I had no idea."

"It's okay."

"No it's not. I let you down. You're pretty much a grown man, and I should have seen how much you liked him. I should have asked it if was okay to give him to the MacAtees as a gift. And if you said no, then we should have kept him."

Virgil nodded. Coal wondered if he had somehow let his boy down, not teaching him the ability to speak his mind, to open up. But he himself wasn't that different when he was Virgil's age.

"If you want to, we'll start looking for a dog for you, buddy. A dog you choose, whatever breed you want—just for you."

Again, the boy's only reply for a moment was a nod. But this time Coal waited. Maybe an uncomfortable minute of silence would wring something out of his boy.

"You know what I've been thinking, Dad?"

"What's that?"

They were almost to the top of the icy Lost Trail Pass now, coming over Highway 93 to start the long, steep descent past Gibbonsville and back into the Salmon River Valley, marked by the entrance into the village of North Fork. A wonderful golden sun, getting ready to set, was striking across the frosty tree tops of the thick forest, once again transforming this place into a magical kingdom, the realm of reindeer, elves, and candy canes hanging from tree limbs.

"I've been kind of thinking about seeing if you would let me train Dobe."

"Train him? How?"

"I don't know. Just ... to do other things."

Coal almost laughed as a silly thought popped into his head, imagining his son trying to teach the pointy-eared Doberman pinscher to put on a little apron, walk on his hind legs, and serve tea, or vacuum the floors—maybe to use a feather duster. After all, Dobe had already been carefully trained to do most of the other things that a dog should know.

Coal went out on a limb and decided to share his silly thoughts with his boy, at the risk of making him feel foolish for suggesting the idea. Instead, Virgil started to giggle, then ended up in a fit of laughter so serious Coal thought he was going to choke. The laughter was contagious, and by the time they got another couple of miles down the road Coal started contemplating pulling over to the side. It was always nice to see where you were steering your vehicle when you went down Lost Trail Pass at breakneck speed, and right now his eyes were full of tears of laughter.

At last, with his cheeks hurting, Coal was able to wipe his eyes dry. "My cheeks hurt," Virgil said. That made Coal laugh a little more, and his heart felt light.

He and Virgil were going to be okay. And in his wisdom he had never had to bring up seeing Virgil's journal entry about how Katie had told Virgil their dad didn't care about them. For Coal Savage, the world was good.

*   *   *

Charley and Martha May Janx drove into downtown Thibodaux to visit Law Puckett at the run-down Thibodaux hospital. It was five in the afternoon, two hours before the end of visiting time as it had been explained over the phone to the Janxes, but the receptionist told them they could only have five minutes.

When they knocked on the door, a faint voice told them to enter in words that were hard to understand. Nervously, Martha May pushed the door open a crack, then a little more. There were two beds in the room, one of them empty. The one next to it contained a man with casts on both of his arms, another on his left leg, and a head and face completely swathed in white bandages so that he looked like a 1930's horror movie mummy, with only his eyes and mouth showing. It was the first time Charley Janx had laid eyes on Attorney Law Puckett.

"Howdy, sir. You be Mr. Puckett?"

"Yes sir, I am," replied the man through stiff, swollen, scabbed lips. "At your service." He looked over at Martha May, and he might have tried to smile. No one could have said for certain.

"Hello, Mrs. Janx. You're lookin' well."

62 pocatellocowboy@gmail.com

Martha May's eyes welled up with tears. "Why thank you, sir. Thank you. You are too."

This time there was no doubt: Law Puckett was laughing. When he got control of himself, he said, in a slurred voice she had to listen to carefully to comprehend, "Please don't do that again, Mrs. Janx. It hurts me to laugh."

"Of course. I'm very sorry, sir."

Puckett flicked the fingers of one hand, trying to wave off her concern. "I'm just havin' fun with you, awright? It feels good to laugh, at least inside. You don't worry now, y' hear? Now what might I do for you good people?"

Martha May would have liked to break down and cry, right there on the spot. Anyone would have known without being told that Law Puckett was here in this condition because of one reason: He had befriended a poor colored boy and his mother when they had no other friends. Had it not been for that, Mr. Puckett would still have been going about his courtroom duties.

"Well, sir, let me tell you: You tolt me about how you might c'd try t' call Bryant's army friend, who lives up there in Idaho an' is a sheriff. We was just comin' in t' check an' see if you was able t' do that yet. Because, sir, they won't let us come in no more t' see our boy. The jail man, that Mr. Mims, he say the jail is off limits to ... our kind."

To anyone who could read eyes, they would have seen that those of Law Puckett grew hard as granite. "He said that, did he? Well, we're gon' see about that," he said with slurred words. He failed to address her first question.

"And ... I hope it's no bother, but ... about that other thing ..."

"All right. Mrs. Janx—Mr. Janx. We are not gonna give up, you hear me? Yes, I did place a phone call to your Mr. Coal Savage, and yes, I did get through. But, uh ... Well, he was out of town." His eyes flickered as he spoke. Martha May's heart fell. It felt like someone had stepped on it. Something had gone wrong.

She almost didn't want to know more, but she had to.

"You gon' talk to 'im again?"

Puckett sighed. "Ma'am, I think ... Well, you know how hard it is to understand what I'm sayin' with my face and mouth all bruised up, right? I wonder, if I give you the number I found for Sergeant Coal Savage ... What do you think about you tryin' to call him yourself? I think you might have better luck—when he gets home, of course."

Martha May stared. Her heart continued falling. There was little hope in Law Puckett's eyes. He knew her boy's army friend, Sergeant Savage, was not going to be any help. He didn't even want to try again.

Trying to look brave, Martha May nodded. "Where is the number, Mr. Puckett?"

"You know what, ma'am? I would shore like it if you would call me Law. That is what my friends call me, you know."

Her throat tightening, Martha May stared at the public defender. His suggestion gave her a surge of happiness, but she knew it could never work. And he must know it too. Her gaze faltered. "No sir. No sir, Mr. Puckett. That would be bad for both of us. But I shore thank you for the offer."

Puckett blinked his eyes a couple of times. He understood. "Martha May—if I may be so bold as to call you that—the number is here in this note pad on my table. I hope you don't mind if I ask you to get it yoreself."

Martha May walked past her husband to reach out a trembling hand and picked up a white pad of paper. There were notes on the pad that must have been made by Puckett's nurse.

"The number says 'sheriff in Idaho' above it. Then under it 'Coal Savage'. See it?"

Martha May bobbed her head. The number was on the second to last page that had any writing on it. She read it back to him.

"Yes, ma'am. That's the one. Take that whole page. And

please try to call him, all right? He might be our only chance."

"You gon' save our boy, suh?" It was the first time Charley Janx had spoken. Law Puckett looked over into his eyes.

"I shore hope so, Mr. Janx. I hope I am."

"He can't go in no cage," Charley pressed on. "He go crazy. He seen what's in them cages. That's no place for a man. An' Slugger, he's a man. He can't go in no more cages."

"Let's try to make the call from here," Law Puckett suddenly said. "Let's see what this army friend has to say."

They called the nurse in, and Puckett told her they hoped to make a long distance call to Idaho. He promised the county would pay for the charges, but she told him just to make the call. It was a very small thing. Mercifully, it seemed the nurse had changed her mind about the five minute limit for the Janxes.

After the nurse left, Martha May picked up the phone and dialed the number. She listened to it ring until a rattling sound came over the line, and then a woman's voice.

Hello, Savages.

"Yes, ma'am. So kind of you t' answer. My name is Martha May Janx, ma'am, an' I'm a-callin' you from Louisiana?"

Oh, yes! Yes! Are you the lady I received a call about on Friday night?

"Yes, ma'am. Yes, ma'am, I b'lieve that would be me."

Well, I wish I could help you. Martha May's heart jumped at those words. She was going to tell her no. *But my son hasn't returned home from his trip yet.*

Martha May stared at the wall, unsure of how to proceed. She wondered if Coal Savage was standing right beside his mother, telling her what to say. She had feared no white man, pretending to be her son's friend or not, would lift a finger for her boy in his time of greatest need.

Can I have my son call you when he comes home?

Martha May pursed her lips. She had heard lines like this before. There was no way she would ever hear back from them. But she at least had to try. Feeling like her heart was being squeezed by a powerful hand, she quoted her area code and phone number to the woman on the other end of the line. And then she made her final plea for help, calling on the love of another mother for her child.

"Mrs. Savage, my boy told me he was a friend of yore son in the war. He's in jail for somethin' he didn't never do. He ain't ever gon' come out, an' he gon' t' prison if we can't find help for him. I'm a proud woman, ma'am, but I'm beggin' of you t' help my boy if you can. There honest ain't no other place I c'n turn."

CHAPTER NINE

Coal pulled the GMC into the driveway half an hour after dark. The sun had been down shortly after they passed the village of North Fork, and after that, down in the depths of the canyon, the world had grown dark fast.

Virgil was asleep beside him, the butt of his new rifle on the floor with the barrel resting between his legs, and the fingers of his right hand curled loosely around it, like a younger boy might in his sleep continue trying to cradle a new puppy. Coal smiled. Thinking back on the trip, even with all it had cost him, he would have paid a hundred times more.

Connie met him on the front porch with a big smile. He had just woken Virgil up, and his boy was gathering all his paraphernalia together in the cab.

"How did your trip go?"

"The best possible, Mom. I couldn't have asked for anything better."

"Oh, wonderful!" She gave him a big hug, then watched Virgil come around the front of the truck carrying his load, with the Remington now back in its box. "Oh! I see a little bribery came into play."

Coal laughed. "Nope. Virgil just needed a hunting rifle, and I got him one. Nothing to it. Right, Virg?" He dropped a hand on his boy's shoulder and squeezed as he stopped beside him on the porch.

"Well, I'll anxiously look forward to seeing that when you get it out of the box, Virgil," said Connie. She looked down at the wooden box in Coal's hand. "And I assume you didn't get left out of the gift-giving either."

Coal laughed. "Nope, I didn't. Just upgrading a little."

They all went in the house, where the dogs did their usual attack. Coal noticed that Virgil seemed to give Dobe some extra special attention this time, as if he were already assuming more ownership of the big lover-dog.

The other kids came running over to greet the wandering travelers, and Virgil went to the living room and pulled his rifle out of the box, showing it off to everyone.

Once everyone was settled and had said their greetings, Connie got Coal to the side. "Honey, you remember that call that came in before you left?"

Coal hadn't given the call another thought the entire trip. "I do now. Who was that?"

"Some attorney."

"Oh, great."

"No, I think it's something you'll want to know about."

Coal frowned. He couldn't think of one attorney, other than perhaps Mike Fica or Bryan Wheat, that he could possibly care to talk to. And his mother had said that was a long distance call.

"So ... ?"

"It was a man from Louisiana. Hang on a second." She went and pulled a notebook out from under the phone and peered at it for a few seconds. "Mr. Puckett? Lawson Puckett?"

"I don't know him. Louisiana?"

"Yes. But about an hour ago another call came in from Louisiana."

"Same guy?"

"No, Son. No. This is why I think it's important. It was a woman named Martha May Janx, and she—"

"Did you say Janx?"

"Yes. Janx."

Coal perked up and came wide awake. Louisiana. Janx. He suddenly knew the connection.

"I had a buddy in Nam at the prison named Slugger Janx. And he was from Louisiana."

Connie swallowed and reached out to touch Coal's forearm. That worried him. She only did that as a way to comfort him, or to prepare him for something hard she was about to say.

"She said her son is in jail."

"What? Jail? I thought he was still in Nam."

"I guess not. He's in jail, she said for something he didn't do, and she said he's going to go to prison if they can't find someone to help him."

Coal's chest constricted. His mind went back to the riot at Long Binh Jail, that hot, muggy, terrible August of 1968. No man had stood stronger and more loyal beside Coal than his friend and underling Slugger Janx. Slugger was a proud, law-abiding man, not the kind of man to commit a crime.

"What else did she say, Mom? Why's he in jail?"

"She didn't say. I just told her I'd have you call when you got back. She sounded pretty desperate."

"Where's the number?" This wasn't something that could wait.

pocatellocowboy@gmail.com

Slugger had stood by Coal in his time of greatest need.

He took the phone and the number up to his room, where he plugged the phone into the jack and dialed it, heart pounding. After only one ring, the phone picked up. There was a distant, hopeful *Hello?*

"Hello. Am I speaking to Mrs. Janx?"

A long pause. *Um, yes sir. Who is this?* In spite of the hope in the voice, there was suspicion too.

"My name is Coal Savage, ma'am. I was with your son in Vietnam."

Oh, dear Lord. Yes! Dear Lord. Oh, thank you, Mr. Savage, for calling me back. Sir, I never dreamed—

Coal cut her off. "Ma'am, my mother said something about your son being in jail. What's wrong? Is he all right?"

No, sir, he ain't all right, Mr. Savage. The policemen, they been beatin' him. They won't let me in t' see him no more. And somebody done beat the attorney man they had t' help Bryant. He's in a real bad way now, in the hospital.

Coal was stunned by the words. "What happened? What did he do?"

Sir, I swear to you, he didn't do nothin'. He had a fight with some kids what was callin' him baby killer an' spittin' in his face. Then some other men who pretended t' help him beat him, real bad. And then the policemen came, an' they beat him too, an' they took him t' jail. He been there ever since, an' I think he's gon' die there, an' they won't let me come in—

"Ma'am. Hang on a second. What's he being charged with?"

The woman, who sounded elderly and frail, told him everything she could think of. Coal listened intently, with a sick feeling in his stomach. His friend, his protector, his buddy, Slugger Janx was being railroaded. His mother was right: He was going to prison, and there was no doubt about it, unless someone came to his rescue. Coal had read all too much about how things were done down South. But this was Slugger Janx, who had remained beside him, shoulder to shoulder, during his darkest days in Nam.

"Ma'am, I'm coming down there."

There was a long pause, at least four seconds. *Pardon me, sir?*

"I said I'm coming down there. Tomorrow, if I can. Will somebody meet me at the airport? I'll be in a small airplane, and I won't be coming through the terminal." Longer silence. "Ma'am?"

Suddenly, Coal heard the sound of the woman's voice. She tried to speak and couldn't, and he realized she was crying. Soon, a man's voice came on the line.

Mr. Savage?

"Yes."

Sir, this is Charley Janx, Slugger's father. My Martha May ain't able t' speak no more right now. Can you talk t' me instead?

Coal laughed. "Yes, sir! You bet I can talk to you."

Coal stayed on the line long enough to get all of the information he felt he would need once he got to Louisiana, and then he said goodbye to both of them, once Martha May finally had control of her emotions, and hung up the phone. He immediately ran down to dig through the phone book and look up a man by the name of Steve White, who was a retired airline pilot and still flew a Piper four-seater aircraft to take tourists and hunters into the backcountry of Idaho, or wherever else they needed to travel. White, originally from Grapevine, Texas, had settled in Salmon six or seven years ago for the small-town environment.

To Coal's delight, White said he had nothing pressing on his calendar for the following two days, and he said he would be happy to meet Coal around seven in the morning and fly him down to Louisiana.

Thibodaux, get the gloves on, thought Coal. *Coal Savage is on his way to pay a visit, and fists are going to fly.*

CHAPTER TEN

Monday, January 8

Retired airline pilot Captain Steve White's Piper Comanche 260 landed too late the afternoon of the following day to deal with anything at the LaFourche Parish court or jail, but at the front of the airport, Coal and White were met by a black man and woman who appeared to be anywhere from sixty to eighty years of age, depending on their genetics and the kind of life they had led.

It wasn't hard to tell by the anxious look in their faces who they were as Coal stopped at the gate, holding his duffel bag. "Would you be the Janxes?"

The woman smiled, and they walked close enough for the man to hold out his hand. But he didn't. "We are! Charley and Martha May," the man said.

"Coal Savage," Coal said, and without hesitation he thrust out his hand. The old man looked down at it, and worried indecision flashed across his face. Finally, he allowed himself to reach out, and they shared a hearty handshake.

Coal turned to Martha May. She was only a slip of a woman, perhaps some hundred and five pounds at most, with pronounced veins in her hands and neck and eight-inch-long bristly, tightly curled hair starting to silver evenly throughout. She wore a yellow dress and scuffed, worn-out brown flats on her feet, with a smile on her face and wrinkles beside her mouth hinting that the smile was an often-used expression.

Without having to think about it, Coal took her in his arms and gave her a squeeze. It took a moment for her to respond, but when she did it seemed to be all the strength she could muster. "Why you wanna go huggin' on a colored woman?" she asked when Coal let go of her.

"Why would I not, Mrs. Janx? I feel like I know you folks already, from everything Slugger used to tell me about you."

Her broad smile crinkled up her eyes, the top of her nose, and her cheeks. "I feel like I know you too. I'm shore glad you come down." She reached out tentatively and patted his arm.

"Your boy is a good friend, ma'am. I know he'd come for me too if he knew I was in trouble."

"He'd try, that's for shore. But we ain't got much money. Flyin' up t' where you are might be nigh impossible."

"You're not doing well?" Coal asked.

The woman searched his eyes. He could tell she was hesitant, maybe afraid he was going to ask her for payment in exchange for his help. "No sir. Not much. But I ... I didn't know where else to turn."

"Well, we're going to work this out, ma'am," Coal promised her. "Can we go see this lawyer?"

"Yes sir, we shore can."

Coal and White climbed into the back seat of the beat-up blue 1952 Dodge Coronet the Janxes had come in, and Charley drove straight to the hospital. On the way, Martha May kept talking, filling Coal in on every detail, the ones she had told him already and a few she hadn't. By the time they reached the hospital, Coal was mad clean through, but even then he wasn't prepared for what he saw in Law Puckett's room.

The nurse tried to tell them they couldn't visit right then, and Coal reached into his shirt pocket and jerked out his badge. "Sheriff Savage. Ma'am, I don't want to sound rude, but I just flew clear from Idaho, and I'm going to see Lawson Puckett, with or without permission."

The woman stared at him, properly cowed. "Can I tell the doctor?" She was asking permission of Coal, which he thought was cute. "Sure. He's your doctor."

When she walked away to find the doctor, Coal turned to the Janxes. He didn't even have to speak. By the look in his eyes, they understood, and without waiting for the nurse to return they marched down the hall to Puckett's room.

When they knocked, there was no reply. Coal pushed the door open and looked in, seeing a mummy that appeared to be asleep on the one occupied bed in the room.

He turned to stare in shock at Martha May. "Is that him? With all the bandages?"

She nodded. "I told you they worked him over real good."

Coal swallowed. He pushed on inside the room, and the Janxes followed. When Coal stood beside Puckett's bed, he looked up and down the length of him, searching for some part he might touch to wake him up, a part that wasn't covered in hard casings. Finally, he reached out and gave the side of his neck a gentle squeeze. The man's eyes jerked open, and his whole body jolted. By the look in his eyes, his first instinct was to jump and run. But this man would not be doing either any time soon.

"Sorry to startle you. Mr. Puckett? I'm Coal Savage, from Salmon, Idaho."

Coal was fairly sure the man tried to smile. "Mr. Savage! By golly, I never really thought you'd come down here. Sir, I wish I could shake your hand."

Between a radical Southern drawl and the man's swollen lips, Coal struggled hard to understand every slurred word. "I wish you could too. I've heard what you tried to do for these people."

A sad look came into Puckett's eyes. "I'm still gonna do all I can. They just tried to make sure that wasn't much, I'm afraid."

"Who's 'they'?"

Puckett rustled his shoulders. It was the best he could do for a shrug. "I'm not sure. The other side. I'm afraid to voice a guess, because if my guess is right, this is huge."

"You're going to have to speak a little slower," Coal said.

A broken laugh escaped Puckett. "I'm sorry. They do say I can talk perty fast, for a Southerner."

"So what's your guess?" Coal asked.

The man sighed. "Understand that I'm going out on a dangerous limb here, but ... I think it was the police that orchestrated the attack. It was either them doing it, or they hired it done. They beat me up, and I thought they were gonna drive over top of me, but I passed out then, and I don't think they did. I think they were just leaving, but I shore thought I was doomed."

"Is there anybody down here I can trust?"

"Oh, you bet! The Judge. Judge Pandra. He's a good man, and if he does anything that sounds off, it's only because he has to keep the peace with some of the people down here if he wants to keep his seat."

"But ... Isn't he the judge that set the high bail?"

"He is. I was miffed too, but he had a reason, and I understood after he explained it. He's keeping the bail high for fear of Mr. Janx being killed if he's released. You have to understand this place, Mr. Savage. Janx battered two white kids."

"Two white kids who attacked him and spat in his face?"

"Forget that part. Just remember 'white kids'. The sooner you see what that means, the quicker you'll understand how to get on down here. It wouldn't matter if them white kids were bank robbers or rapists—it ain't the place of a Negro to touch them. That's all there is to it."

Coal clenched his jaws. He wasn't going to make a big debate out of all this, but he wondered what made the average Southerner tick. And how had attitudes not changed after more than a century since the end of slavery?

Puckett cleared his throat. "Savage, does the name of this town mean anything to you? You ever heard it before?"

"Not that I remember, except maybe from Slugger."

"Well, then let this sink in. This place is the home of what they call the Thibodaux Massacre, back in 1887. There was a big strike against the sugar plantations, and the white paramilitary group down here set upon the Negro camps. Killed somewhere between thirty and fifty Negroes—men, women, and children. Somewheres around three hundred came up either wounded, missing, or dead. And believe me, things ain't changed a whole lot around here. That's what you're dealin' with, and you best not ever forget it if you wanna keep your hide. The only thing more hated down here than a Negro is a nosy northerner sticking his iron in the wrong fires."

Coal nodded, but he didn't skip a beat. "I guess I need to go to the jail first thing tomorrow and put up the bail."

Puckett stared up at him. It was hard to see any expression in his face when all Coal could see was eyes and mouth. But from those two things Puckett seemed amazed. "You understood the amount, right? It's five thousand dollars. And if Mr. Janx fails to appear, it's forfeit. Gone. And if he stays here, in order to appear in court, he's probably going to get killed. Or at least hurt a lot worse than he already is."

"I'll get the five thousand," said Coal. "We'll see about the rest."

Coal started to turn, but Puckett's voice stopped him, and he faced him once more. "There is one other man might be on your side, Savage. There at the courthouse. Name's Chris Kay."

"Another lawyer?" Coal asked.

"Not a lawyer. Deputy." That revelation surprised Coal, after all he had heard. "Just remember: If there's anybody else around, you prob'ly aren't going to get anything out of him either. Man like him's gotta walk on eggshells down in this country."

Tuesday, January 9

Coal had gotten his own room at the hotel, with Steve White in a different one. He got up early and went downstairs to wait for the Janxes. They were already waiting in their old Coronet on the street, afraid to come into the hotel, since they claimed it was a white establishment.

As Coal got into the front seat with Charley Janx, the old man said, "You really sure you wanna do this, Mr. Savage?"

"Why wouldn't I be sure?"

"Sir ..." The old man started into traffic. "You gotta understand, these folks hate coloreds. And they hate folks who like coloreds. But maybe even more, they hate folks from the North. What Lawyer Puckett said yesterday's the truth: They all gonna be again' you. Ever' last one."

Coal smiled grimly. "From what I understand, the feeling will be mutual."

Charley nodded and continued driving, expressionless. Coal could only imagine the fear that must be inside him.

Ahead, Coal spied the dark top of the roof that had to be the courthouse. He looked at Charley and Martha May, both of their faces painted in bold colors of fear.

Coal didn't know if it was going to be a good day or a bad day, but it was sure about to be a day.

CHAPTER ELEVEN

The imposing courthouse of LaFourche Parish at 201 Green Street, constructed of stone mostly covered in cloud-white plaster, in the Beaux-arts style, stood lofty and austere over the street, pretentious as a television evangelist among the dilapidated offices and shabby apartments of old town, with their brick walkways and pots of long-dead flowers sitting out on windowsills. Pairs of massive, fluted columns, bloated with pride in themselves, rose up on either side of the front courthouse doors and in front of three large windows with domed tops to form a shaded portico. They served to support a grand gabled pediment jutting out over the row of four wide steps that would lead one up onto the porch and through the black maw of the eight-foot-tall front doors, just now standing open as two men in light-colored suits passed through. On the front of the portico, standing out in plastered relief from the face of the structure, four numbers proclaimed the birth of the building as 1856.

The American flag, ironic symbol of liberty and justice for all, rose on its slender steel pole to the right of the sidewalk, and two leafless oak trees, like powerless sentries, stood guard on the drab lawn in front, dormant and gray, stripped of aroma and color, their skeletal branches sad now, and standing naked and shamed while they waited for spring to return.

Charley Janx parked his car right in front of the building instead of around in back only because Coal told him to. He certainly didn't like it, and as he threw it into park he glanced around to see if anyone was watching, his eyes large and frightened, a villain in the act of some dastardly crime.

Coal looked at Charley. "Do you want to come in, or stay put?"

"I want to come in, but I'm afeered it's gon' bring you trouble."

"What about you?" Coal looked in the back seat at Martha May.

"I wanna come in. That's my boy in there."

Coal nodded. "Then let's go in. It's about time for something to change down here. Maybe we can start now."

The three of them disembarked, and Martha May came and reached out for her husband's hand, giving Coal a surge of unexpected emotion. Once more, they were stepping into the realm of LaFourche Parish's white folk, a place their kind didn't often dare to venture. They had an escort this time, but he was an outsider, and he would not be thought of more fondly than they were.

The front sidewalk was made of flawlessly laid red brick in the shape of a large T. They took it at a brisk walk, then up the stone steps they went, and as they pushed inside they paused. The musty smell of stone and old plaster and wood, of more than a century of Southern justice meted out, of old books and sweaty, pompous attorneys and courtroom observers and frightened defendants all descended upon Coal and the Janxes from every corner and every shadowed nook. Across from them on the wall, an overbearing oil painting in a gold frame depicted some self-important figure in a white three-piece suit and black tie, staring down smugly at those who would dare enter the forbidding shadows of his kingdom. He was reinforced by the nearby photographic portraits of Richard M. Nixon and Spiro Agnew.

Martha May didn't wait for Coal to decipher the directory inside the door. She just pointed the way to the basement. And they descended into the jaws of LaFourche Parish justice.

The first door at the bottom was deep brown wood, with an opaque window two feet wide by three high. Above it in black cast iron letters was one word: JAIL. Coal looked at the Janxes. They couldn't hide the pinched look of fear on their faces.

"You can wait out here if you'd like."

"No sir," blurted out Martha May. "No sir." She set her jaw.

Coal shifted his eyes to her husband. "Charley?"

"I'll go with my woman."

With a nod, Coal turned the ornate brass door knob, and they stepped inside.

A counter made of the same wood as the door stretched along fifteen feet of the inner sanctum of the jail before a break where a swinging door hung a foot back from the line of the counter, which then continued on down to the end of the room.

A man wearing a light blue shirt and black tie, with black hair parted in the middle and pomaded down flat to either side stood up from behind a desk and looked them over. He hadn't missed the 1970's memo about giant sideburns, and a Clark Gable mustache tried to give his homely face a dapper look, but failed. He looked up—way up—at Coal, his eyes only darting over at the black couple before deciding he wouldn't deign to offer them a greeting.

"Good morning, sir. May I help you?" Spoken in a proper Southern drawl.

"I hope so. You have a Bryant Janx in your jail and I need to see him."

The man's gaze faltered. Darted toward the Janxes once more, then back. He hadn't really needed to be told why Coal was here, since he came in with Charley and Martha May. All this was obvious in his eyes. He was operating merely on formality.

"It isn't visiting hours yet, and apparently no one has told you, but those two aren't being allowed in here anymore. And ... who might you be?"

Coal had a feeling the man was trying to decide if the Janxes had managed to find their son a real lawyer, since his public defender had become *predisposed.* The fleeting notion to tell the man that was just what he was crossed Coal's mind. That would sure throw these people for a loop. But his better sense warned him not to. He didn't want to lose his credibility from the very start, and if they asked for his credentials he most certainly would.

"Sheriff Coal Savage." No need to tell the man sheriff of where. He glanced down for a moment at the brass name tag pinned to the black pocket flap of the man's blue shirt. "Officer Leary?"

"Yes sir. Sheriff? You don't mind if I see your ID, do you?"

With an affected look of patience wearing thin, Coal pulled out his wallet and let it fall open to reveal his badge and ID. He had left his uniform badge at home, since wearing it here seemed tantamount to impersonating an officer on duty.

"You would have to agree to be searched, sir."

Coal looked down at the man. He spoke only with his eyes for a few seconds, and he meant for his eyes to say a lot. "Search away."

The man blinked rapidly a couple of times. He licked his lips, and his glance swept the room. He wanted support from his own kind, and there was none to be had.

"Oh, never mind. Since you're a peace officer."

"What about them?" Coal jerked his head toward the Janxes.

The man turned to stare at them, his expression a mixture of hatred, repulsion, and fear. "They're with you, so ... Well, just come on in. But ..."

The man paused too long. "Yes?"

"Well, I would just ask that if any other officers come in you go along with me when I tell them I searched the three of you."

Coal wanted to let a smile out, not a friendly one, but one of disdain. He didn't know whether to like the man for passing on the search or to look down on him for his fear. But he certainly didn't mind not being pawed over by him.

The deputy's eyes dropped to Coal's belt, where his new Smith and Wesson filled its russet-colored holster. "I'm supposed to relieve you of any weapons before you go in there."

Coal met the man's eyes squarely. "I won't go in the cell. And you can go back there with me."

The man's eyes jumped toward the outer door. He must be wondering how far out his compatriots were. "Well, I s'pose that'd be all right."

He went and unlocked the door into the jail, allowing the Janxes and Coal to pass in front of him, then shutting the door behind as he followed them through.

In the cellblock, one bare light bulb hung down from a wire twisting out of the ceiling. Wherever the light from the bulb didn't touch, the jail lay in shadow. It smelled strongly of old stone, faintly of aged urine and excrement and sweat and fear, all mixed into a potpourri that included the distinct odor of chlorine bleach.

Martha May marched down to the very last cell, where the darkness was deepest. Slugger must have recognized the tread of her feet, for he was already standing by the time they got there, and as Coal came up he saw those dark hands he remembered so well come up to curl around the bars of his cell door.

"Hello, Son." Martha May's voice was shaky with emotion. Some of it seemed like happy emotion, however. "I brought someone to see you."

When Coal came into sight, Slugger jumped a little back from the bars. He stared for a few seconds, and Coal stared back, too angry at the sight of Slugger's haggard, bruised face to speak.

"Sarge? Sarge, is that you?"

Coal found his tongue and tried to seek out good emotions inside himself. "It sure is, buddy. It's me."

"What—" Slugger stopped and looked over at his parents, then let his eyes shift to the jailer, and quickly away. "What you doin' here?"

"I'm getting you out."

Slugger stared at him. The silence was thick as molasses pie.

His eyes went again to the jailer, then to Coal.

The quiet was too much. Slowly, Coal, and then the Janxes shifted their full attention over to Leary. "Is there a problem?"

The jailer cleared his voice. It echoed against the ungiving walls of the cellblock.

"Well, yes sir. That is, the judge just this morning revoked bail."

CHAPTER TWELVE

The day was cloudy and gloomy, but even so, the upper level of the LaFourche Parish courthouse seemed bright and beautiful in comparison to the dungeon below, as clouded light streamed through sky lights in the roof.

Jailer Leary had warned Coal that court would soon be in session, and by the flutter of activity upstairs, and the people fidgeting on the hard wooden benches in the hall, he guessed that much was true. But he also guessed this session wouldn't take long, since most of the activity in the hall centered around two groups of people. Two groups of people, so possibly only two defendants. How long could it take?

Still, Coal's impatience was vast when he thought of his friend, a man who should have received a hero's welcome home, stuck down in that dungeon of a cellblock. He looked at his watch. Just shy of nine o'clock.

Looking over at the Janxes, Coal jerked his head for them to follow him, and he walked to an important looking door, its deep brown wood contrasting sharply to the yellowing white of the plaster wall in which it was set. On the milky glass of the door were

82   pocatellocowboy@gmail.com

stenciled the words in black: COURT CLERK. Taking a breath to
calm himself, putting a little oxygen in his system that he hoped
would help him keep his anger at bay, Coal pushed through the
door, bringing the Janxes in his wake.

A blonde with a page boy haircut and a navy blazer over a
frilly-fronted white shirt, pushed dark-framed glasses up on her
nose and bolted up out of her chair as Coal stopped in front of her
desk.

"Miss. Sheriff Savage. Is the judge available?"

"Umm ..." The girl, for that was what her obvious early twenties made her to Coal, glanced at a clock on the wall behind him.
"No sir, he's about to start court."

Coal didn't let that deter him. "It's urgent business, and it
shouldn't take more than a minute."

The girl looked over at the Janxes, then hurried her eyes away.
Apparently, people down here thought their retinas might burn if
they looked at black people too long.

A door down the way from the girl's desk opened, and a wrinkled, stoop-shouldered man whose little remaining hair was smutty
gray passed through and gaped at Coal and the Janxes, perplexed.
"Amy? Court's about to start."

"Judge Pandra?" Coal ventured a guess.

The old man stared up at him through washed-out blue eyes.
"No, sir. He's in his office—about to go into court. You'll need to
wait outside."

Coal sensed a huge relief from the girl, Amy, because now she
had reinforcements. But he detected no strength, only bad temper,
from the shriveled old man he assumed must be the bailiff.

"Listen. I came all the way down here from Idaho to see the
judge, and I need to see him now. Please tell him Sheriff Coal Savage is here, and I promise I won't take two minutes of his time."

"Well, he won't see you," the old man sputtered.

Coal's senses heightened. This impatient old man was weak.

He would cave in.

"I'm not leaving this office until he does."

"Then you'll be thrown out," said the old man, but his eyes bounced to Amy, then around the otherwise vacant room, obviously wondering how he was going to make good on his threat.

The old man suddenly turned and left the room, and a moment later a much larger, younger man in a deep gray suit entered from the same door, the old man following him like a monkey after a tinker.

"Sir? You're going to have to wait in the hall."

Without these two men and Amy in the courtroom, it was not likely that the judge would have gone in yet either, and he suspected his honor's office lay behind the solemn-looking door directly back of Amy's desk. Coal took a big chance and raised his voice.

"I'm not going until we can see the judge. He can afford two minutes."

"Well, I think you *will* leave," said the big man, putting a hard sound in his voice as he started forward. He didn't seem to realize just how large Coal was, and how large the revolver on his belt, until he got closer, where he paused. Now he had to save face. He had spoken too big in front of two fellow employees, and, worse yet, the Janxes.

"Go out in the hall. You can see the judge after court." His voice was loud, but there was no power behind it.

"I'll see him now," Coal pressed, and he started around Amy's desk, hard put not to notice the fear that came into the girl's eyes.

Without warning, the dark door behind Amy's desk opened. In the doorway, his hand on the polished brass of the knob, leaned a man clothed in a black robe, with blond hair going much to white, curling around his ears and onto his forehead, thick as polar bear fur. "Folks? What seems to be the problem?" The judge, all five-foot-ten, perhaps one hundred seventy pounds of him, was overtly addressing everyone in the room, but Coal understood that the words were directed at him.

"Good morning, your honor." His words cut off whatever the old man started to say. "I'm really sorry to bother you, but I needed to see you before court started. I'm Sheriff Savage, from Lemhi County, Idaho."

The judge's still-brown eyebrows lifted ever-so-slightly. "As I thought you might be." He offered the Janxes a reserved smile. "And these would be the parents of our jail guest, Mr. Janx, I assume."

The Janxes stood frozen until Martha May found her voice, taking a timid step forward. "Yes sir, your honor. I'm Martha May Janx, an' this here is my husband, Charley Janx. Pleased to meet you, sir."

"And you as well," replied Judge Pandra, and his smile widened, just by a touch. He let his eyes pump across Amy, the old man, and the big man who Coal presumed to be a court marshal. "Go on in, folks. I'll be in shortly. Please inform the court that there will be a brief delay."

Turning again to Coal and the Janxes as Amy and the court officials filed toward the door, Judge Pandra looked Coal up and down. "They grow them pretty large in your part of the country, don't they?"

Coal chuckled. "Not that many, sir. Thank you for seeing us."

"My pleasure," said the judge formally, turning back to his chambers so that he appeared to be nothing but a flowing black curtain topped by that head of white-gold hair. "Won't you come into my office?" he spoke over his shoulder.

Coal and the Janxes trailed inside, where beautiful wood made an otherwise stiff, formal office seem warm. Venerable-looking tomes with tan and red, embossed spines lined up in perfect order on one long shelf of a bookcase, with other shelves weighed down with similar books of black, or deep brown, all with gilt lettering.

No Mister Rogers songbooks in here, thought Coal wryly.

A coffee pot between two bookcases filled the room with homey aroma, hiding most of the acridity of long-extinguished cigars and the faint scent of cologne Coal recognized as the brand Amy had been wearing.

An exquisitely embossed carpet of burgundy, black, gray and tan shades showed absolutely no trace of dust or debris, and the walls, unlike most in the courthouse so far, were not of white, but of a deep, rich beige, almost tan, with a mahogany wainscot, and red oak chair rails separating the two.

"Do we need to sit?" questioned the judge as he turned.

"No sir. I promised I wouldn't take long."

"Fine." The judge remained standing. "I assume you already guessed, but I'm Judge Pandra."

"Yes, sir. I guessed."

"And I may help you in what way?"

"They told me downstairs that you revoked Slugger Janx's bail?"

"Slugger? You mean Bryant? Yes, I did."

"Could I ask why?"

"Quite simply, to keep him alive. I can't allow him out of this jail if he has no way out of this parish, and as far as I am able to ascertain he has no way out." The judge stopped and swept the three with a studying glance, resting last on Coal. "Does he?"

"I was Slugger's sergeant at Long Binh Jail, in Vietnam—USARVIS. The military prison where we housed our own troops. We worked together for almost a year, your honor, and we became like brothers."

A warm look came into the judge's eyes. "I'm thankful to hear of it. Very heart-warming."

Coal nodded. "The short of it is I'd like to take Slugger home to Idaho with me."

Judge Pandra raised an eyebrow. "Do tell. And you shall take

full responsibility of this man? I am told that he has a bit of a temper."

"Sir, if you will pardon my saying so, I would venture to agree
that he does, when he's been spat on and called a baby killer. That
man should have come home a war hero. Two wars ago he sure
would have."

Judge Pandra nodded. "As it happens, I agree with you. I was
in that war you speak of, and yes, I came home to parades, and a
hero's welcome. And ... Well, that is not what our young men got
this time around. Sheriff Savage, correct?"

"Uh, yes sir. Coal Savage."

"Well, sir, how does two bits sound to you?"

"Pardon?"

"Two bits. Twenty-five cents."

Coal cocked his head. "I'm not sure I follow you."

"On the condition that you will sign a paper stating your intent
to take Mr. Bryant Janx home to Idaho with you, where he will
assumedly be safe from harm, I am hereby re-invoking bail for
him, in the amount of twenty-five cents." Coal stood there staring.
He was having trouble registering the judge's words. "And you do
understand that if Mr. Janx doesn't appear in my courtroom on the
date of his hearing, I am required to sign an arrest warrant for him,
correct? And that all bail money would be forfeited, and you will
not be entitled to receive one penny back?"

Coal continued to hold the judge's eyes. Was this man for real?
"You did say twenty-five cents," he said by way of confirmation.

The judge nodded. *"If* you're taking him to Idaho."

Coal nodded, unsure if he should let the grin he was feeling
cross his face, or if this judge was too stern for that. "I'm taking
him back to Idaho."

Judge Pandra put out his hand. Coal shook it, and it was as
warm as his voice and demeanor, yet also just as stiff. "I will make
a phone call down to the jail. You can put up bail there."

CHAPTER THIRTEEN

Wednesday, January 10

The following morning as the Piper flew high over what Steve White informed them were the yellow prairies and brown winter fields of Kansas, Coal sat in the front passenger seat, Slugger Janx peacefully asleep in his exhaustion behind him.

He had to chuckle every time he thought of the expression on the face of Jailer Leary, who had still been on the phone with Judge Pandra when they got down to the jail. By that time, there was a second jailer with him, and that slightly larger man than Leary stared at his co-jailer as he heard Leary's words to Coal: "So I guess you're here to bail out Bryant Janx. The judge says that will be a total of ... twenty-five cents." If Coal was not mistaken, it almost looked like the man with Leary was attempting to hold back a smile. That was when he noticed the name on his badge: Kay. This had to be Chris Kay, the decent deputy Lawson Puckett had told them about.

It was worth every moment of Coal's time, and every penny he was putting into fuel for the Piper Comanche and into Steve White's pocket for his time and trouble. White had told him he was doing it for free, other than the cost of fuel, but Coal simply couldn't bring himself to allow that, and he told him so. White finally gave in and told him he would bill him when they returned to the Salmon air strip.

The blue side of their departure from Thibodaux was watching the tear-filled goodbye between Slugger and his parents. Unlike his trip across the ocean as a soldier, this time they were sure he would not be killed in combat, yet also knew that even as he lived and breathed, they would never be with him again. Coal had to keep thinking about jailer Leary's partner to keep the tear-stained face and the shaking, frail frame of Martha May Janx from his thoughts. The man had turned out indeed to be Deputy Chris Kay, and he followed them out of the jail and to the street, where he shook hands with Coal and told him he was glad there were people like him in the world. Of course Kay didn't dare shake hands with any of the Janxes, but he did sneak in a nod toward them, and a smile, before sweeping the area to see if anyone was watching him, then turning quickly to retreat to the big courthouse.

It was late in the day when the Comanche made a swing to the north, to parallel the Lemhi Range the rest of the way on into Salmon, and thirty minutes later they touched down on the little runway. Slugger Janx by then had been wide awake for a couple of hours, and staring out the window at the frozen landscape below, or at least what he could see of it through the scudding gray clouds.

While the engines were still whirring, with the plane parked in front of a small white hangar, they disembarked into a world that could not be much above zero and pulled out their luggage as Steve White unlocked and threw the door up to his hangar, then got back in and pulled the plane all the way in. He performed all his procedures to make sure he was ready for the next flight while Coal and Slugger stood by in the shelter of the hangar, which wasn't much warmer than outside.

After White had shut the hangar up and locked it, the three of them, with their breath puffing out around their faces in crystalline clouds, carried their luggage to the parking area beyond the white and green single-wide trailer house that served as the airport's headquarters. Coal's GMC was parked next to White's red Jeepster

Commando. They threw their luggage into their respective vehicles, and Coal turned to White.

"Thanks again, Steve. What do I owe you?"

"Well, you already paid for every fill-up so far. I'll fill it up the rest of the way tomorrow and send you the bill. How does that sound?"

"Great. And your time?"

"Oh, right. So ... Two bits."

Coal blinked. "What's that?"

"I said two bits. Twenty-five cents?"

Coal laughed. "Right. No you don't. How much?"

White shrugged and turned to the front door of his Cherokee, throwing it open and starting to climb in.

Coal pressed him. "How much, Steve?"

"I told you." White plopped down on his seat, rolling down the window because he knew Coal wasn't going to leave him alone, then shutting his door to create a barrier between them.

"Come on, Steve. I'm not paying you twenty-five cents to take me all the way to Louisiana and back."

White fired up his engine, letting it idle for a moment. Finally, he looked up at Coal. "Fine, then. Don't pay. But see if I ever take you flying again."

With that, he stepped on the gas and pulled away, leaving Coal standing there feeling like an idiot—not to mention a freeloader.

He turned and looked at Slugger. His friend looked like hell, with one eye swollen all the way over, the other halfway, both cheeks bumpy and bruised, a gash on the left side of his forehead, and his lips still puffy and scabbed. He had his arms folded across his chest and was shivering all over. But somehow, through unspoken pain, Slugger was smiling.

"I never knew there was so much stuff that cost two bits, Sarge. Know what else?"

"What?"

"I hope your truck has a good heater. You never told me it was gon' be colder than a polar bear's toe up here."

They drove into Salmon, and as they hit Main Street and stopped, Coal looked over at Slugger. "Hey, you hungry?"

"Jeez, man. You kiddin'? I could eat a bucket of turds."

Coal laughed. "I guess there's a reason you wanted to come to Idaho, if that's the fare down in your neck of the woods."

"Sarge, stop clownin' around. If you was my side o' this face, you'd know how bad it hurts t' laugh."

"Oh, make no mistake about it, Slugger: I'm on *my* side of your face, and it still hurts."

They laughed together, and Coal turned left and pulled to the curb in front of the Coffee Shop. He pointed north up the street. "A good friend of mine owns this place, but there's another joint called Wally's a couple of blocks up—and a young lady over there who's cute as a button—but I'll start you out with some Coffee Shop grub. You know, this is actually a five-star restaurant."

Slugger turned and stared at Coal, trying to see humor in his face. "You serious?"

"I am. You don't think we can have a five-star restaurant in Salmon?"

"I never thought about it, but I guess I'd a said no." Slugger's eyes swept the quaint little town. "And I never seen no five-star nothin' before anyhow. Sure not down in Thibodaux."

"Not even in Hanoi?" asked Coal with a wink. "Come on. Let's go see if they serve any five-star buckets of turds in here."

They went inside, the sound of the door chimes being drowned out by the clamor of voices and laughter in the restaurant. Before anyone could come to seat them, Coal, who was watching Slugger's face, became aware of a gradual hush falling over the place.

He had been about to ask Slugger if something was wrong, but the suddenly overbearing quiet drew him to turn and glance about the room. Every eye, without exception, was staring toward them.

And Coal was fairly certain that not one of them was on him.

It was high time to break the sober silence. "Hi, folks. I'd like to introduce you to a new face in the valley—this is Slugger Janx, visiting from Louisiana. Slugger was with me in Vietnam."

Eyes shifted around the room, one patron looking at another, everyone trying to catch the reaction of his neighbor. A few people recovered quickly enough to nod at Slugger. Some recovered only enough to lean to the side and speak in whispers to a neighboring diner.

From way at the back of the room, Coal saw a man in a cowboy hat stand up, and he recognized Joshua Olschewski, the saddle maker. Joshua threw down a napkin on his chair and strode up through the long room, dodging tables. When he was close, he threw out a big, strong hand. "Howdy, Mr. Janx. I'm Joshua Olschewski. But you c'n call me Josh." His eyes skipped around Slugger's battered face.

Slugger slowly gave Josh his hand, and they shook heartily. It was only then that Josh turned to look at Coal, and he touched his hat brim, then stuck out his hand. "Hey, Sheriff."

Coal greeted the man and shook his hand, then watched as he strode back to his table, where an attractive brunette sat in Levi's and a plaid turquoise shirt.

In the room, no one else made a move to rise or speak to Coal or Slugger, but slowly the sounds of conversation began to return, albeit more subdued. After a few more seconds, Tammy Hawley came from the other side of the restaurant. She seemed to make a point of keeping her smiling expression level as she looked at Coal, but it was obvious she had already heard the news in the other side of the restaurant: There was a black man in Salmon, Idaho.

"Hi, Coal." Tammy's bright-toothed smile was warm and welcoming as always. "It's sure good to see you." Without an invitation, she threw her arms around him, and he accepted the embrace gladly, holding on a little long because he wasn't sure he wanted to see how her demeanor changed when she turned to Slugger—if she did at all.

He soon had to chide himself for ever questioning this sweet woman, however, for she had no sooner let go of him than she turned and gave Slugger the same big smile. "Hi. I'm Tammy. Welcome to Salmon." And she held out her hand to Slugger.

Eyes shifting over to Coal, Slugger quickly looked back at Tammy and took her hand in a gentle grip. "Name's Bryant, miss. But most ever'one calls me Slugger."

"Okay, Slugger. It's good to meet you. Come on. Let's get you two a table if we can find one."

Four men abruptly stood up from a booth at the front of the room, and the one of the bunch who looked like their leader, a heavy-set man with four rings of wrinkles around his bull neck and a thinning head of short black hair, said, "We're leavin', miss." He jabbed a wad of bills out toward her. "It's all there, an' yer tip." The man didn't smile, and his dark eyes glanced over at Slugger, swept him up and down, then looked over at his fellow guests, sending them toward the front of the restaurant with a sideways jerk of his head.

As they were passing through the door, muffled by the door chimes Coal thought he heard one of the men say, "I guess that's about the last time I'm comin' in this place." Unfortunately, by the glance Slugger shot Coal, he had heard as well.

So had Tammy. Obviously embarrassed, she tried to cover the uncomfortable moment with her big smile and small talk. "Well, Coal, if you don't mind standing there for a sec, I'll just clear this table off, okay? So what have you been up to?"

She glanced at him a couple of times as she was stacking plates and scooting them all forward on the table.

"Not much." Coal's smile wasn't as easy to beckon as Tammy's, since he was still gravely affected by the overall sub-dued tone of the big room and unable to pretend joviality. "Just normal sheriff stuff."

"Nice. Hey—I was sure glad to hear about Jim. That was pretty scary, huh?"

Coal nodded. "Yeah. You never know what's going to happen in this valley."

Now the next table over was vomiting out its crowd of diners as well, and Tammy tried to smile at them, pretending not to notice the large amount of food remaining on their plates. They trooped past her in a voiceless cluster to wait together for a moment by the cash register. Then most of them, speaking in low voices, went outside, leaving only one behind, holding his wallet. Coal thought they might head to their vehicles and start them up, but instead they milled around outside the door in the ice-cold air.

Tammy rang the diner up, then came back to move all the plates from the first table to the second, and she ran a rag across the table and benches to clear them of crumbs. She summoned back her huge smile for Coal and Slugger, which sometimes seemed bigger than the whole of her face. "All right, you two. Have a seat and I'll be right back to take your orders. Do you want me to start you off with something to drink?"

Coal met Tammy's eyes. She was always friendly, but today she was going the extra mile, trying to make up for what the room had become. Coal and Slugger ordered water, and Tammy went back to the kitchen.

More and more people were starting to stand up throughout the room. Coal didn't care. No one could tell them how long to remain. Maybe they were done eating. But when four newcomers entered through the front door and stood there for only a moment, said something in a whisper to each other, then turned to go, it was too much for Coal.

Even as Tammy was approaching with her little order pad and a pen in hand, and Jay walked past Coal and Slugger, making his way to the checkout counter, Coal spoke up to the newcomers from his bench in the booth: "There's an empty table right here, boys."

His words forced three of the four to turn back, while the fourth effectively hid behind them. Coal recognized one of them as Danny Shea, one of the county commissioners.

As the four men stood there dumb-struck, Tammy had time to reach them. "Yes, guys, come on in. I'll get this table cleared right up for you."

Even as she spoke, another waitress hurried up from the back. "Don't worry, Tam, you just take Coal's order. I'll get this table." The second waitress Coal didn't know hurried to clean up the table, while the four men at the door, apparently too embarrassed now to make a further scene by leaving, stood there in cold silence.

A booming voice came out of the quiet on the other side of the restaurant. "What's this I hear about a nigger in here?"

Following on the heels of the voice, a mountain of a man loomed into Coal's view. It was six-foot-eight Bigfoot Monahan.

CHAPTER FOURTEEN

It had been some time since Coal laid eyes on Paul Monahan, the man referred to in the valley as Bigfoot. He couldn't deny that the man crossed his mind now and then; after all, they shared quite a history. But for some reason he hadn't entertained the thought of ever running into him again, since Bigfoot worked clear over in Leadore, and Coal didn't get out that way often.

Hearing Bigfoot's booming voice now, and seeing him in person, set Coal back on his heel. It wasn't the compassionate Bigfoot swabbing the blood of battle off Coal's face with a wet rag that came to mind, but the Bigfoot who once had looked into his eyes like a hungry lion, ready to tear off his limbs.

"What the hell is that?" Coal heard Slugger say. The words broke him from an almost trance-like state.

Without looking at his friend, Coal said, "That's what they call Bigfoot."

"You're jokin'. I thought that was a myth."

For some reason, that made Coal chuckle. But the look in Bigfoot's face as he marched their way was not humorous. Coal kicked Slugger's foot under the table and motioned with his head for him to stand up. Slugger wasted no time in complying, and Coal did the same.

To almost everyone in the restaurant, Coal cut an impressive figure. No one, probably not even Bigfoot, would call him small. But somehow Bigfoot always made him feel as if he were shrinking, and the closer Bigfoot came, the more powerful that feeling.

Bigfoot Monahan stopped just four feet from the slack-jawed

Slugger, with Coal yet another three feet away. With his paws hanging seemingly relaxed at his sides, he looked Slugger up and down. The expression in his pale eyes was unreadable, but Coal remembered the same look in the eyes of a caged cougar in a zoo he had taken Laura and Katie to when Katie wasn't yet a year old. That cougar didn't seem to care about anyone else, only tiny Katie, and the look in its eyes sent a chill over Coal's body he remembered to this day.

Coal drew on his knowledge of how many in a warrior society, particularly American Indians, respected bravery, and even if they hated someone as an enemy, they might accord him respect and spare his life if he showed himself to be bold. He wished Slugger had read the same thing, but his friend made no move at all. At least he didn't turn and run under the piercing gaze of Bigfoot.

"Hello, Paul. How are Beverly and Butch?"

For a moment, it didn't seem to register in Bigfoot's brain that Coal was addressing him. Coal saw his right hand flex and tighten. He wondered if he should shove Slugger out of the way, for if there were one thing he knew about his friend, he might very well be afraid, but he would fight like a bobcat in spite of it. And although he had seen Slugger perform well in a fight, he wasn't sure how he would do in a fight against a juggernaut.

All talk in the room had ceased, and every eye was glued to the real-life movie screen before them. Bigfoot finally drew in a huge breath, and his eyes pivoted over to Coal.

"They're fine."

"Good."

Bigfoot's lip twitched when his eyes bounced once again off Slugger. "Why's this in here?"

"Why? *This* is Slugger Janx, Paul. He's a friend of mine from Vietnam. I brought him here to show him how good people in the valley are to strangers."

Bigfoot nodded. His eyes sliced like razors across Slugger,

strafed Coal, and then returned to imbed themselves in Slugger. But he spoke to Coal.

"You better keep it in a cage then. Animals runnin' loose in a town like this get hurt."

Coal stood tall, like a trapper of old facing down a war party of Blackfeet.

"That's not too neighborly, Paul."

Bigfoot's nostrils flared as he stared at Slugger, then again, wider, when his eyes burned into Coal's face. "Stop callin' me Paul. And I ain't tryin' to be neighborly."

Bigfoot stepped forward, his eyes zeroed on the front door. Sensibly, Coal and Slugger each pivoted on one foot, making them look like swinging doors being shoved aside in a Western movie. Some might have said they resembled the Red Sea, being parted by Charlton Heston's Moses.

Bigfoot strode to the front, and Tammy scrambled after him and met him at the counter. Bigfoot looked down at her. "Left my money on the table ... *miss*. With yer tip."

Tammy nodded. "Thanks, sweetie. Have a good day, okay?"

Something changed in Bigfoot's eyes, almost imperceptible except to a man watching as close as Coal was. The big man looked down at Tammy Hawley, and his normally cold, fierce eyes, for one moment, looked at the same time warm and a little sad.

"You too," he replied, in a much softer voice, then turned and pushed outside into the cold. Like any furry bear, he wore no coat.

No one in the room spoke for a minute or so. When they commenced again, it was in subdued tones. Coal motioned toward the table, and he and Slugger sank back into their seats as Danny Shea and his three companions slid into the next booth.

Seven or eight people waited at the counter to pay now, and Jay Castillo rang them up as fast as he could while still trying to make each patron feel appreciated. Jay wasn't the type to put on airs. He simply cared about people, and that was a big reason customers always returned to the Coffee Shop.

The other waitress Coal didn't recognize came hustling in from the other room carrying a black and red buffalo plaid coat, like Coal's blue one, only larger. She looked about, an almost frantic look in her eyes. "Is he gone?"

No one responded, so Coal, looking at the size of the coat, cut in: "You mean Bigfoot?" So much for his thought about furry bears.

The woman turned and looked at Coal, nodding. "He must have been pretty upset when he left."

Coal raised his eyebrows. "Yeah, apparently. Why don't you give me the coat. He lives out by me. I'll take it back to him."

"Wow, okay. That's pretty nice of you after the way he was acting."

"Oh well. They say you catch more bees with honey, right?"

The waitress, a pretty blond woman who appeared to be in her mid-fifties, pushed glasses down the bridge of her nose a little ways. "Sure. But you catch more flies with manure."

With the half-serious look on the woman's face, it took Coal a moment to realize she was playing with him, and he let out a laugh. "I guess that's true. So the question is whether Paul Monahan is a bee, or a fly."

The woman grinned and held out her hand. "I'm Jodie Beaudoin."

Coal enjoyed the woman's warm, firm grip, introducing himself and Slugger and taking Bigfoot's coat from her, throwing it over on the bench. "It's great to meet you, Jodie. It's always nice to find a fellow connoisseur of sharp wit."

Jodie Beaudoin laughed, gave his forearm a squeeze, and headed back to the other side of the restaurant.

Pot roast as good as any Coal had ever tasted finally arrived, with hot biscuits and homemade strawberry preserves on the side, and a small salad. Coal watched Slugger, with his battered lips, gingerly put down all his food, until nothing remained on his plate. He even scooped up some of the juice from the roast and licked it off his finger.

When he was finished, he smiled at Coal, making the light in his good eye almost disappear. "Doesn't get much better, Sarge. Thanks."

"No need to thank me, buddy. I'm just glad to have you here."

Slugger nodded. "Me too. I think."

After paying for their meal, Coal led the way back out into the cold, and he and his friend hurried to the pickup and climbed in. Coal started it up, and they sat there waiting for warmth to come.

"You really gonna go give that man his coat back, Sarge?"

"Of course."

"You're crazy. He hates you."

Coal thought for a moment back on his past with Bigfoot. Unless something drastic had changed, they had seemed to be on fairly decent terms when they parted. He didn't voice the real reason he figured Bigfoot had acted the way he had. He didn't want to think about it.

"We'll see. His hatred might turn to love if he gets his coat back." Coal laughed. "So where are we going to put you up?"

Slugger shrugged. "Sarge, you know I ..." He stopped, trying to hold Coal's gaze.

"What?"

"Well, you know I ain't got nothin', man. No money."

"That's just great. How are you going to pay me back?"

Slugger stared at Coal. A confused look came over his face. Finally, Coal couldn't hold back a laugh. "Come on, soldier. You're my guest up here. I wouldn't let you pay for anything anyway. The town is yours. You want to drive around a while and pick a hotel? We'll worry about money after you get settled."

"I ain't gon' be no charity case." Slugger's face was resolute.

"Good. I wouldn't expect you would."

"Then ... Is there some place I c'n get a job?"

"We'll look. But right now, you need a pad." Coal's first thought was to take Slugger home to the Savage boarding house, as he had come to think of his mother's place. But he didn't know if Slugger would be comfortable there with all the strange faces, and besides, he had already put Virgil out enough, asking him to share the twins' room while Ray Christian took his over. It wasn't until later that something struck him hard, and it gave him serious pause: Was there any other reason why he didn't take Slugger Janx back home? While he was driving Slugger around to look at every available hotel and apartment he knew of in town, Coal couldn't help mulling over that thought.

It was mid-afternoon before Coal finished showing Slugger around. He decided last of all to go over to Lemhi Valley Realty. The sound of sucking air as he closed the door seemed to be what brought realtor Harvey Cupper out of a room in the back. "Oh, hey, Coal! What can I—" Cupper jolted to a stop as his speech faltered. He glanced over the black man standing there in his Army green four-pocket fatigue shirt and blue jeans. It took him a moment to find his voice again. "What can I do for you?"

"Harvey, this is my friend Bryant Janx. We were in Nam together. Most folks call him Slugger. Slugger, this is Harvey Cupper." Neither man moved to shake hands, and Coal tried to dismiss the suspicious look in Slugger's eyes. "Harvey, I'm trying to find Slugger a room. Know of any apartments for rent?"

"Uhh ... Well, shoot. I'm not sure I do." Cupper seemed more pale than normal.

Coal stood for several more seconds, waiting. "Is there any way you could look through your listings? Just in case?" It seemed stupid that he was having to tell a realtor his job, but Cupper was frozen in place.

"Oh. Yeah, I guess."

The heavy-set Cupper ran his hand back through his silvering blond hair. It seemed to be without conscious thought that he flipped open a heavy white binder as he fumbled a Saratoga out of a pack on his desk and lit it with a silver Zippo. There was an almost scattered look about Cupper as he thumbed through pages in the binder, and to anyone looking at him from behind, with the smoke puffing out his mouth and nose, it might have looked like he was catching fire.

The realtor stopped and studied a picture and text for a moment, then tapped it a couple of times with his heavy forefinger, reaching up with his left hand to slide the Saratoga out of his mouth, twist his lips, and blow smoke to one side.

"Philip Lawson might have a little apartment still available in his basement. Leastwise he's never told me it was rented."

"Philip Lawson the lawyer?"

Cupper nodded, looking up only at Coal. "Yes sir, that's the one."

Coal frowned. He recalled the name only because Lawson was the same man employed by Bud and Linda Miley when they were basically kidnapping two innocent girls who had recently lost everything in life they held dear.

"There's nothing else?"

With a shrug, Cupper said, "I can make some phone calls if you want. Is there a number I can call you at later?"

"I think I'll get Slugger a room over at the Stagecoach, but why don't you call the house if you find something?" He gave him the five-digit phone number.

Cupper sucked so deeply on the Saratoga it looked like the tip was going to burst into flame, then a second later shot smoke out both nostrils like an angry cartoon bull. He tapped the down-bending button of ash into a glass tray near his hand as he finished writing the last digit of Coal's number. Then he looked up.

"All right. I'll give you a call if I find anything. Oh—any price range I need to ask about?"

Coal gave a shrug. There was no need consulting the dead-broke Slugger. "No more than fifty a month, if you can manage it."

Cupper nodded, sucking in his upper lip, then nailing the cigarette into its hole once more. He gave one more very pronounced, brisk nod, then stuck out his hand to shake Coal's.

"I'll let you know." He didn't even look over at Slugger.

They left, and two minutes later Coal pulled up in front of the Stagecoach Inn. They tramped inside, stomping a little ice off their boots at the door. A stiff-looking older lady behind the counter fixed her eyes on Slugger as they walked toward her. At the last second, those pale brown eyes darted either way, seeking assistance—or a way out.

"Welcome to the Stagecoach. How may I help you?" Her voice was dry and scratchy. If a laboratory skeleton could talk, this might be its voice.

"One room, ma'am."

The woman pulled her mortified eyes off Slugger and deposited them on Coal's face. In that moment, it was as if her face melted in relief.

"One ... For both of you?"

Coal had to laugh. "No, ma'am. Sorry, I guess we haven't met. I'm Sheriff Savage. Coal Savage. I've already got a house."

The woman made a valiant attempt at smiling. Coal was pretty sure icicles broke and fell off her eyebrows. "Oh. So no then. So ... only for ..."

"Any problem?"

The woman's face blanched. "Well, no— I mean, not that I know of, other than ... Um, sir, do you mind if I make a quick phone call?"

"I guess not. About what?"

She stared, and her mouth came open, like a fish left on a bank, sucking one last time for air that wouldn't come. "Well, I'll need to talk to my manager and—"

Coal heard a pleasant voice behind him. "What do you need to talk to me about, Lorna?" The front door had opened without Coal hearing it, which apparently went for Lorna as well. He turned to see Julie, the hotel manager. In a horizontally striped, sleeveless sweater over a wide-collared white shirt, and a dark blue skirt that ended some way-too-many inches above shapely knees and calves, she made Coal's lower jaw come unhinged.

That disarming smile and black-framed glasses that in her school days might have earned Julie the nickname of "Four-eyes" but now only gave her a distinctive, sophisticated air and accentuated the beauty of her clear blue eyes and long, dark lashes rendered Coal helpless for a moment. It must have been something else known only to Lorna that rendered her helpless as well.

"Well, I—" Lorna's eyes jerked over to Slugger, then returned to Julie.

The manager, looking for a moment a little confused, turned her eyes to Coal. "Hi, Coal. Can I help you?"

"I was just trying to get a room for my friend."

Julie looked at Slugger. Her smile widened. "Sure. Just any room? For one night?"

"I don't think we're particular. Unless you want to put him in one on the river. And yes, probably one night. I'm trying to find something more permanent around town. By the way, this is Slugger."

Julie reached out her hand without hesitating. "Hi, Slugger. I'm Julie."

"How you do, ma'am? Pleased to meet you."

"Same to you. So yes, let's put you in one of the river rooms. You'll like that."

She went on to make small talk, while Lorna fumbled to fill out whatever paperwork she had to, then paused and waited for Slugger's attention.

When everything was settled, Julie smiled again at Slugger. "Well, it sure is nice to have you here. I hope you can get used to the cold. I bet it's pretty warm back in Louisiana."

"Pretty hot," said Slugger, with a battered grin. Coal knew the words had a hidden meaning neither of the women would catch, for the small talk hadn't delved into Slugger's ugly recent past.

They went out to the truck, and Slugger got his bags. Setting down the one in his right hand, he looked at Coal. "Sarge, I don't really know's I c'n thank you for everything. I promise I'm gon' pay you back, though. Somehow."

"You're paying me back just by being here, my friend. I still owe you for what you did in Nam."

"Shoot! Don't even talk about that," Slugger replied. "What you did for me was worth that ten times over."

After leaving Slugger at the hotel, Coal drove straight back to Lemhi Valley Realty and marched inside. Harvey Cupper had seen him coming. He tried to suck his current Saratoga down his throat into his navel. "Hi, Sheriff, I—"

"Is there a problem with my friend?" Coal shot out.

"Huh?"

"Is there an issue finding a place for Slugger Janx?"

"Well, no, I— I don't see what—"

"Oh, come on, Cupper. You looked at him like he had the plague. Do you know that man would have given his life for you, or any other person in this town if they needed him? He should be a war hero. I brought him up here hoping to find some peace for him from all the protestors down where he's from. Now up here where vets are honored he still gets treated like a pariah."

"Hey, Sheriff, I ..." Coal stared at him and waited. "I didn't mean anything."

Coal calmed himself. He had said his piece, probably too loudly. He realized only now that Cupper's secretary was one desk away, trying furiously to ignite a piece of gum by the friction of rapid chewing. She had a look of someone wishing they had gone home early for the day.

"Did you find any rooms? You didn't happen to call Lawson, did you?"

Cupper cleared his throat. "I did, actually."

"What'd he say?"

"Um ..." Cupper's eyes slipped momentarily away, telegraphing his forthcoming lie. "He's changed his mind about renting. He's going to use the apartment as a shop."

Coal stared. He calculated carefully how to reply. "All right. I'll be expecting a call soon. There must be some better place in a town this size. Maybe the other real estate office has more listings." That was his subtle way of telling Cupper he might have to steer business away from Lemhi Valley Realty if he didn't find satisfaction here. He hoped Cupper was smart enough to decipher it.

He drove straight up to the courthouse with a vendetta, looked up Philip Lawson's office number, and dialed it.

Hello. Lawson law office.

"Yes, Mr. Lawson? This is Ezra Tweed." Even in his irritation, Coal patted himself on the back for coming up with such a unique name off the cuff. "Someone told me you might have an apartment for rent."

There came a long pause. Lawson's suspicion would be heightened, since if Cupper was telling the truth this was the second phone call within half an hour about his apartment for rent.

Well, yes, that's true. Just a little basement apartment with a kitchen and half bath.

"Well, I hope it burns to the ground."

Coal hung up feeling the clash of humor and guilt of a kid making prank phone calls.

Was this how Salmon, Idaho, was going to treat a war hero, because of the color of his skin? Somehow he had believed he knew his hometown better.

CHAPTER FIFTEEN

When Coal finally left the office that day it was five-thirty. He had called his mom and told her not to make anything for supper because he had a surprise. He, Coal Savage, actually had an evening free, and he was going to treat the whole family to rib eye steaks and mashed potatoes and gravy made with his special recipe.

He hadn't bothered to ask yet, but he planned to go get Slugger and bring him home for supper as well. The experience should be an eye opener for Connie, Cynthia, and Sissy. His own children, having lived in Virginia and having known Tony Nwanzée, as well as plenty of other black children in school, wouldn't think a thing of it, but the other three, well, there was a good chance that Cynthia and Sissy had never seen a black man in person, and Connie couldn't have seen many. She hadn't ever been beyond the borders of Montana and Idaho, as far as Coal knew.

Many people had just gotten off work, it appeared, for the curbs were packed. Coal had to park a ways down from Saveway, and as he was walking toward it he saw a familiar face step out of M. H. King's department store, and then one, two, three more of them.

It was Kathy MacAtee and her three daughters, Milo, Sara, and Jen. Coal felt his face light up, and he started toward them. Considering all they had shared together, he thought he would get a similar reaction from Kathy and the girls, but all of them seemed a little reserved as he came up to them.

"Hi, Kathy," he greeted as he got close. "Hey, girls."

"Hello." Kathy didn't call Coal by name, nor by any of the pet names she often had for him. Even while cursed with the blindness of manhood, he caught that.

He struggled looking for something to say. It didn't seem like Kathy had any intention of carrying the conversation forward.

"You girls just out shopping?" He scanned along the four of them, making a point to make eye contact if they were willing.

"Yeah. We got thinking breakfast for supper would fun, so we came to get some bacon. So ... the stew was good."

Coal stared at her, puzzling. He felt a half-smile on his lips. It had come to him unbidden as he tried to figure out why she seemed to think he should know what she was talking about.

Suddenly, Coal's heart shot into his throat. It had good timing, because if it hadn't, something would have slipped out of his mouth that he would have felt bad about, with the three girls standing there.

He put his hand to his forehead the same way he might have done with a bad headache. He read the half-hidden look of hurt and disappointment in Kathy's eyes as if there were words printed there. He had had a dinner date on Monday with Kathy and the girls. But he was in Louisiana.

"Oh, my heck. Kathy! Monday! I'm so sorry."

"It doesn't matter. There probably wouldn't have been enough anyway." The words of a scorned, hurt woman if ever Coal had heard any.

Coal scanned all four of the accusing faces and came back to Kathy's. "I really feel stupid, but please let me tell you what happened. I got a phone call Sunday night that a friend of mine from the war was in big trouble down in Louisiana, and early Monday morning I flew down there to get him out of jail. He was in a real bad way. Girls, I really feel terrible. I got so caught up I just forgot to call you."

Now he stood there. He had broadcast bread out on the water and now had to see if anyone would at least nibble at it. He had nothing else to offer.

He was looking solely at Kathy now, but from the corner of his eye he could see the girls, one by one, slowly turn their eyes up to their mother to see how she was digesting his story.

Kathy's stone face began to falter, and Coal saw ripples in the water. She was nibbling at his bread. She wanted to eat it, he could see. She just had to swallow the bitter pill he had given her by standing her and her girls up Monday night.

Common courtesy, friendship, and forgiveness between friends finally dictated the smile that came over Kathy's face. "Hey, honey, don't worry about it. We can set another time. Is your friend all right?"

There was the term of endearment Coal had been missing. He knew he could raise his head up out of the swirling waters of the toilet and suck in a big breath of air. He grabbed onto both sides of the figurative porcelain rim, slippery as they were, and started paddling—fast.

"He's better now. It's a long story, Kathy, but I'd like to bring him over for you and the girls to meet sometime. I'm really sorry I forgot you, though. I was sure looking forward to that stew."

Forgiveness and understanding were complete, and Kathy sucked in every morsel of bread he had thrown out for her when she stepped close and gave him a bear hug, squeezing tight as she said, "I'm so glad you're okay, Coal. We were really worried about you Monday."

Holding her and smelling the wonderful sent of Agree shampoo in her hair—which he wondered why he would even know!—he said, "Why didn't you call the house?"

"I don't know. Stubborn, I guess."

"It sure would have saved me some real embarrassment—and you a lot of worry, it sounds like." She looked up at him, and he added, "Not to mention probably being pretty put out for a while."

She smiled ruefully. "Yeah. Sorry. I just thought you found

something else more important to do."

"I would have been there. But it really sounded like my friend Slugger was in bad shape. I had to get to him."

"Well, I'm glad you did. I know how much your friends mean to you. We'll look forward to meeting him. Do I dare try to set another appointment, or should we just wait for you to call?"

Coal knew she didn't intend that to cut him, but it did. It was his own fault. "Why don't you let me make sure Slugger gets settled in, all right? Then I'll give you a ring."

"Sounds good." She stepped closer and took his arms, her faced tipped up to him. Just for a second, he imagined she was expecting him to lean down and give her a kiss on her parted lips. And there was a second when the carnal part of him thought of doing it. She sure looked beautiful right then. But his sensible side knew he would be hurtling over a line from which he might never be able to return.

Coal managed not to stop and talk to anyone at the store, and he headed out of town imagining the smell of grilling ribeye steaks. He had just one thing to do before starting to cook.

He drove past Savage Lane, and farther down the road he pulled off at the home of Bigfoot Monahan. He stopped in the driveway and cut the motor, then put his hand on Bigfoot's coat, which lay on the seat beside him.

Other than the incident at the Coffee Shop, the last time he had any dealing with Bigfoot Monahan they seemed to be on good terms. Before returning to the valley, nothing could have surprised him more. But now, thinking back on the way Monahan had looked at him and Slugger in the restaurant, he had his first moment of pause. Should he be doing this? Maybe he should hang the coat on the mailbox and leave.

But that seemed a cowardly way of doing things, and Coal was anything but a coward. Besides, it would be good to know how things lay between him and Bigfoot Monahan.

Stepping out of the truck with the coat in hand, Coal walked briskly up the concrete steps and rapped on the door. The front room drapes parted an inch or so, and after half a minute more the front door cracked open. It was Beverly, not Bigfoot, whose face shone through. Hesitantly, she pulled the door open the rest of the way.

"Hello, Sheriff."

Coal doffed his hat. "Evening, ma'am. I don't suppose Paul would be home."

She shook her head. "No sir. He—" She stopped and looked toward the highway. "Now he is."

Coal turned as the old red station wagon pulled off the highway. It passed the pickup and came to a stop in front of the porch. Coal faced the station wagon, Beverly Monahan forgotten behind him.

Bigfoot loomed out of his car, towering over it. His eyes bored into Coal's. "What's goin' on?"

It was time to ward off trouble the fastest way possible. Coal held up the coat. "You left your coat at the restaurant."

The big man's eyes lowered to the coat. He stared for a few seconds, and then his eyes flickered. "Oh. I ... Yeah, I guess I did have it with me."

Coal nodded. "So I figured I might as well swing it by before I head home."

Bigfoot looked at him grudgingly. At last, he slammed his door and came around the car. He seemed to grow to Goliathan proportions as he came up the steps, then stopped close to Coal, taking the coat from him.

For a few seconds, Coal thought the big man was just going to turn and go in the house without saying anything. After a moment, Bigfoot nodded. "Well, I appreciate you goin' to the trouble."

"No trouble at all, Paul. By the way, I just wanted to tell you that guy I had at the café, he's a friend of mine. We were in Nam together."

He had watched Monahan's eyes harden the moment he knew what Coal was talking about. "Well, somethin' you oughtta know too. I growed up in a place where there was a lot of them. And that's how I learned to fight. Because I was forced to. I got a word for them people, and I expect it ain't a word you'd like t' hear. I hope we understand each other. Evenin', Sheriff."

Before Coal could think of a reply, Bigfoot Monahan turned and stepped into the house, shutting the door behind him.

With a sigh, Coal went back to the truck and fired it up, satisfied that he had done all he could. He was home with his rib eye steaks by six-thirty. He told Connie what he was planning, including his intentions of having Slugger come over and meet the family, and of course she agreed heartily.

The potatoes had been boiling for ten minutes, and the gravy was already simmering, when the phone rang. Coal looked over in time to see Connie frown to herself as she walked over and picked it up. With a wire whisk, he kept stirring the gravy but watched his mother from the corner of his eye. He also kept his ears open, listening past *Adam-12* on the television.

"What? Oh, no! That's terrible! Yes. No, thank you for calling. Yes, I'm sure he'll want to know. Thanks again. Good night."

Connie turned to Coal as she was hanging up the phone. He was staring at her and waiting.

"Honey, there was some trouble down at the Stagecoach. That was Bob Wilson."

Coal managed only to swear in his own mind. Might as well keep the clutter from invading his children's minds as well.

"What happened?"

"A fight. With your friend."

Pressure was building in Coal's head. He'd have to get out in the truck in a hurry in order only to offend his own ears. Reaching out, he flipped off the stove and strode to the phone, looking up the

Stagecoach in the phone book and dialing their number.

Someone said hello after only two rings, and he barked, "Sheriff Savage here. What happened with Bryant Janx?"

Oh, Sheriff! I'm so sorry. There was a little trouble in the hall. You might want to come down here. The police are still here.

"Who's this?"

Odette Wilkinson.

"All right, Odette. Thank you. I'll be right down. See if you can hold Officer Wilson until I get there."

Coal turned to Connie, who was watching him with her fingers laced together in front of her. "Finish up the stuff and put the steaks on, would you, Mom? I have to run to the hotel. If I bring Slugger back with me, then great. If not, we're going to have to eat without him."

"You'll be back soon, Son?"

"As soon as I can. I'm not going to let this spoil our supper."

Flying down the highway, Coal ran through a dozen possible scenarios in his head. Of course he couldn't know if any of them were near the truth. It was just his mind's way of staying occupied.

He flew up crossways in front of the entrance doors, slammed on the brakes and set the emergency brake, turned off the truck and got out. Bob Wilson's baby blue police car was the only one there, and it sat cold and quiet a ways in front of the truck.

Inside the lobby, Bob turned from sipping a cup of coffee at the sound of the door opening. Thick eyebrows settled over his dark eyes, and he took a long sip of coffee as Coal walked close.

"Damn, Coal. Looks like you brought a hellcat to town. Who is this friend of yours, anyway?"

"He's from Louisiana. The best friend I had with me over at the military prison in Nam. They call him Slugger."

"Huh. Good name for him."

Coal cringed inside. "Great. What happened?"

"Well, according to the two other guys involved, he came up

and called them "whitey," then just started picking a fight with them, for no obvious reason."

"They're lying."

Bob stared at Coal. His face was mild. "Could be. You're that sure?"

"I am. Where's Slugger?"

"Gone."

"Gone? What do you mean gone?"

"Just gone. These guys said it looked like he got cold feet and took off. Headed up the highway, north."

"Why would he do that?"

Bob shrugged. "Search me. I thought maybe you'd know."

"Do the other guys have a room here?"

"Yeah. I told them before I let 'em go you'd probably be coming to have a chat with them."

"Good. Room number?"

"One twelve. I'll go with you."

Coal almost smiled. He knew it wasn't that Bob didn't trust him. He *did* trust him—completely. To lose his cool.

"Come on then." He walked down to room one twelve and knocked. The half-minute it took to answer the door was the half-minute of someone trying to steel himself for an unpleasant conversation—at least that was Coal's take.

A man with bushy dark sideburns contrasting a blond head of hair pulled the door open. He appeared to be in his early twenties and had a newly split lip. "Hi."

"Hello. I'm Sheriff Savage. Come out and talk to me. Someone else in here?"

The young man nodded, then turned his head. "Burt, come out here."

Another man, this one with medium brown hair and a clean-shaven face that didn't help him look more than sixteen, when in reality Coal guessed him closer to twenty-one, came out of the bathroom and edged closer. His left cheek was red and swollen, and it was pushing that eye nearly shut. "Yeah?"

"Coal Savage. Out in the hall. I need to talk to you."

The two men obeyed. Coal turned to Bob. "Take Burt with you, would you? I'll talk to ..." He looked at the blond one.

"Daren."

"Daren," echoed Coal. "I'll talk to Daren."

When Bob and Burt were out of earshot, Coal pierced Daren with unhappy eyes. "Tell me what happened tonight."

"Well, like I told the other officer—"

"No." Coal held up a hand, much like a wall in front of young Daren. "I don't care about what you told him. Now I want the truth."

"Huh?"

"The truth. Capiche? I want the truth. You've had plenty of time to think about it. Now before you say anything else, let me tell you I got pulled away from a rib eye steak for this, and a night with my family. I'm already not very happy. Don't make it worse."

The man blinked at him a couple of times. "Hey, man, we were just having a little fun."

"Fun? Name-calling fun?"

"Yeah, I guess."

"You guess? How far did that go?"

"Listen, man, do I need a lawyer?"

"You're going to need a doctor," Coal said with a lowered voice. "I want to know how you set that man off. He doesn't start throwing fists over nothing."

Resignation washed over Darin's face. "Well, I saw his shirt—army, you know? And I just kind of asked him if ..."

"If what?"

"You know I was jokin', of course. I asked him if he had to kill any babies. That's all."

"That's all? You must not realize how many times he's had to listen to that crap since he stepped off the plane from Nam. Hearing that one time is bad enough. Two, or three, or twenty—how would you like it? How about every single time you meet someone he says, 'Hey, you with the butt-ugly sideburns." Coal picked the make-believe jab especially for Daren.

"Well, hey—"

"Hey, nothing. You don't like it, do you?"

"Man, I want a lawyer." Daren glanced down the hall, his face reddening. "Where did Burt go?"

"You don't worry about Burt. What else was said to that black man? What did Burt say?"

"Well ..." He glanced once more along the hall in the direction Burt had disappeared. "I guess he's the one that said ..."

"What?"

"He said somethin' like, 'I hear you niggers were the worst baby killers of all. Is that true?'"

"He said something like that, or that's what he said?"

"I guess that's what he said."

"And then Slugger hit him. Right?"

The man had to digest Slugger's name for a moment. "Uh ... Yeah. Yeah, that's when he hit him. No warning, no nothin'. Listen, man, we didn't want a fight. We were just havin' fun."

Coal stepped into Daren a little closer. "Fun, huh, Butt-ugly sideburns? Fun? How fun is this?"

"Hey, man, back off, all right?"

Coal took a deep breath, but he took it quietly. He didn't even want Daren realizing he was trying to calm himself down. "I'll be talking to Slugger later too, and I've never heard Slugger tell a lie. So is there anything else you'd like to say before I let you go?"

"No, not really."

Coal started to turn away.

"Wait. So ... you know this guy?"

"I know him. I was in Nam with him. He could eat four or five punks like you for breakfast and not even burp. You're lucky you can even talk."

Coal walked off without another word and found Bob and Burt just outside the lobby. "I'm done with Daren. I think he crapped his pants." He turned and looked at Burt. "Now it's your turn." He looked back at Bob. "See ya, Bob."

Taking the cue, Bob gave Burt a measuring glance, then shrugged and walked through the lobby and out the front door. Burt was at Coal's mercy.

"Any reason why Daren would hang you out to dry?"

"What?"

"Let me word that another way: Is there any reason you can think of that unless Daren's lying through his teeth he would blame this whole thing on you?"

"Wait—he blamed *me?*" Burt stood up straighter.

"Was he lying?" Coal purposely avoided a direct answer. So far, he hadn't actually said anything that was a lie.

"Hell, yeah, he was lying! He started the whole damn thing! He's the one started askin' that guy if he really sat on the porch all day eatin' watermelon an' fried chicken. Then he starts in t' callin' 'im a baby killer and crap. He told you that was me?"

"Nope. I never said he did. I just asked you if there was any reason he would blame you."

It took several seconds for Burt's at least slightly inebriated brain to realize he had been tricked. "Hey, man! I made all that up. I knew you were lyin'!"

"Yeah, you did. By the way, did Officer Wilson ask you if you wanted to sign a complaint?"

"We *did* sign a complaint," countered Burt.

"I bet if you go in to the courthouse tomorrow you find out your memory's wrong. I'll bet you never signed one at all."

"What are you talkin' about? I guarantee I—"

"Shut up," growled Coal. "Get out of my sight."

With that, he turned and looked over at the desk clerk, touching a finger to his hat brim before he walked out the front door to find Bob.

Bob was standing in the darkness smoking a cigarette. He saw the red tip of light before Bob materialized in the shadows. Coal went up to him.

"You let them sign a complaint against Slugger?"

"Yeah. I only had their story, and he ran off."

"Yeah he ran off. Bob, you should see this guy. He's spent several days bein' beat up by thugs and cops down in his hometown. He didn't have any reason to expect any different here."

"Really? By the cops?"

"Yeah. And by the way, I got the real story out of those two punks."

Bob stared. "They flipped over?"

"Yeah."

"They started it? He didn't hit them first?"

Coal stared back. The reality was that Slugger had snapped. He had struck first, just like he had been trained to do to fight a deadly enemy in Nam. Discern an enemy from a friend, then strike them before they can strike you.

He lowered his voice, feeling a little humbler. "Would it make any difference if I told you you and I would probably have hit them first too?"

Bob pulled the cigarette out of his mouth. "Would you?"

"Probably."

Bob raised something in his left hand and shook it, making it flutter. "You think I should have let them sign a complaint?"

"A couple of trouble-making drunks? Against a loyal, hard-fighting vet? I guess you do what your department tells you to. I sure wouldn't have."

Bob only stared for a moment more. Finally, he put the cigarette back in the corner of his mouth and tore the ticket in half.

"Good enough for me. Do I expect them to come down to the City filing a complaint against me now?"

"I doubt it. I doubt you'll see those two again. Now what about Slugger?"

"What about him?"

"How am I going to find him?"

"I wish I could answer that. All I know is he walked off. It's damn cold out here, and all he had was his Levi's and that shirt. Maybe he'll be back."

Coal thought about that for a moment. It only took a moment. "Yeah. And maybe he won't."

CHAPTER SIXTEEN

After calling Jordan Peterson on the radio and meeting him at the Stagecoach for a briefing, they set out to locate Slugger Janx. Coal had also made the requisite call to Connie and the kids: In light of the situation, there was no coming home, not until Slugger was found. Coal was going to be eating cold steak tonight.

Even if Slugger had taken off running, after figuring out the entire time lapsed from the time of the call to now, Coal knew his friend couldn't have gotten four miles away, at the outside. And with the temperature sitting at about three degrees Fahrenheit, and Slugger being from nearly at sea level, and probably wearing his army boots, even two miles was a stretch.

So Coal and Jordan drove out together for about three miles, then slowly started to work their way back, this time stopping to knock on doors as they went.

When Coal, making his way down the left side of the road, got all the way back to the Shady Nook and asked the first waitress he saw if she had noticed a man of Slugger's description, she shook her head. But a man at a nearby table called out to Coal, making him turn. The man had short, slick-looking black hair, more or less a military cut, and a tattoo of a dragon on his left shoulder, peeking out from under his short sleeve. Coal remembered him as Adam Manetti, and he had been in a jail cell when Coal first returned to Salmon.

"Hello, Manetti."

"Hey, Sheriff."

"Did you see something?"

"Well, I didn't really *see* anything, but when I pulled in I could hear somebody cussin' and bangin' around toward the back of the place. Sounded like some ticked off drunk."

"You didn't go check it out?"

Manetti chuckled. "It ain't really my issue, boss. I just came in for some food and a drink. I ain't goin' back and get in a fight with some lunatic an' end up back at the jail with you." He gave a crooked grin.

"Sound reasoning. Thanks for the tip, anyway."

"Any time, man. You treated me square. It's the least I c'n do."

Manetti turned back to his table, where there were three other tough-looking characters, and Coal wandered to the back and found the manager, a forty-year-old named Cal Griffin, the cook people are warned not to trust because of their thin build. Griffin couldn't grow sideburns, so he was out of vogue, but he had a wonderful Clark Gable mustache, deep brown eyes, and long black lashes.

Griffin grinned when he saw Coal. "Hey, brother! You don't have to come back here to order, you know."

Coal returned the grin. "I wish I had time to visit, Cal. I'm here on business."

"Yeah? What's up? Can I help?"

"Maybe. Say, what kind of outbuildings do you have back at the rear of the parking lot? Any?"

"Umm ... Just the shed, I guess—where we keep the de-icer and snow shovels and what-not."

"Is it locked?"

"Normally. But with the yahoos we have around here, who can say?"

"All right, well, there might be somebody back there."

"Who?"

"It's a long story. I'm looking for a guy, and one of your patrons said he heard some banging around back there. This guy's got to be looking for shelter. He wasn't dressed too warm."

"You want some help or something, man? Don't be gettin' hurt on my place now!"

"Thanks, Cal. I'm sure I'll be okay. It's a friend of mine."

Going back out to the car, Coal got Jordan on the radio and asked him to stand by in the parking lot but be ready to jump and come running. After all, there wasn't even any proof that whoever was making noise at the back of the Shady Nook was Slugger Janx.

He pulled his flashlight out, turned it on, and started toward the rear of the building, glancing back only once, when the headlights of a car entering the parking lot streamed across him before the car stopped and they were extinguished. It was Jordan in the LTD.

The shed behind the restaurant hardly seemed big enough to draw one's attention. But to a freezing man it might look inviting. Besides, maybe Slugger was being smart. After all, the smaller his hiding place, the easier it would be for his body heat to take the ice out of it.

He shined the light on the hasp. There was a padlock still attached, but the hasp itself was broken loose from the door frame. "Slugger! Hey, Slugger! It's me, Coal. You in there?"

No reply.

"Buddy, you aren't in trouble. We're sorting that mess at the hotel out. Just come on home with me. I was right in the middle of cooking you a steak dinner. You hear me?"

Again, silence. Coal swore. He motioned for Jordan to come in. When the deputy got to him, he motioned him over to the opposite side of the door, then held a finger to his lips in the universal signal for silence.

At the door, Coal waited for a moment, taking in a deep breath of the icy air that almost made him cough. "Slugger, I'm opening the door. I'll take you home where it's warm. Nobody's going to hurt you."

He eased open the door and shined his light inside. Other than some bags, a couple of buckets, and two snow shovels, with random small tools on a shelf, the place was empty. Coal swore again.

Shutting the door, he looked at Jordan and shook his head. He put his light on the hasp and lock. The damage was recent, but it was anyone's guess how recent.

In a quiet voice, Jordan said, "Hey, boss, there's one place across the street where nobody was home. And they had some outbuildings."

"Did you search them?"

Jordan frowned. "Right. No, I didn't search them."

Coal gave up a half-smile. "Okay. I don't blame you. Well, let me go talk to Cal about this lock, and then we'll go over there."

After going into the Shady Nook to report the condition of the lock on the shed, Coal met Jordan back outside, and they drove over and parked in front of a little white house that stood with vacant-looking black windows staring out in sullen silence. Coal went up on the concrete stoop and knocked hard a few times. When there was no answer, he tried the door after looking for damage.

With no luck there, they went around back. A quick check of the door and windows showed no damage to them either.

Coal swept the outbuildings with his light and let out a sigh. One of the buildings was a garage. Another one just a ways from it looked suspiciously like a hen house. Coal thought about the chickens they used to keep in a coop he and his father had built. It had a lot of straw on the floor, and maybe some thirty chickens that would gather up and roost in it at night. He remembered that it was closed in, much like this one, and it always seemed appreciably warmer inside than out. It was a place he could have gone for shelter if someone had locked him out of the house and barn.

Coal knew Slugger had brought his Colt .45 with him from Louisiana. He also had a good knife, a Nguyen Dan Bowie-style fighting knife, made right there in Nam. Coal had been with him when he purchased it from a G.I. who was headed Stateside. Coal couldn't just walk up in the dark on any place where Slugger Janx might be hiding, alone and afraid.

"Slugger! It's Coal!"

Again, only the battered side of the chicken house heard his voice, and Jordan, who stood beside him. But this time Coal's guts told him Slugger was inside. Calmly, he told him the same things he had said to the empty utility shed behind the Shady Nook.

"I'm coming in there with you, bud. We've got this all figured out. Come home with me."

As he spoke, he was moving. He decided for safety he should make sure Slugger knew Jordan was out here as well. He sure didn't need him thinking his only friend was trying to trick him.

"Hey, Slugger, I've got a friend out here with me. His name's Jordan. He's pretty harmless." He turned and winked at Jordan, although he wouldn't see it in the dark. "I just needed him to help me look for you."

After several seconds, Jordan leaned close and whispered, "Am I missing something? How are you so sure he's in there?"

Coal shrugged. "My guts, I guess. Just a hunch. We'll talk about it sometime. For now, why don't you just hang back? I'll go in alone."

He moved forward, talking to Slugger all the while. "This

stupidity is over, bud. No one's going to hurt you. Those guys you had trouble with, they signed a complaint, but I talked my cop buddy into tearing it up. Understand?"

A shadow loomed suddenly up between the chicken house and the garage. It was a big, dark shadow, darker than what lay behind it. Only the olive drab shirt and blue jeans could be seen by the light of the stars.

CHAPTER SEVENTEEN

"Slugger."

The reply came back after several seconds of dead silence. "Yeah, Sarge. It's me."

Coal took a tentative step. "Are you all right?"

No response.

Coal looked back at Jordan. "Hey, bud, I've got this. You can head out."

A hesitant: "You sure?"

"Yeah. Go ahead." What he wanted to say was, *Damnit, get out of here before this blows up!* Something was going on with Slugger Janx deeper than anything Coal could guess.

They both watched Jordan go get in the LTD, fire it up, and back out onto the highway, then drive toward town. Slowly, Coal turned to his old friend.

"All right, brother. It's just us now."

The shadow stared. "I can't come out there."

"Why?"

"Sarge, these people here no diff'rent from back home. I don't belong here."

"Where do you belong then?"

The silence was dead, and cold, and ugly.

"Nowhere. I got nowhere to be. They gon' get me anywhere I am."

"Slugger, that isn't true. For starters, we'll get you some new clothes. You can grow your beard out. We'll forget all about the army, okay? That's all over now."

He had moved almost up to his friend, and Slugger just stood there, his hands hanging at his sides.

"It ain't ever gon' be over, boss. An' it don't matter. I c'n change clothes all I want. I'll still be a nigger."

"Hey. Stop it, man! You're anything but that. You know better."

Slugger's voice was soft and listless. "Tell *them* that, Sarge. They'll never let me be."

A chill went over Coal. "Do you have your .45 on you, buddy? And your knife?"

He thought he might have seen Slugger nod. He made no sound.

"Hand them over to me, all right?"

"You takin' me t' jail?"

"Of course not. I'm taking you to my house. We're all good people there. You'll be safe."

"I ain't gon' mess up yore fam'ly too. No."

"This is an order, Private." Coal spoke in the softest voice he could find.

Slugger started all of a sudden to laugh. It was soft at first, but it began to build to a roar, then choked to a stop. "Yore damn pig-headed, Sarge. I always wanted t' tell you that."

"So why didn't you?"

"I couldn't. Not with them stripes on your arm."

Coal chuckled. "Come on, bud. Give me the gun, all right?"

He was surprised when, without reaching up to his belt,

Slugger brought his hand out in front of him. In the cold light, Coal caught the contours of the Colt lying across his palm. He had had it in his hand the entire time. Again, the chills passed over him as he took the gun and put it down his belt behind his back.

"What about that knife? That Nguyen Dan knife?"

Slugger leaned way down and worked the right leg of his Levi's up. Coal heard the grating of metal on metal, and then the knife was between them, butt toward Coal.

"There ain't no other man on God's earth I'd give these to, Sarge. Nobody nowhere."

Coal believed him.

It was a dead silent drive back across the highway to the Stagecoach Inn, where Coal went in alone after locking Slugger in the truck at Slugger's insistence. He informed them at the front desk what he was doing and that he would deal with Julie the next day, then went to his friend's room and collected his clothes and toiletries into his duffel bag, bringing it back out to the pickup. He laid the bag in the bed of the truck, then climbed in and headed home.

The eerie silence didn't break for miles, and Coal didn't try. There would be plenty of time for talk. Now was a time for thoughtful silence.

On a whim, Coal turned off the highway at Maura's place. Since Jordan was working, tonight seemed safe. He caught the shine of some of the horses' eyes out in the dark as they gathered at the fence to see who was here and why. But it wasn't until he opened the door that he could hear the dogs barking. Maura had taken them inside, and he didn't blame her, on a night like this.

As the porch light came on, Coal looked over at Slugger, who was watching him. "This is a friend's place, buddy. If I can get her to come with us, I hope you don't mind company."

"Yore truck, Sarge."

The front door opened, and Maura stepped out on the porch. The pickup was still running, but he had cut the headlights, so he could only see her by the pathetic yellow bulb she used for a porch light.

The slamming of the pickup door was unusually magnified, probably by air that swarmed with ice crystals.

"What are you doing sneaking around in the dark?"

Coal laughed. "Just sneaking around in the dark. I thought I'd peek in your windows and see if I could catch you getting undressed or something."

It was Maura's turn to giggle. "Do you wanna come in?"

"To see you getting undressed?"

"Oh, knock it off. You're pressing your luck." She paused. "Hey. Do you have someone with you?"

"I do. It's my friend from Louisiana. So no, I can't come in. I actually just stopped to see if you've had anything to eat."

"I just sat down to a lovely cold sandwich and some delectable Campbell's condensed soup. I'm not sure how I could ever break away."

"Oh. Never mind then." Coal grinned. Just for a second, this almost felt like old times, trading wit with Maura.

"Now cut it out. What were you thinking of?"

"Well, I was actually making supper tonight, and I bought an extra ribeye, just in case. And ..." He froze.

Maura stepped away from her door, pushed the dogs inside, and shut it softly, turning back to him. She folded her arms tightly across her chest, and even though he was fifteen feet away he was pretty sure he saw her shiver. Or maybe that was him.

"Are you inviting me to supper, Coal?"

"That depends."

She cocked her head. "On what?"

"On what your answer would be if I did."

"It would be what the heck took you so long."

"Then yes, I'm inviting you to supper. Right now. If you'll ride with us. And about what took me so long, stupidity, I guess. That's what my mom tells me, anyway."

"Well, she's right." No laugh followed. Coal wasn't sure she was joking. "Let me get my coat."

"Hey!" His voice stopped her and turned her around. "Can I borrow your phone real quick?"

"Well, no." She giggled at the look on his face. "Of course you can. Come on." She waved him in.

While Maura got her coat on and stood by the door, Coal dialed home and told Connie he had a couple of strays he was bringing home for supper. He caught Maura rolling her eyes at him, and that warm feeling once more filled him up inside. Just for this moment in time, it felt like nothing had changed between them.

Before they stepped outside, Coal reached out and took Maura's elbow. "Hey."

She turned back to him, looked down at his hand, then back up into his eyes. "What?"

"I thought I should warn you. I don't know if it makes any difference, but just so there aren't any awkward surprises, my friend Slugger is black."

Searching his eyes for a moment, she shrugged. "I don't know why it would make any difference."

It was the perfect answer. They went out, and as Slugger saw Maura coming, he started to open his door until Coal raising his hand stopped him. Slugger then saw they were both going to the driver's side, so he shut his door again and waited.

Coal flung his door open. "Slugger, this is Maura. Maura, Slugger. Or you can call him Bryant."

Maura reached across the seat and put out her hand. For a moment, Slugger only stared. Coal could imagine the confusion and even possibly fear that must be going through him. At last, he took the hand and shook. "Sarge was lyin' to you, miss. Only my mama and the preacher calls me Bryant. I allus been Slugger."

"Okay. Don't ever call me any names he tells you for me

either."

"Oh, brother." Coal poked her in the ribs. "Just get in, would you? I'm turning into an icicle out here."

Coal was amazed how in the last few minutes of their ride Maura got Slugger talking. She never asked him about the war or about what had brought him to Salmon, and he wanted to kiss her for that. Well, maybe it would be more honest to admit he just wanted to kiss her, period. But her questions for Slugger were about Louisiana, his family, and, once she found out about his mentally retarded brother, Baby, she asked many questions about him. Slugger opened up and kept on talking, and by the time they pulled into the yard at home he had a new-found sense of hope for his friend.

Coal opening the front door was an invitation to the twins to run to him screaming, "Dad! We're starving!" He crouched down and swept them both into his arms.

"Starving? Didn't you guys eat?"

"No!" Wyatt said. "Grandma was making us wait."

"Oh, man! I *bet* you're starving! Jeez, you must be half dead by now." Both boys giggled as Coal let them go and stood up to push the door open wider. Maura had come in behind him and went straight into greeting the family, but Slugger was standing behind the shelter of the door. A jarring vision of Boo Radley hiding behind the door on *To Kill a Mockingbird* flashed into Coal's mind.

"Come on in, Slugger. I'd like you to meet my family."

Slugger came out of the shadows, his skin reflecting the lights from the kitchen, and the dimmer ones from the TV and the living room lamps. He stood in silence, waiting for someone else to speak.

Both Dobe and Shadow had come over, and they threw all politesse aside and began sniffing Slugger's legs up and down. Connie was making her way across the room when Slugger looked over at Coal. "Man. Great dogs. Is it okay if I pet 'em?"

"You bet. Dobe. Shadow. Be good." There was no doubt in the dogs' minds what that command meant. To them, it was tantamount to "sit," which they both did, on the instant. Then they stayed there allowing Slugger to stroke them all over and scratch behind Dobe's sharply upright ears.

"Oh, man. Wow, Sarge. I used to have me a dog. Gosh, they're beautiful."

Slugger bowed his head down to Shadow so they were almost nose to nose, but not before Coal thought he saw the glitter of a tear on his cheek. He held up his hands in a silent sign begging everyone else to wait and be still. For the children, that was no problem at all. All of them were hanging back anyway. It was Connie who had to be shushed, because she was doing her typical hostess thing and champing at the bit to get to Coal's friend.

Slugger finally straightened up, and his eyes went around the room. There was something completely different about him now, a phenomenon Coal could only explain by his friend's interaction with the dogs. His eyes settled on Connie.

"Howdy, ma'am. You've gotta be the woman Coal told me about all those times. You're beautiful just the way he said."

Connie laughed. "Well, doesn't that beat all. Coal! Well, I don't know about that, Mr. Janx, but he sure has talked about you an awful lot too."

Slugger's eyes darted toward Coal, then back again to Connie. "Ma'am, would it— I mean, I would shore like t' shake yore hand, if that'd be all right."

"Oh, not in this house, Mr. Janx!" Connie chided. She stepped close, and to Slugger's obvious surprise she put her arms around him. She held on for so long that he finally brought up his own arms and gingerly encircled her with them. If he could have blushed, Coal knew he would be as red as the blood in his veins.

Coal introduced everyone else, and it filled him with pride to see Katie, Virgil, and Cynthia come forward and shake hands with

Slugger. Then Wyatt and Morgan of course had to have their turn. Sissy was the only one who wouldn't come near the stranger, and after Maura had finished hugging on her and gone down the hall to wash up, Sissy had retired to the cowhide couch. Now she had her back pushed up against the far arm of it, her feet pulled up under her, holding tight to her lower legs. She was staring Slugger down like a monster straight out of a Saturday night horror movie. Coal would have been shocked to see her any different.

Finally, Coal looked at Connie, as they made their way toward the kitchen in a wave. "Now what's this crap I hear about you making everyone wait to eat?"

Connie gave him a mock angry look. "Now you watch yourself. I was hoping you'd get back sooner than you thought. It was just a few more minutes."

Coal grinned and hugged her to him with one arm. "Okay. Thanks, Ma. Hey, why don't you get everyone seated? I'll see if I can get that little critter off the couch."

Coal went back to Sissy, who kept her eyes on Slugger for as long as she could, until Coal was just too much in the way. He was only four feet away when she finally looked up at him, and she got up and fairly leaped off the couch and threw her little body against him, burying her face in his shirt. This little girl sure knew how to wring the emotions out of a tired old man.

He pried her loose and brought her up high so he could press his cheek to hers. "Hey, Sis. How was your day?"

"Fine." She had learned that response from the twins.

"Well, good. Hey, listen. Listen to me." He pulled away and looked into her face. "I brought a really nice man home with me to see you and the family and eat supper with us. I know he has really dark skin, doesn't he? But you know what? He's just like me. It's okay if you don't talk to him right now, but I think you're going to like him. Do you know what his name is?"

Staring solemnly into his eyes, she only shook her head.

"Slugger. His name is Slugger. Can you say that?"

"Sugger."

Coal grinned. "Yeah. Slugger." He hugged her again. "If I let you sit right next to me, is it okay if we go to the table?"

Sissy peered past Coal's shoulder, seeking out Slugger. After studying him with her big eyes for perhaps twenty seconds, she looked back up at Coal. Her nod was slow, but it was sure. Coal kissed her cheek and squeezed her tighter.

This place sure housed a motley group. But they were a family.

CHAPTER EIGHTEEN

Connie was dishing out mashed potatoes when Maura came back down the hall and scanned the table. The last empty chair was conveniently right next to Coal—his mother's doing. She came over, and the whole time Coal was expecting some dig about being forced to sit by him. But nothing witty was forthcoming.

Before she could take her seat, Slugger, who was seated to Coal's left, jumped up because Coal had his arms full of Sissy, and came over to grab the back of Maura's chair and jerk it out from the table. "Excuse me, miss. There you go."

Maura was taken completely aback, and she stared at Slugger in amazement. "Wow. Thank you, Slugger. I'm not used to that kind of treatment." The comment cut Coal deep because he realized she was right—he had never pulled a chair out for her.

"Don't mention it, miss. You're welcome."

Slugger pushed her chair back in as she sat, then went back and sat down, glancing at Coal, who scrambled to save face. "Well, you know, Maura, I *was* Slugger's supervisor, after all."

She raised an eyebrow as high as it would go. "Hmm. Then it's a wonder he even knows how to sit at a table."

Coal broke out laughing. "Oh, wow. I guess I know where I stand with you. Besides, you're the tough girl that wouldn't even let me open the car door for her not that long ago."

Maura shrugged. "Touché."

After that, everyone started eating, but it became quickly obvious that Sissy would never be comfortable where she was, seated with Coal, and so close to Slugger. She kept fighting to move farther and farther over to Coal's right side, until Maura came to the rescue and took her onto her lap.

"Wow, Coal, the steak is delicious!" Cynthia exclaimed.

"Thanks. I just went and rustled it fresh before I came home."

Everyone laughed, and the joking set the tone for the whole meal. When it was over, the kids settled down in front of the television.

The adults stayed at the table talking, until Maura reached out and touched Coal's sleeve. He looked over at her, now that he had a good excuse. He had been forcing himself not to until now.

"Hey. Can I talk to you for a minute?"

"Sure." He looked at Connie and Slugger. "We'll be back."

They got up, and Maura walked to the front door, with Coal following. When she made to grab her coat, he said, "You know it's almost zero out there."

"Oh. True. Then where can we go?"

"Up to my room? Or Mom's."

"I'm not going to your room! You never know what you might try once the door shut." She was trying to hang onto some of the mood from earlier, but Coal wasn't buying it. He smiled, but only out of patience.

"All right, woman, that's enough. Since when did everything become a joke to you?"

Maura's face colored a little. "Sorry. You're right. Your room is fine."

They went upstairs, and Coal didn't even have to look back to know if there was one set of eyes on them it would be his mother's. In the room, he shut the door behind Maura, and she stopped and looked around.

It was a typical man's den of a bedroom, with a bison hide spread across the bed, the mount of a huge mule deer buck on the wall at the head of the bed, positioned so when Coal was lying on his back he was looking up at its neck, chin, and the ears and fat, gnarled antlers. From his rack of hats to his guns, knives, guitar, and a pair of Wranglers lying in a heap on the floor, this was the kind of place a man would keep. Maura scanned it but said nothing.

"Sorry it's a mess," Coal said.

"One pair of pants on the floor? That's not a mess."

"Okay. So ... What did you want to talk to me about?"

"Jordan."

"Jordan? What's he doing now?"

Maura tried to smile. "Coal ... He's not doing anything. But does it bother you? Me and Jordan going out?"

It bothered the hell out of him.

"Why would it bother me?"

She tried to hold his gaze but dropped hers after a moment. "I don't know. I just thought ... Oh, I don't even know what to say."

She started to turn back toward the door, but for some reason he had expected that, and he caught her arm. He turned her back toward him. "Hey. Hey. I know you've been trying to plan a time for us to talk for quite a while. Now I need to say something: If you're like me, even when you finally have the chance, it always seems easier to keep things inside. But if you're like me you'll hate yourself for it later. Am I right?"

She nodded, trying to hold back a little smile. "Yeah. You're right too much of the time."

"That's my line. Now come on. What did you want to say? You

might never get the chance again."

"You remember Christmas Eve?" Of course he remembered. It was the first and last time they had kissed. But he knew her well enough to know she wouldn't come right out and say that.

"I'll never forget it."

"Well ... Did anything change after that?"

"Like what?"

"Like between you and Kathy, or Annie." He knew those words had taken all her strength to get out.

"No."

She nodded. "Nothing has changed with me and Jordan either."

"That seems pretty important for you to have me know. Are you really sure? Because it's all right if it did. We're both adults."

"But Coal ... Okay, please stop. I'm trying to tell you something."

He almost laughed, but he forced the urge down. "I know. I guess I'm not helping, though."

"No, as usual."

"If I just don't say anything at all, would it help?"

"No. It would be worse."

"Then what can I do?"

She looked up at him. For a long time, their eyes were locked. She almost looked like she could have passed out. "Coal, I know we aren't tied to each other or anything. I know you have your life, and I have mine. But ... Sometimes I just ..." She shook her head and looked down. Taking a deep breath, she looked back up. Then she blurted out, "Sometimes I just want to ask you to kiss me again. So I'll know nothing has changed."

He wanted to smile at her to reassure her. But right now he couldn't smile if he had wanted to. Instead, he leaned close to her, took her in his arms, and walked her backwards right up until her back was pressed against the closed door. Then he lowered his face, and their lips met once more, as they had that wonderful

Christmas Eve, and as they held each other gently they softly explored each other's lips. And they were Coal and Maura again—not quite lovers, but then not quite merely friends either.

And the world was a brighter place.

Friday, January 12

The next trouble was only two nights later, out in front of the Owl Club. Coal had taken Slugger to town with him after supper, where they enjoyed a shake at Wally's and visited with sweet Karen Richardson and her father Wally, whenever he got a chance to get out of the kitchen.

Coal had only stepped back to the kitchen for a minute to say hi to Wally's wife Beulah and tease her for a minute, which turned into five or ten after he complimented her on her locally famous flower arrangements, on display in the front of the restaurant. If Coal was in a hurry, he made the mistake of giving Beulah a hug and then telling her the flower arrangements were masterpieces, which opened a flood gate. Beulah loved to talk about her flower arrangements—even if Coal knew nothing of the art. All of a sudden, he heard the front door chimes and the excited cries of young Karen.

Turning away from Beulah and Wally, Coal rushed back out into the dining room, now empty except for Karen, who had apparently just come back in.

"You've got to go help Slugger!" Karen said, although the words came out as something less intelligible.

Coal grabbed her shoulders. "What happened?"

"I went for a walk down the street with him, just to show him around. Some men came out of the Owl Club and started a fight! They—"

Coal didn't hear the rest of it. His ability to hear shut down as he raced for the front door, threw it wide and turned to see a fight going on at the Owl Club. It was too close for him to get in much of a run. He reached the fight in two seconds and grabbed the first available person by the coat collar, jerking him backward as hard as he could.

Coal saw the man stumble backward, hit the edge of the curb, and start to go down. Yelling out that he was the sheriff, he grabbed the next one to his left by the arm, which was set to go into action, and spun him around. His repeated shout that he was the sheriff didn't register on this man, or maybe Coal simply didn't want it to. With the back of his hand, he knife-sliced the man in the left side of his neck and as soon forgot him, knowing he would be out of the fight.

Turning, he roared out again, and the tiger that was Slugger Janx erupted out of the midst of three men who were on him at once, throwing two of them to the side and leveling the third one with a blow to the jaw.

Coal grabbed one of the other two by the collar and rushed him backward to slam him into the glass at the front of the Owl Club. "Settle down!"

Testosterone and adrenalin were a potent soup, seeming to fill the air, as six men, some of them wobbly, came to a standstill on the sidewalk. The seventh, the one Slugger had just hit in the jaw, lay prone on the sidewalk, unmoving. The one Coal had struck in the neck stood against the building, trying to hold himself up with both hands on the edge of the windowsill.

"What the hell's going on?" Coal growled.

No one spoke for several seconds. Each man's eyes bounced around the circle, expecting someone else to speak. When no one else did, a skinny man in a heavy work coat and work boots said in a whiny voice, "This guy pulled a knife on us."

Coal zeroed in on the man. "What's your name?"

"Lynn. Jamie Lynn," the man wheezed.

"All right, Lynn. You say he pulled a knife on you?" By now,

Coal was faintly aware that the three Richardsons had come up behind him. He turned and sought out Karen, beckoning her to him and putting a comforting arm around her shoulders. "Karen? What did you see? Did he pull a knife?" Coal was afraid of the answer. All he could think of was Slugger's big Nguyen Dan fighting knife.

"I didn't see that," Karen said. Her fear lay all over her like a coat of paint.

"Then what did you see?"

"They just started calling him names, and— I don't really know," she blurted, visibly shivering. "Then they were just fighting."

"All right, honey. That's fine." He released her back to Wally and Beulah, then turned to scan the group. "All right. Where's the knife?" He feared they were about to show him Slugger's knife.

There was silence for a moment, and then the man Coal had chopped in the neck wobbled over and held out a folding sheath knife with a four-inch blade, which was closed. Coal took it and turned it over in his hand. This was a high-quality knife, a Gerber. There wasn't anything to say it didn't belong to Slugger, but Coal had never seen it before.

"Is this your knife, mister?" Coal held it across his palm, looking at Slugger. He purposely didn't call his friend by name, hoping to avoid this circus of men claiming favoritism.

Still breathing hard, and with blood oozing down from one corner of his mouth, Slugger stared at the knife. He looked up at Coal. "Man, I ain't never seen that blade before."

Coal's eyes scanned the group of fighters. His sharp eye noticed that the man who had produced the knife had a sheath on his belt. He couldn't see if there was anything in it or not.

"Anybody else have any weapons on you? Guns? Knives?" He scanned the group and from the corner of his eye saw the man with the knife sheath casually raise his hand just enough to pull the bottom edge of his coat over his sheath. That was about all Coal needed.

"So did anyone else see this man pull this knife?"

The others glanced around for a couple of seconds before one of them, then another, agreed that they had seen Slugger pull out the knife in question and accost one of them. Soon, all heads began to bob. It was unanimous: This was Slugger's knife.

"All right." Coal looked at Slugger. "I guess I've got to take you in, Mister. I'm keeping your knife—as evidence. Do you have any other weapons on you?"

Slugger stared. He weaved his head from side to side.

"Raise your coat."

Slugger complied. To Coal's surprise and satisfaction, Slugger had left both his pistol and the fighting knife at the house. He made him turn around, so the charade would be complete, then pulled a pair of handcuffs from his back pocket and walked over to him.

"I'm going to have to cuff you. Put your hands behind your back." As Coal was snapping the cuffs, he looked around at the others. "All right, I guess you boys can go back in the bar, or whatever you planned on doing. I'll handle this from here."

None of the fighters was sober enough to think about signing a complaint or even giving his name. They started to disperse, most of them going into the owl club. The man who had produced the knife lingered longest, and Coal caught him licking his lips as he looked toward the pants pocket where Coal had slipped the folded knife. "Thanks for your help, sir." He was being facetious as anything, but that man didn't know it.

Coal turned with his hand on Slugger's right arm and led him down the street to the pickup, where he opened the door and helped him in, shutting it soundly behind him. He turned knowing the Richardsons would have followed him. By now, a quick scan of the sidewalk showed only one of the brawlers left outside, a man who stood a ways down by a dark-colored car, smoking a cigarette as he looked toward Coal and the others. He was well out of ear-shot.

Coal looked at Karen, who was still shaken, her face pale and her teeth clattering together. On a whim, he put a comforting hand up to the side of her face. "Hey, Karen. You did a good job tonight. Thanks."

She nodded. "You're welcome. Is Slugger going to be okay? I know that wasn't really his knife. Those men started the whole thing."

"He'll be fine. This is all for show. I do have one question, though." Coal already figured he knew the answer. "Who threw the first punch?"

Karen looked toward Wally and Beulah. She seemed loath to reply. Finally, she drew a breath and pursed her lips. "It was him. It was Slugger. But those men were saying some awful things to him. Really awful."

"I'm sure they were. Thank you again, Karen."

"So he's not going to jail?"

"He's not going to jail. I'm taking him home."

Coal drove down to the Texaco and turned in, stopping the truck in the dark lot. He got out and went around to Slugger's side, ordering him out. When Slugger was standing on the concrete, he turned him around and unlocked the cuffs, taking them off and slipping them into his hip pocket. Slugger rubbed his wrists as he turned back around. It was plain he wanted to speak, but he held back.

Coal reached into his pocket and pulled out the Gerber knife. He hefted it in his palm, then held it out to his friend. "I guess this is your knife."

"Coal, I swear that ain't my knife. I've never seen it before."

"Listen, buddy, seven men swore that was your knife. Whose word am I going to take—the seven, or the one? Take your knife back. It's too bad he didn't give you your sheath too."

Slugger's confusion vanished, and his face broke into a grin. "Oh ... Oh, man, yore slick, Sarge. Yore real slick."

Coal met the grin. "Well, don't let that get around."

Slugger took his new knife and got back in the truck, and Coal went to the other side and started home. It wasn't until then that Slugger said what he had been holding back.

"Hey, Sarge?"

"Yeah, buddy?" Coal kept staring at the highway, bright in his headlights.

"I'm sorry, man. Real sorry."

"About what?"

"About ... You know. Man, I can't seem t' stay outta fights. I'm afraid yore gonna be sorry you ever brought me up here."

"You swung first, didn't you?" said Coal. "Since we're playing true confessions."

"Yes sir, I did."

"Why?"

Slugger leaned back in his seat and sighed. "Man. Sarge, the things they were callin' me. They ... I'm sorry. I shouldn't a come here." After a silence of several minutes, Slugger's quiet voice filled the cab again. "I thought it'd be different up here. Sarge, when's it ever gonna stop? When am I ever gonna find a place where I belong?"

CHAPTER NINETEEN

Saturday, January 13

Saturday had been good for the Savage household. There were no emergency calls, and the worst thing to deal with was Virgil's dilemma: He was back in the twins' room again, as Slugger Janx had taken over his. But if that bothered Virgil, it never would have shown. He spent at least half the morning bugging Coal about shooting his new rifle, until Coal finally gave in.

They were being treated to a wonderful warm spell of one degree above freezing that day, which was phenomenal considering the zero degree temperatures just two days earlier. So the family made an outing of it, all of them bundling up to go out and throw lead at some targets.

Connie took it upon herself to call up Maura because she seemed to remember her mentioning she wasn't scheduled to work. At least those were Connie's words. Coal knew there was no "seemed to remember" about it. This fact would have been securely locked in his mother's memory.

Setting up targets, Coal let Cynthia and Katie shoot first, knowing they would soon want to get back in the car where it was warm. To his surprise, Cynthia preferred the cold to sitting in the truck, as long as she could have a gun in her hands. Much to Virgil's chagrin, she even outshot him, although in the boy's defense she didn't do it with his new .30-06, but a .22.

Coal almost got a taste of the same medicine when Maura took her .38 special out and shot a twelve-inch group at fifteen yards. "Wow. Do you always shoot like that?"

She gave him a pseudo-smug look. "Maybe. At least when I'm showing off."

"Well, I'll admit you're one great show-off."

He took out his new .44 magnum and deafened the family putting six holes into a six-inch circle at the same fifteen yards as Maura. He thought he was being quite chivalrous when he didn't look over at her afterward.

She saved them all from the deafening silence. "Huh. Well, I guess next time I decide to show off, I'd better practice first."

"Maura," cut in Connie, "I got this from *The Andy Griffith Show*. One thing you always have to remember if you're trying to catch a man: Never outshoot him."

Coal laughed. "Don't listen to her. You can outshoot me—if you can outshoot me."

The twins took a turn with a Smith and Wesson K-22 while Coal helped them steady their hands. Even though he was helping them, they both pleasantly surprised him with their careful squeezing off of six rounds, especially Wyatt. He had let them shoot from ten feet, because he didn't want to hurt their confidence, and each boy shot two bull's eyes out of their six shots.

Finally, Slugger got out his .45. He had to be a smart-off and went back to twenty-five feet for his turn. His group was much bigger around than Coal's, but to his credit all of his rounds were also in a span of maybe ten seconds less than Coal's. Coal shook his head. He sure wouldn't want Slugger shooting at him! He told him as much.

"Sarge, if you ever see me shootin' at you, you c'n bet it's Armageddon."

"Good. All right, it's getting cold out here. Anyone want to go home and see if Grandma can make us some hot chocolate?"

*   *   *

Coal spent the rest of the day reloading .44 magnum rounds in a workroom he and his father had dug out when he was twelve in the basement beyond where the weight room was now and rocked in to make it a permanent part of the house. For company, he had Slugger, two dogs, his new, very welcome shadow, Virgil, and a beautiful woman named Maura PlentyWounds. He couldn't guess if Connie was more pleased that Maura had descended into the dungeon with him and the guys, or upset that she didn't stay upstairs to partake in a game of Life with her and the girls. The twins and Sissy, meanwhile, spent their time roving between the television and the basement, but none of them could seem to wrap their little minds around the tedious chore of pouring powder into casings and crimping bullets down on top.

Later, with one hundred rounds of downloaded forty-four ammunition in cases, and forty practice loads for the ought-six, the anti-social foursome trekked upstairs to try their hand at the board game *Clue,* known originally as *Murder!*

In spite of his general shy-ness, it would have been hard to disguise Virgil's glee at winning two games in a row. Then it was back to *Life* again, and Coal had to excuse himself. Games one could win only on mere luck weren't anything that interested him. He would rather sit in front of the television and watch *Emergency!*

One of the few times he listened to the clamor at the game table, Coal frowned at Slugger Janx's words: "Man, I sure wish real life could be as easy as this. Blue men, pink women, and nobody better than anybody else."

The words played over and over again in Coal's mind throughout the rest of the afternoon and into evening.

It was eight-thirty when Coal jerked at the sound of the phone ringing. *Leave us alone!* Those words were spoken only in his head as he concentrated on the TV and pretended not to hear until Katie got up and answered it.

"Dad, it's for you."

Inwardly, Coal groaned. He was snuggled up close to Maura on the cowhide couch, with Sissy in his lap. Getting up out of this state of bliss was difficult for him not only physically, but emotionally. "Who is it?"

Katie put her hand over the transmitter. "Kathy MacAtee, I think."

Coal's eyes sliced over toward Maura but didn't make contact. "Is she okay?"

Katie just shrugged. Politely, she kept holding the phone, when Coal could see she would rather set it down on the desk.

Coal sighed and transferred Sissy over onto Maura's lap, then climbed out of the lap of luxury and went to answer the phone.

Hi, Coal. Okay, I know the plan was for you to get settled with your friend before we tried for supper again, but ... Okay, buster— seriously, how long is that going to take?

Coal laughed. "I'm sorry, Kathy. Well, apparently longer than we thought, huh?"

Apparently. Well, the girls are really champing at the bit to show you all King's tricks, so I told them I'd call—even though I think they'd have better luck getting you here than I am.

Coal winced. "Hey! That's not fair."

All's fair— Kathy stopped herself short. *So ... I'm making stew in the morning, and I think by six o'clock tomorrow night all the flavor will have time to sink into every morsel. It would sure taste good with some fresh wheat bread and strawberry preserves I put up in September. Am I tempting you yet?*

"You've done tempted me," replied Coal. "You say six? You think the girls will be able to break away from *The Wild Kingdom?*"

I'm positive of it! They have their own wild kingdom going on here!

After hanging up, Coal squeezed down into his spot between Maura and Cynthia again. He sighed, making a point of not looking at Maura. She was going to draw her own conclusions anyway. He was positive she had heard every word of his side of the conversation.

Later, the kids were in bed. It was around nine-thirty, and *Barnaby Jones* was droning along on the television. Maura reached over and grabbed Coal's leg, giving it a little shake. "I probably should get going."

Even though Ken had worked his magic, it was beginning to seem like Maura's old International, Ebenezer, was still broken down, but the reality was that either he or Connie always seemed to come up with some reason why Coal should go fetch Maura from her house rather than make her drive herself. He sighed and got up, then held his hand down to Maura, who took it and let him help her up. When he tried to release his grip on her warm hand, she held on for a few seconds longer, then gave his fingers a couple of squeezes.

They got their coats, Maura said good night to Connie and Slugger, and then they stepped out into the night. It was just about right at freezing outside, and their breath came out in puffs of steam and filtered into the still air. The sky was black as pitch, and stars by the thousands crackled like tiny campfires in the vast heavenly expanse.

Maura was quiet as Coal opened his door and let her slide in before him. She seemed to sit closer to him than normal, in fact so close that a feather could not have been slid down between them. Neither of them spoke until they were almost to the house, when Maura drew in a lung-filling breath, then let it sigh out. Coal waited.

"Hey, so ... You're going to Kathy's, huh? Tomorrow?"

"Yeah, I guess. She's really been wanting me to try her stew."

"Good. You'll like that." She seemed genuinely happy for him.

Coal pulled off the highway into her yard and stopped, setting the brake. "What about you? Do you have plans for tomorrow?"

"Ha! No, nothing really. I might go for a ride."

Coal's heart jumped a little. That sounded great: a cold saddle against his backside. It had been too long.

"I wish I could go with you."

"Hey." She reached out and gave his leg a squeeze. "Now we decided this together, right? It's okay to see other people."

His heart caught in his throat. Sure, it was okay. He thought that. He wanted to say it. But part of him wanted only to be with Maura.

He sighed. "It'll be all right."

She had not taken her hand off his leg. She squeezed again and leaned her head over against him. He couldn't see her expression now. "Coal?"

"Yeah."

"Kathy MacAtee lost her whole world not very long ago."

"I know."

"She's got to be lonely and trying to figure out what she's going to do, how she's going to take care of those girls all by herself. How she's going to carry on for the rest of her life, being so young, and still beautiful."

Stop it, thought Coal. *What are you trying to do? You aren't helping anything.*

"I'm sure you're right." *And that's why you aren't supposed to be okay with my going over there for supper,* he thought.

"She doesn't have anyone else. You don't have any choice but to be with her."

Damnit, was she reading his mind? Or was she fishing for something? He wasn't sure how to take her words. *You don't have any choice but to be with her* could be understood two very different ways.

"Do you think any man would take on three teenage girls who weren't his own?" he asked. It was an innocent question, but when she replied he realized how it might have sounded.

"I don't know. Would you?"

CHAPTER TWENTY

Sunday, January 14

Slugger was not ready to attend church. He had left his own church behind, and his Baptist minister, and back there in Louisiana there were plenty of people his color with whom to mingle. Here, he would be the Savior's almost literal black sheep, and that he could not bring himself to be. So he stayed home with the dogs and the horses while Coal accompanied his family again to Sunday services, which was getting to be a nasty habit.

Perhaps even nastier was the habit of picking up Maura PlentyWounds on their way. But that was what they did.

In church, she sat once more next to Coal, holding Sissy on her lap, and as she sang "God Be With Us 'Til We Meet Again" at the end of the service, Coal closed his eyes to the beauty of her voice, and just for a moment he was back in time, back with Laura, when their love was new and the world seemed spotless and golden. Was he ever going to find a way to shake those memories? A way to move on and be whole again?

After church, Maura came to the house for a crockpot roast, potatoes, and carrots, probably far too much like the stew he was going to turn right around and eat at Kathy's that evening.

A golden sun was out, and the sky a bold, crisp blue. It had topped freezing, again by one degree, and after dinner, when everyone else was settling down on the chair and couches, Coal saw Maura pause at the picture window, staring out at the glory of the day, and the shining fields of snow up on the Beaverhead Mountains.

He walked over and said something stupid he hated to hear when anyone else said it: "Penny for your thoughts."

Maura let out a giggle, which he thought was a bit of an over-reaction.

"Was that funny?"

She unfolded her arms and poked him in the ribs. "No. Sorry. It just didn't sound like anything you'd say."

How funny she would think that too.

"Okay, it's not. Normally. I guess I should have said, 'What're you thinking about, chick?'"

"And I would have called you a pig."

Coal laughed. "Well, I guess I am that—in more ways than one. I assume since you're spending all this energy poking fun at me you have no intention of getting back to my question."

She looked at him, her face unreadable. But he knew Maura enough to know she was trying to decide between being her some-times sweet self and being sarcastic and cutting and funny.

Sweet-self won.

"I was thinking what a beautiful day it would be for a ride."

"Yeah?"

"Yeah. I know, it's silly."

"Silly why?"

"Because of the cold."

"Cold! This isn't cold. It's thirty-three degrees, and no wind." In fact, he couldn't remember the slightest breeze blowing here in days.

She scanned the mountains. Her eyes right then could have been the wondering, enchanted eyes of a child, and they were made a bolder blue by the sky reflected in them. Finally, she reached down, as if it were perfectly normal in front of his family, and took his hand. "So ... Do you think we could?"

"What?"

"Cut it out! Do you think we could ride?"

It was time to stop with the wisecracks. "Sure. I'd be up for it."

And so they rode. They went up Lemhi Road, with the dogs running out before them, and thankfully they only had two horses left on the Savage property, because no one else was able to ride along.

The day seemed too pristine and crisp and wonderful for talk, so Coal held back as long as he could, watching his breath puff out away from his mouth in gouts of tiny crystal, and watching the sunlight and shadow interplay on Maura's golden hair.

Finally, he couldn't hold back. "Hey."

She looked over at him, her eyes sparkling. "Hey."

"I was thinking about something."

"You do that a lot."

He chuckled. "That's funny. Most people tell me I don't think *enough.*"

"Well, I didn't say you think about the right things—or that your thoughts are correct."

That made him shake his head. Sometimes he wondered how he and this woman ever held a normal conversation. It was always this banter, or something serious and angry. At least it seemed that way.

"So if you'll stop joking around for just a second, can I tell you what I was thinking?"

She giggled. "Okay."

"It's been a while, but one time you told me you had a place you wanted to show me. Do you still?"

"I do."

"When are we doing that?"

"I want to wait. 'Til it warms up."

"Oh." His heart fell. "I feel warm."

"Me too. But the weather doesn't. You'll know why I waited, Coal. Trust me."

"Okay. I'll trust you."

They rode two miles out, then finally turned around and rode back, watching the interplay of light and cloud shadow along the frosty farms and fields, and the rooftops of barns, sheds, and homes scattered through the valley.

A few hundred yards from the house, Maura said, "I kind of wish you didn't have to go to MacAtees' later." That was a bold admission from the woman who held her deepest thoughts close to the vest.

"Why?"

She looked at him and frowned. "Oh, gee. Let me think. Come on! Because I'm having fun. It seems like we just don't get to have days like this very often."

She was right. And deep inside, he sort of wished the same thing. But wasn't it Maura herself who had said Kathy needed him? Just last night?

"Do you want me to cancel?" It disgusted him to admit to himself, but if she had said yes, he probably would have, and he didn't like being that kind of man.

She thought for a moment and finally gusted out a heavy sigh. "No. No, that wouldn't be nice. I'm just being selfish. But ..."

She didn't finish her thought, and the gravel crackling under Cody's and Bolt's hooves now was the gravel in Connie's driveway.

"But what?"

She glanced over at him, lost her steel, and looked away. "Well, maybe sometime we could plan a Sunday like this just for me. Well, I mean for us."

*   *   *

Coal Savage hated to think of his life as a romance novel. He felt like it fit him more to be in an action-adventure story, or a

Western, with the sun at his back, facing down an angry lynch mob. Better yet, riding into a beautiful sunset, leaving behind the woman who had tried her darnedest to tie him down.

But anymore it was starting to seem more like what he deplored. Romance. Romance. Romance. It was enough to make a man's man nauseous.

Yet was any of it truly romance? Maybe not. Maybe he was just being the big, lone gunman, the only one in the valley who could protect the scared, lonely widow—or divorcée, as the case might be. And maybe Coal Savage was an idiot. If the people in this county only knew the stupid things he thought about sometimes, they would probably laugh at his attempts to keep the law.

He pulled the GMC into the MacAtees' dark yard, feeling bad that he longed to be back with his family, and with Maura. But Kathy needed him. Maura had said it, and he knew it. In a way, her daughters needed him as well. How was he supposed to walk away from that?

Kathy came out to meet him, lit beneath the yellowish porch light, and for once the jeans she was wearing didn't have the ugly flare to the legs. She was sporting good old-fashioned Wranglers, looking like the real rancher lady she was supposed to be. She was also wearing Coal's favorite shirt of hers, a mix between buffalo and shadow plaid, blue and black in color, that did something magical to set off her rich brunette hair and chocolate-colored eyes. He thought back and wondered if he should ever have told her how much he liked that shirt. It made him feel weird things for her, the only recently widowed wife of his best friend Larry.

"Hey, buster," she greeted when he got out of the truck and slammed the door. She swept him with her eyes. "Wow. It's so good to see you, Coal."

And he couldn't deny that it was good to see her too. They met in a crushing embrace under the sickly yellow light. After fully half a minute in her arms, Coal had to say something about ordinary things to break a spell. He looked up at the light bulb. "We need to get you a better fixture, and a good flood light." He didn't add the rest of his thought, that he didn't like her and the girls being out here so far from neighbors without a man around to scare off bad guys.

Kathy giggled, and he frowned at her. "What?"

"What? You think of the funniest times to say stuff."

"What's funny about that? You need a better light."

"I guess. But I would have rather stood there and held onto you for another five minutes than to hear about my bad lighting. In fact, I kind of like my light. Maybe I keep it for mood lighting." She winked at him.

Coal laughed. "Fine. I'll put another one in beside it then, so you'll have a choice which one to turn on. You know, not every guy who comes up here in the dark is a knight in shining armor."

"Well, maybe I'd rather turn on my knight in shining armor than a brighter light."

Coal stared at her, too shocked to laugh, too stunned to cuss. Awkward. This was his best friend's wife!

Laughter. The best medicine. He had read that in *Reader's Digest,* so it must be true. He belted out a laugh that echoed across the hard-packed yard. "You're a funny woman. Well, you always turn me on, Kathy, so stop worrying about it."

Of course he was speaking in a voice that would leave no room for her to doubt that he was only being playful. Except that by the deep look in her eyes, and by the way she reached out and gave his hand a squeeze, then said, "I'm so glad you're here, Coal," he wondered if she realized he was only trying to keep it light.

Knight in shining armor? Ha! He was more like the jester.

"Me too. Let's get inside before I freeze me rump roast off."

She laughed and pulled the door open with the hand that wasn't still hanging onto his and led him into a warm house full of gleeful girls and barking golden retriever.

Kathy had not exaggerated anything. Her daughters had really worked wonders with King, and Coal was impressed with the display of commands and fun tricks they had taught him. If Virgil ended up so accomplished when he started working with Dobe, it was going to be something to be proud of to say the least.

It was King and the girls who ended up saving the night for Coal, and keeping him on track, and his mind and heart where they needed to be. He couldn't deny one thing: Now that Larry was gone, he was seeing Kathy in a whole new way. He had never doubted why his best buddy had chosen this woman for his wife, but because he *was* his best friend, there had always been a reserve in Coal that would never have let Kathy be attractive to him. Now, the more he saw of her, the more he realized how beautiful she was, and how much he really did enjoy being with her. Those thoughts disturbed him to no end, however, and that was the devil of it all. There was simply too much at stake for Coal to jump into another relationship. Perhaps, down deep, it was because he felt like such a failure from his first marriage. Perhaps he would never be able to let down his guard again and start over in a new relationship, with all the unknown challenges and problems any long-term relationship between a man and a woman was bound to have.

Maybe the crux of all Coal's problems, why he had such difficult issues trying to make realistic decisions concerning Kathy, Maura, and Annie, was that, at the heart of it all, he was a yellow-bellied coward.

With the memory of a long, loving embrace lingering in his mind, along with the unfulfilled promise of a kiss he knew without a doubt could have been his for the asking, Coal drove home ten miles an hour slower than the speed limit.

By the time he reached the house, finding it dark but for the glow of a fire in the stove, he knew nothing more than whatever he had started out the day knowing.

Coal Savage had four choices: Maura PlentyWounds; Kathy MacAtee; Annie Price; or the lonesome, heart-breaking life of a man who would let his haunting past rule whatever was left of his future.

It was a bitter admission he would make to himself alone that his past had sculpted him. He was scarred, and he was scared, and it was going to take one hell of a woman ever to change that.

CHAPTER TWENTY-ONE

Monday, January 15

Outside of guarding the over seven hundred American military malcontents and criminals who populated Long Binh Jail, and then traipsing the jungles of Vietnam on search and destroy missions, Slugger Janx had no noteworthy skills. Or at least none that might put him on the top of anyone's hiring list in Salmon, Idaho.

So when Coal took Slugger job hunting, it was with the blatant understanding that any work he could land was likely going to be fairly mundane, probably dirty, and, for certain, physically de-manding. Also, his job was going to depend more upon someone owing Coal a favor than on any qualification he could show.

They purposely avoided anything in food services, saving those places as a last option. Places like McPherson's and King's were also at the bottom of the list. Instead, they went seeking hard-ware stores, lumber yards, feed stores and the like. Because Slug-ger was at least temporarily going to have to use Coal's old blue Chevy pickup for his transportation to and from work, Coal was also careful to put all local businesses at the top of his list. That cut out mining and timber jobs that would have paid better and that his friend probably could have adapted to fine.

Because they couldn't expect any of the jobs on the list to pay very much, Slugger had to agree that at least for a while he would remain at the Savage residence. That was no problem for anyone there, even Virgil, who by now had become accustomed to moving in and out of his bedroom. No problem, that is, except for little Sissy, and Sissy would probably have an issue with anyone new who came to live with them.

Coal started out taking Slugger to Lemhi Lumber, on the corner of Shoup and St. Charles Streets. The owner, a friend of Coal's, wasn't in, so they spoke with the manager, whom Coal did not know and who treated Slugger, it seemed, with much less respect than he deserved.

They tried the hardware stores after that, then Economy and Home Lumber, neither of which had any interest in hiring and didn't waste any time letting it be known.

When Coal began feeling desperate, he made his last stop the same as his first, at Lemhi Lumber. This time his friend Joe was in his office, and he called Coal in as soon as he heard he had come back.

Joe Taylor was an odd-looking sort, who stood over six feet tall but had a torso that looked as long as his legs. Short-cropped blond hair gave him a military look that he came by honestly, as he had done twenty years in the Navy, and unless he was clowning around with someone, which he often was, he bore a perpetual look on his face like he had just sucked too long on a lemon. He grinned when Coal pushed open a plain-looking wooden door and walked into the cluttered mess Joe called an office.

"Hey, Coal! What's going on?" His eyes flickered a little as he saw Slugger step in behind Coal, but he didn't look over.

"Hi, Joe. How's Danni and the kids?"

Joe waved a hand dismissively. "Oh, you know Danni! Spending all my money so fast I think I'll be a hunnerd before I c'n retire from her. An' the kids, well—growin' up. Hard to believe Joey's fourteen now."

"You got an early start," said Coal with a smile. Then, not to leave Slugger's presence unexplained for too long, he turned and jerked a thumb at him. "Hey, Joe, this is a good friend of mine, Slugger Janx. We were in Nam together."

Without hesitation, Joe reached across his desk to offer his hand. "Hi, Slugger. Is that your real name?"

Slugger looked sheepish and wiped at his bad eye, which now was starting to heal up but still sometimes leaked fluid. "No, it's Bryant, sir, but nobody calls me that."

"All right. Slugger's good. Good to meet you. You know, Coal an' me go way back. *Too* way back, I think sometimes!"

Coal chuckled his agreement. "So Joe, we stopped in here first thing, but I have to say, and no offense, but your manager didn't seem too thrilled about Slugger."

"Oh yeah? I sure don't like to hear that. Well, I'm here now. How can *I* help you?"

Coal drew a deep breath. "So after we left here we pretty much hit every place we could think of locally, and all of them gave us a big no. Slugger's really in need of a job. He's living with us right now, but he's still going to need spending money—you know, for gas and things like that. I don't suppose you might have anything going on here that you could use a good worker for—a guy that does his work and never complains."

Joe stood up straighter, putting his hand to the lower part of his face and letting his eyes drift down as if reading something important on his desk that pertained to Coal's request.

In a few moments, he looked back up, this time straight at Slugger. "If it started out on a temporary basis, would that be enough?"

Slugger gave a big shrug. "Yes sir, I think so. Sure better than any other offers I've had."

Joe waved a hand across the front of himself. "And I'm talking maybe even as much as twenty-five, thirty hours, straight off. Sometimes maybe not quite that, but something, anyway."

Slugger nodded. "Sir, I have to say I'd be mighty grateful to you."

"All right. Yeah, sure, I'll give you a try." He stuck his hand out again. "Let's get you some paperwork to fill out, shall we?"

*   *   *

That evening Coal picked Slugger up from work, and he was nearly overjoyed to hear his friend speak of his experiences that day. There were a few standoffish customers who came into the lumber yard and didn't seem to want to deal with him, but Slugger tried to be positive and had told himself it was only because he was a stranger, and had nothing to do with the color of his skin. Coal hoped he was right, but from what he had encountered himself since bringing Slugger to town, he wasn't going to be so generous. As Slugger told all about his day, Coal made the decision that as soon as they both had time he would start taking him around to as many friends and friendly acquaintances as possible, to make sure the town knew who Slugger was to him, and that he was responsible for his being here.

After supper, Slugger settled in with the kids and Connie to watch TV, with Sissy using Connie as a shield to keep her out of Slugger's sight. Coal watched for a while, and it made him smile to see Sissy peeking around Connie whenever she thought Slugger's attention was elsewhere and staring at him. This was taking some getting used to for her, but Coal had a feeling Slugger was going to win that little girl over sooner than he had. Sissy was like a moth emerging from its cocoon.

Coal felt restless. He wasn't in the mood to watch TV. He was more in the mood to watch Maura. When he was positive the children weren't going to notice his absence, and it was getting near their bedtime anyway, he told them good night, advised Connie not to wait up for him, put on a clean shirt and his best jeans and drove to Maura's. He had no particular plans for the evening other than simply to be with her.

But when he slowed down to make the turn into her yard, he saw a sight that made him stop and swerve back onto the highway: Jordan's car was parked in front of her house.

With a sigh, he kept driving. Now what? He couldn't go back home, at least not yet. He wasn't in the mood for a barrage of questions from his mother. Should he go to a bar? He wasn't much of a drinker, and he felt out of place with a bunch of drunks anyway.

Then he realized where he was, and once more he slowed the truck. Annie Price's place was just ahead, to the left. Was she working a night shift, or was she home? Keeping the pickup out on the highway this time, he stopped almost directly in front of Annie's. There was a light on inside, but a very dim one. Yet her car was parked out front, and she had no other vehicle.

He sat there in the highway in a state of indecision until he saw headlights coming up behind him. *Turn in or gun it,* he told himself.

He turned in. He was longing for female companionship, and Maura was occupied. Annie, on the other hand, always seemed more than happy to see him.

His knock on the door brought no answer. He tried again, louder. It was only ten minutes after eight. Surely she wouldn't already be in bed.

Another knock, and this time he thought he heard a faint voice.

Cautiously, he tried the doorknob. It was locked.

He knocked again, and again he thought he heard the voice.

Worry began to creep into the edges of his mind. Whoever was in there speaking in reply to his knocks wasn't very good at making herself heard. But what if that was because she was hurt? What if fate had somehow guided him here tonight, and he was the only thing between Annie and a long, terrible night? What if she was too injured somehow even to answer her door?

He had to make a choice, and to him he made the obvious one. Going around back, he stepped up the wooden staircase to the landing, carpeted with ugly green indoor-outdoor carpet. Reaching out, he grasped the doorknob, and this one turned. Feeling a little awkward, he pushed the door open a couple of inches and spoke into the half-dark:

"Annie? Are you okay?"

"No! Coal, is that you? Please go away."

CHAPTER TWENTY-TWO

Coal was suspended for a moment in that place of disbelief just before reality comes crashing down. Was that actually Annie Price who had spoken? And did she truly realize who he was? He found it impossible to believe. Something was very wrong here, and even though the voice had given a very plain command, Coal had to delve into this deeper. He was having flashbacks of learning about Laura's self-inflicted death, and warning bells told him he could not walk away from Annie.

He pushed the door open wider, then waited. What should his next move be? Did he dare rush in to wherever Annie was? What if she was not alone?

He shoved his hesitation aside. "Annie? Are you okay?" He didn't even realize he was echoing his own words exactly.

"Coal! Please! I said go away. Don't come in here."

In the words of one Admiral Farragut, "Damn the torpedoes; full speed ahead!" Coal had no choice. He wasn't going to turn around and leave only to come back here tomorrow to take a death report on Annie Price.

"I can't leave, Annie. Are you decent?" Coal felt his heart pounding harder and faster than it had in some fights he had been in.

"No! Coal, I'm not. Just go away."

"I'm coming in there, Annie. If you're not covered, you'd better get covered."

He stepped inside and shut the door behind him. The house felt way too warm. He walked over and looked at the thermostat. Eighty-six degrees! Dialing it down, he looked around the room. He noted that there were no dishes, either on the counter or in the sink. Not that this would normally mean anything, because Annie tended to be a tidy woman, but it seemed like if she weren't feeling good, and she had eaten at all, she wouldn't have taken any time to clean up afterward.

On the floor by the front door, he saw Annie's coat and shoes, not laid there in any kind of order, but simply tossed.

"Coal," he heard the voice from the bedroom again. "I don't want you here."

What was happening? The more Annie bade him leave, the more Coal was driven the opposite way.

"I have to make sure you're all right, Annie. Please understand."

He started down the hall, where her voice was coming from. It was dark and foreboding. It put him in mind of the tunnel, surrounded by sticky web, of a spider.

A moan rose from down the hall, and Coal started moving faster. A vague warning made him draw his .44. He didn't want to, but he had seen so many strange things in his life in the military and FBI. He had to be ready for anything.

He reached Annie's open door. Now he could smell the odor of some kind of alcoholic drink. There were two switches for the hallway light, and the second one was in sight now to Coal's left, just outside the bedroom door.

"Hey. Annie. Please forgive me. I can't leave without knowing you're all right."

Coal reached over and flipped on the hallway light. Its dim glow formed orange swatches of light and deeper shadows on the wrinkles and mounds of Annie's bedding and the bulk beneath.

Keeping the door open, Coal eased into the room. He could see Annie had drawn the covers up over her face. He scanned the room, saw no other threat, and holstered his revolver before Annie could see that he had drawn it.

"Annie? What's going on?"

Silence. Deafening, ugly silence.

He walked to her bedside, then stood there contemplating the still form beneath the covers. She didn't even appear to be breathing. A rush of panic came over him.

"Annie? Annie! Answer me or I'm going to pull the covers off."

A sound of weeping started suddenly from beneath the blankets and grew louder and louder as Coal stood there with a feeling of sick dread filling his entire being. Was this the same Annie he knew, the Annie full of fun and smiles and a zest for life?

Taking a big chance, he eased himself down onto the edge of the bed. He took a deep breath, then started speaking, in a much quieter voice.

"Hey, girl. Hey. Whatever's going on, it'll be all right. Okay? I'm going to make sure you're fine. Then if you want to stay here and try to sleep, I promise I'll go. Deal?"

She kept crying. It was a forlorn, heart-breaking sound. What had happened to the real Annie Price? This was the sound of some-one affected by illicit drugs. Or at least if it were someone besides Annie Price, that was what Coal would have guessed. But Annie? No. That wasn't something she would do. Then again, did he really know? Did he really know Annie at all?

Coal was in way over his head. The only thing he knew was that he couldn't leave here. At least not yet. He had seen broken people before—most recently his own wife. He could never be responsible for walking away from that again.

"Annie? I'm here for you, all right? You didn't hurt yourself, did you?"

She was able to stop crying just enough to get a sullen-sounding "no" out. But in her state he wasn't sure the word meant anything.

"I'm going to turn on your light. Just for a minute." He didn't wait for a reply but flipped the light switch and carefully looked around the room, specifically seeking for pill bottles or drug paraphernalia. He switched the light back off and went to the bathroom, looking for the same things. After that, he carefully went over the entire house, then returned to Annie's bedside.

He sat down on the bed and listened to her sob herself into eventual quiet. After she had sniffled for a while and it seemed to be done, Coal said, "Annie, I can hold you if you want. I'll stay and hold you as long as you need me to. Would that make you feel better?"

A long silence followed, and then the weeping began again. But this time she threw off the covers and struggled up to a sitting position, and Coal leaned into her and took her in his arms. She lay her head on his arm and cried until he didn't think she could cry anymore. And then she went on crying.

Annie Price was as broken a person as anyone Coal had ever seen.

There was no remaining in the awkward position both of them had found, so finally Coal eased her back down onto the bed and turned to pull off his boots, then lay beside her. Almost instinctively, it seemed, she rolled over onto her right side, in a fetal position. Coal waited until she had stopped moving, then adjusted his own position and moved up close behind her, laying his left arm across her body and drawing her tight into him. Then, for close to an hour, he stayed there, listening to her breathe, and sometimes shake with a residual sob. The whole situation reminded him eerily of another such time, only that time it was with Maura, in his mother's bedroom.

Finally, her breathing evened out. She lay still. Taking a chance, Coal got up off the bed and went into the other room, picking up the phone to dial home. He told Connie he wasn't going to make it home, at least for a while, and that he just wanted her to know he was all right. He had an emergency that needed to be handled, and it was something very sensitive that he simply would not be able to talk about—perhaps ever.

Then he returned to Annie's bedroom and crawled back onto the bed with her, spooned her, rested his arm across her body, and eventually he, too, fell asleep.

CHAPTER TWENTY-THREE

Tuesday, January 16

It seemed like a long time since Coal had heard the wind blowing in the valley. But it was the wind that woke him up in the deep dark of pre-dawn. With his left arm still holding Annie close into him, his right one numb, he felt her warmth and listened to her quiet, steady breathing. He was glad she was finding much-needed sleep.

He wondered how her mental state would be when she woke up. And what had brought on such a great depression the night before. He almost didn't want to know, but there was that part of him that still wondered if he could help. Within limits, he would do whatever he could for a woman who had been so dear to him since his return to this valley.

The wind outside wasn't strong, but it was there. It reminded him of someone trying to learn to whistle. He carefully eased over onto his back, inviting the blood to start flowing in his right arm again, and stared up into the darkness.

When dim daylight began to creep around the edges of what ended up being a small blanket Annie had nailed up over her window, Coal sat up on the edge of the bed and pulled his boots on. He had no idea if Annie was going to be in the mood for breakfast, but he knew he was, and he could eat enough for the both of them if forced to.

Going to the kitchen, he stared at the near emptiness of the fridge. He opened the door to the freezer compartment and frowned at a stack of TV dinners. Salisbury steak? Chicken fried steak? Oh, the choices in plastic food. Wearing the frown as permanent attire, he pulled out three of the dinners and turned one over to check for the cooking temperature, then got two pans out of the oven and turned it on to bake. Not waiting for the oven to pre-heat, he shoved all three of the partitioned aluminum foil trays onto the middle shelf, set the timer, and went to doze on the couch after opening the blinds just enough for the overcast sky to light the room dully.

He heard rustling down the hall, and then the bathroom door closed. After a few more minutes, the toilet flushed and the sink water came on. He sat on the couch, expecting Annie to head from the bathroom back to bed. She surprised him.

He heard the thumping of her heels in the carpeted hall, and soon she stood there at the edge of the kitchen. She wore only white panties and a tee shirt, something he would have known had he been the kind to explore in the night.

The look in her eyes as she scanned the room was a little disconcerted. When she spotted him on the couch, her face immediately went into crying mode, and she rushed across the room to him. He got up to meet her and took her in his arms while she cried, this time very softly. It didn't take long for the crying to turn to sniffles, and she started moving her head around, sort of the way a dog does when it's trying to dig itself a deeper, warmer bed. Her warmth felt good against him.

"I'm going to have to turn the heat back up if you don't get some pants on," he said softly. That made her giggle.

"I know. Sorry. I thought I was turning the heat on by *not* having pants on."

He laughed, happy to hear her joking around. Hopefully that meant she was coming out of her funk. He was tempted to give her bottom a slap. He didn't.

She looked up at him, her face like that of a beautiful woman who had been forced to stay awake for three days and cry. But "beautiful woman" were still the key words.

"You sure had me worried. You okay?"

She gave a hard little shake of her head and squeezed her eyes shut, forcing back tears. "No. Coal, I'm so embarrassed. I didn't ever want you to see me like this." Her eyes opened as she tried to meet his gaze again.

He took one hand from her back and put it beside her cheek. "Hey. Everybody gets to break down sometimes. Even tough guys."

She giggled again. "Tough guys like me?"

"Yeah, just like you."

Annie looked into his eyes, and her lips parted. As she started to come up on her tiptoes, the oven buzzer went off.

Another rueful little giggle. "That's how my life goes." She dropped her hands from his back. "What are you cooking me? I'm starving."

Coal smiled. That was the best sign yet. "Well, I guess I'm cooking something that only remotely resembles food, but it was all you had."

She looked at him quizzically.

"TV dinners."

"Oh, yum."

He laughed and went over to turn off the buzzer, then used a dish towel to take out the meals and set them on the stove top. He had to admit they smelled pretty good, but he didn't have to admit it out loud. "Disgusting stuff. I wonder what they make it out of."

Annie had followed him and put her hand on the small of his back, giving it a little caress. She breathed in the aroma he was guiltily enjoying. "Well, I don't care. They're fast and easy. You know, my mom doesn't hang around here and cook all my food for me."

"Ouch!"

She gave out another giggle, a sound that, in spite of his lack of good sleep, made Coal very happy, and she poked him in the ribs with her finger. "Come on, Sheriff, let's see what they taste like."

"I'm half afraid to!"

Annie sat at the table eating in small bites. She still hadn't gotten dressed, but at least now she was covered by the table. Still, the vision of her shapely legs kept coming back to him and could not be completely erased.

Chewing a spoonful of carrots and green beans, she studied Coal for a moment. Thoughts were bouncing in her eyes, very close to the surface.

"Hey."

"Hey."

"I'm really embarrassed about last night."

"I don't want you to be. I just hope I made the night a little easier for you."

"You did. I'm sorry I sounded so grumpy. I don't know what came over me."

"Let's forget about it."

She sat looking at him contemplatively for a while, then made a little flourish toward him with her fork. "Well, hey—at least I finally got you in bed, right?"

"You're a naughty girl. You know nothing happened, though."

"Damn. I was hoping you had a confession for me from after I fell asleep."

"I'm sure that's what my mom's waiting for too."

"Ouch. I'm sorry, Coal. She's going to hate me."

"No she won't. She doesn't know where I spent the night, and I'm not telling her—or anyone else."

"Why?"

"Why? Why would I? I'm not the kind of guy to use things against people—especially people who mean a lot to me."

She dropped her eyes to her almost empty tray as they filled up with tears again. Finally, she looked up, blinking rapidly.

"I'm glad I mean a lot to you. You mean a lot to me too."

*   *   *

When Coal left Annie's, the sun was broken silver across the Beaverheads, peeking through a small window in the clouds that obviously would not last long. That thought brought Annie back to mind. He hoped the silver lasted a little longer for her.

As he neared Maura's place, his stomach tightened, and without thinking about it he slowed the truck down. When he came abreast of her place, he saw only her Travelette in the yard, and a gust of air escaped him. He drew in another deep breath and drove on. He didn't know where Jordan was, but he wasn't at Maura's for breakfast.

After going back to the house to get his workout, shower, and put on new clothes, Coal forsook breakfast in hopes of dodging the expected grilling by his mother. As he made it down the stairs from his room and headed for the front door to pick up his coat and make his escape, he heard Connie's voice from behind him, drawing his name out twice as long as normal with an accusing tone.

Coal didn't swear. He was duly proud of that accomplishment. He turned back. "Yeah, Mom?"

"Are you leaving?"

"Oh, uh ... Yeah, I need to go feed the prisoners."

"Uh-huh." Coal hated the way her voice sounded. This was going to be ugly. He looked past Connie, noticing Slugger standing there at the sink for the first time. Slugger was watching Coal intently, and in a glance Coal read his mind: *Oh, man, I would not wanna be you right now.* Funny thing was Coal didn't want to be himself right now either.

"Do you need to talk about last night, Son? The kids were sure worried."

Meaning his mother was worried. He tried to keep calm.

Maybe the destroyer would pass him by if he made himself small and hard to notice. "No, Mom, not really."

"You weren't at Maura's." Her voice was so matter-of-fact as she casually knifed some of her disgusting Blue Bonnet margarine onto a piece of white bread she might as well have told him she had read in the paper it might snow next week.

He stared at her. "Maura's?"

Adding strawberry jam on top of her margarine, she pretended to be involved in the conversation only because she had nothing more important to do at the moment. "Oh, yes—Maura. You remember her. Little blond thing?"

Coal gave her a sarcastic smile. "Very funny. Okay, spit it out. What do you want to know? And how do you know I wasn't at Maura's?"

"Well, I had to go to town, and ..."

"Caught yourself there, didn't you? You went to town? I didn't even leave here until eight o'clock."

"Okay, I drove over there to see if you were there."

"What time was that?"

"I don't know. Maybe eleven."

"You were driving around at eleven o'clock last night?"

Connie's face flushed a little. "Well, I was worried."

"Okay. I'm sorry. No, I wasn't at Maura's. Jordan Peterson was."

She stared back at him blankly. "Jordan wasn't there. Maura was alone."

"Really? His truck was there."

"No, it wasn't. And Maura was by herself. I talked to her." A smugness had come into her face and voice this time. Inside, he cringed.

"It was eleven o'clock, and you talked to her?"

"She was up. Yes, Coal. I wanted to know if she had seen you. She was up listening to Merle Haggard on her record player, so we sat and talked for a while."

By now Coal's mind was racing. Several thoughts buzzed around in his skull like flies that had suddenly realized they were trapped inside a dark, smoky box. Jordan wasn't at Maura's! His mom was checking up on him late at night! Maura was listening to Merle Haggard! Merle was one of Coal's favorite singers, but listening to him at eleven o'clock at night, and all alone, was a sure sign that either Maura wanted to become depressed or she was already depressed and looking for someone who had it worse.

But the main thing was—Jordan Peterson had not spent the night at Maura's. And neither had Coal.

The second most important thing was that now Maura knew Coal had been gone, and that he had not come home. *Thanks a lot, Mom.* He didn't say it, of course, but he wanted to in the worst way.

He had to stop this interrogation—in fact the entire investigation—right now. "Mom, I can't talk about where I was. I'll only tell you it was vitally important for someone, and that I didn't do anything to make you ashamed. Okay? Now I'll see you tonight."

Her heard her voice behind him as he shut the door and headed out to the truck. When he heard the door open behind him he had to hold his temper in check, waiting for his mom to call out. Instead, it was Slugger yelling out to ask him if he minded having company on the way to and from work. It turned out Slugger had been scheduled for an entire day at the hardware store, so he figured he might as well save some gas. On the seven-mile drive to town, Slugger was silent, and Coal was thankful. Two grown men, both savvy to the world, knew when it was time to shut up and enjoy the drive.

After dropping Slugger off at the hardware, he picked up a couple of breakfasts and went on to the jail. Personally, he still wasn't hungry.

Young Victor Yancey was getting ready to go home, and he

had nothing to pass on about the prisoners. Victor didn't drink coffee, and Coal was loath to talk him into it, because he didn't need another rookie trying to make coffee he would have to dump in the toilet later. He got out the Folger's and set a pot to brewing, then took the two breakfasts he had bought at Wally's, both in paper bags, back into the cell block.

Ray Christian—he still had a hard time thinking of him as Rey Medina—sat up on his bunk, blinking to clear his vision. "Mornin', Coal."

Coal only nodded in reply. He looked over at Angel, whose bandaged hand was on top of his wool blanket. The man still wore his black sunglasses, even in bed, and Coal had a notion that struck him several times a day—to go tear them off and stomp on them. He could hardly bear being in a room with a man who always had to hide his eyes.

Coal slid the breakfast into both men's cells, then turned to go. "Hey." He turned back to Ray, who had spoken. "You ever going to talk to me again?"

"What's to say?"

Ray gave a sad frown and shrugged. "Nothing, I guess. See you, man." With that, he lay back down on his bunk and pulled the covers over his face. His food sat on the floor, forgotten.

That afternoon, Coal was cruising back toward town from a visit to Leadore when he heard the radio speaker open. *Salmon dispatch calling Sheriff Savage.*

Unable to hide a weary tone to his voice, he picked up the mic and said, "Savage."

Flo said, *Coal, you're going to need to get back to town as soon as possible.*

He swore. Who wouldn't have expected him to? "What now, Flo?" He made no attempt to use proper radio procedure. In the sticks, no one cared.

A disturbance by the high school. And ... The pause went too long, and then he heard the speaker click off. When it came on again, she finished: *It's involving your friend Mr. Janx.*

And Coal swore again, and it didn't sound good, but it didn't feel bad.

CHAPTER TWENTY-FOUR

As Coal neared the city limits, he called Flo back, and she directed him to the police department. He stopped at the city building and went down to the basement, where the police had their operations.

Chief Dan George had his back to Coal when he walked in, and his hat was off. His gray, almost white hair made thin streaks down the back of his head.

"Hi, Chief."

George turned to him and dragged in a deep breath. "Hello, Sheriff. Glad you could make it."

"What happened?"

"Oh, boy. Want some coffee first?"

Maybe some Jim Beam would be better, Coal thought. "Um, sure."

The chief went over and pulled out a blue porcelain mug. He looked down into it, frowned, then blew in it and wiped it on his shirt. Another time, the man's antics would have made Coal smile. He watched the black liquid flow steaming into his cup and took it with thanks when it was handed his way. He took a tentative sip, and then another.

"Somebody down here knows how to brew java."

One corner of the chief's mouth coming up was all he could

muster for a smile. "Thanks. That's Bob, I think. So Coal ... Man, we've got a real problem."

The moment Coal had been waiting for. "Okay. I figured. What was it this time?"

"Well, it's kind of a double-edge sword this time. Your boy was going for some lunch, and—"

Coal jerked his hands up. "Hold on. *My boy?*"

George searched Coal's eyes. It was the first time Coal had seen uncertainty in them. "Well, you know what I mean, your friend Janx."

"All right. Friend. That sounds better."

George looked at him queerly. It was almost like he was afraid to go on.

"Sorry, Dan. I'm a little on edge. It's just ... Yeah. Slugger's my friend. He's not my *boy.* I've got three boys.*"*

"I apologize," said George with a nod. "Anyway, to make a long story short, Mr. Janx was on his lunch break, and I guess he saw an out of town bus, and it was full of Negro kids, coming through for some tournament or something. Some of the local kids were giving them a hard time, and I guess things got a little out of control. They started pelting the bus with rocks, and ..."

"High school kids?" Coal asked, growing angrier than he had expected to. "Why?"

"I don't know, Coal. Jeez. Being kids."

"That's not being kids. What the hell kind of town is this?"

The chief let out a long sigh. "Take it easy. They haven't seen that kind of thing around here, you know? It's something new to them."

"New? So do our kids throw rocks at everything they see that's new? If Raquel Welch came through in a bikini, that would be new. But I bet they wouldn't stone her."

The chief's lips had gone tight. "Okay. I get that. I'm not say-ing it's right, Coal. It just is. Will you let me finish the damn story?"

Coal swore. He reached up and pulled off his hat, setting it on top of a bookcase and sucking in a deep breath. "Dan, I'm sorry. I've been up most of the night. Go ahead, and I'll shut up for a while." He walked over and pulled a chair around, dropping onto it and taking another long sip of his coffee.

"I know this can't be easy for you, bud. You brought this guy here—this friend of yours. You probably figured the valley would be good to him, and you could give him a new start in life. I totally understand. But some things change hard."

Coal nodded. "So what did he do?"

"Well, I guess the short of it is he lost his cool. He flew into those high school kids, a lot of words were thrown around, and then the fists started pounding. And I guess that boy—that friend of yours—carries quite a wallop. He broke Jerry Wannaman's son's nose, and there's a couple others that are going to be wearing marks for a few days."

Coal brought his free hand up and massaged his forehead vigorously, giving himself time to think. What was he going to do with Slugger? How was he ever going to fit in here? That was his first thought. His second thought, which he wouldn't dare voice, was *Good for him!*

"Where is he now?"

"He's in the back. In cuffs."

"Did he fight you?"

"Well, he started to. Till one of my boys drove his club into his neck."

Coal grimaced. "Is he hurt bad?"

"Oh no. No, it only stunned him, long enough for us to cuff him up. That's a big, strong man, Coal." George leveled his eyes on Coal. "He could kill somebody. And someday I think he will."

"I don't know what to do, Dan. If you knew what he'd been through down where he's from—even at the hands of the police—

you'd probably understand this more. He probably thought once you got cuffs on him you were going to beat the hell out of him. That's how they did it down in Louisiana."

George frowned. "I'm sorry about all that. But whatever the past is, now he's been battering underage kids, and Wannaman's going to have some hospital bills he's going to expect to have paid—by somebody. I don't see a choice but to cite Mr. Janx into court—and that's if you really think he shouldn't go cool off for a few days in jail."

Massaging the back of his neck, Coal let his mind go over everything he had heard. "Where's this bus of Negro kids?"

"At the school, I think. Bob and Tim Lacey are over there to keep the peace."

"That's pretty sad, don't you think—that anyone has to be there to keep the peace? I thought this valley had better folks in it."

"I know. Prejudice is all over the country, Coal. It's not something you can stamp out in a day."

"So what happens in the meantime? Slugger's got nowhere to go, Dan. He was being spit on by the anti-war crowd down there in Louisiana, called a baby killer, beat up by rednecks and cops both, and his life threatened. He'd be better off if he'd been killed in Nam. He really is like a man without a country."

In the end, there was no way to keep Slugger from being cited with several counts of battery. Coal understood that, but he was also determined not to let the rock-throwing incident lay quiet either. His friend had acted in an inappropriate way for good reason. Those boys responsible weren't going to walk away without some stripes of their own.

Coal went and got Slugger out of the back, using his own key to remove the handcuffs and turning to hand them to the chief. "You all right, buddy?"

Slugger looked up at him. "All right? Hell, I don't know whatchoo mean. There ain't no 'all right' in this world."

Coal had no reply for that. "Come on. You're coming with me."

Slugger's look was defiant. "To jail?"

"No. If you were going there I'd have left the cuffs on you. We're going back to work."

"Ha! I'm an hour late. That man ain't gonna take me back there."

Coal, feeling more frustrated than Annie had made him, motioned toward the door. "Just come on."

They went out together and got in the pickup, driving the little ways to Lemhi Lumber, where they got out again and went in the store. Coal was half afraid to look at Slugger. There was one young man who was ready to take on the world, and Coal wondered if he had a smile left in him.

Joe Taylor came out of his office when they called him, his long arms swinging at his sides. He stopped and looked back and forth between Coal and Slugger.

"Sorry Slugger's late, Joe."

Taylor held up his hand, giving a little wave in front of his face. "No apologies. The police chief called and told me what happened." He turned his eyes to look at Slugger, but the black man had his gaze on a shelf of goods, with no intention of looking at his boss.

"Slugger? You all right?"

That drew Slugger's eyes. "All right? Why wouldn't I be all right?"

Joe raised his eyebrows, looking over at Coal. "Easy now, son. I'm on your side."

"Ain't nobody on a nigger's side." There was a growl to Slugger's voice.

"I don't like that kind of talk in here, so—"

"Aw, who you think yer foolin'? This place ain't no different than no other place. I'm a nigger here, out there"—he jabbed a finger toward the outside of the store— "and ever'where in this here country. I'm a nigger, I'll always be a nigger, an' ain't no one can ever change that. An' no white man sure ever gon' to."

"Slugger!" Coal growled. "Outside!"

When Slugger whirled and stared at him, Coal just stared back. Finally, Slugger turned and stalked out, and Coal almost had to run to catch up. When they got outside, Coal thought Slugger would keep on walking, but he whirled on him.

"What?"

"What? You've got to be kidding me. Slugger, we've been friends for a long time. I'm trying to give you a chance here, and Joe Taylor's one of the nicest guys in this town, and retired military to boot. If you should be treating anybody like a friend it's him—and maybe me. What are you trying to do? You've only got so many chances."

Coal thought he saw Slugger's eyes moisten right before he looked away, staring up the street. He worked his jaw muscles for a few moments, and then Coal saw him blinking to clear his eyes before he looked back.

"I don't know what to do no more, Sarge. There ain't no place for me nowhere. You shoulda seen them kids throwin' rocks at that bus—an' all 'cause them kids was black. No other reason."

"I wish I could make everything better, buddy. I wish I could change the world and make everybody treat everybody else right. But I can't. It's going to be up to you to find the people who are your friends and stick to them. And Joe's one of those people. You've gotta give him a chance."

Slugger stood staring back at him for a moment, then picked up his hands and threw them back down violently. "He ain't gon' take me now! Not after what I just did in there. I'm done, Sarge. I gotta go ... I don't know, find me some place. Some of my people."

"I *am* your people, Slugger. My mom is your people. And my

kids. Those guys think the world of you. And I know Joe well enough to say he's not done with you. You've just got to relax. The whole world isn't your enemy."

When Slugger's eyes teared up again, he stomped his right foot and turned partway around, throwing his hands again. He brought his left hand up and wiped angrily at his eyes, keeping them directed away from Coal. "Man, Sarge, you just don't ... You don't know what it's like. You ... You just don't know."

And Slugger was right, of course. He really didn't know. And he would never know. "I only know I'm your friend, Slugger, and you have to trust me. We'll get through this thing. We'll get through it together."

"That judge gonna throw me back in jail."

"We'll see. I don't think he will. He's a fair man."

"To white folks."

"He's a fair man—to people. Come on, Slugger. Let's go back inside. Let them see the kind of man you really are."

This time, Slugger was meek as he followed Coal back into the hardware store and they found Joe Taylor working the counter. He eyed Slugger carefully, then looked at Coal.

"Slugger's ready to come back to work, Joe." He didn't ask for the option.

"You good, Slugger?" Joe asked.

"I'm good."

"Did you get something to eat?"

"No, sir. Never had time."

"All right, then you just go get some food in you and be back here in an hour. I can hold this place down okay. Sound good?"

"Sounds good. Thank you, sir."

"No need to thank me. I can't have my guys trying to work on an empty stomach, you know?"

Slugger nodded and made a genuine effort to smile at Taylor, and then he and Coal went outside. Coal walked him down to

Wally's, where he bought him a burger, fries, and a huge, decadent Coca Cola. He downed his food swiftly at the counter while cigarette smoke whirled in blue wreaths all around them.

Slugger was friends with Coal, an important, popular man, a generous man, and for Slugger, life, for once, was good.

CHAPTER TWENTY-FIVE

The rest of Tuesday floated by like a dream for Coal. The day went so easy, in fact, that he was able to trade the pickup for the LTD and pick all the children up at school. It might have seemed a simple thing to a civilian with a normal job, but seeing the girls' faces light up when they saw him, and then the grin that Virgil tried to hold back but couldn't was worth more than gold to Coal.

He was so happy in that moment that he decided it was high time they all went over for hot cocoa and a donut at Wally's.

Before he could pull away from the school, Katie whirled on him. "Dad! Did you hear what happened today?"

He gave her a confused look, throwing the truck back in neutral. "No. What?"

"About Slugger! A school bus came to town with a whole bunch of Negro students, and some of our boys started throwing rocks at the bus and calling them names, and—"

Coal let out a sigh. "Okay. Yes, honey, I did hear about that."

The wind obviously knocked out of her sails, Katie stared at him for a moment. "You did?"

"Uh-huh. I had to go get him from the police and take him back to work."

Katie looked around at Cynthia and Virgil, then returned her eyes to her father. "What's going to happen?"

"I'm not sure. He'll have to go to court. I know that much. I guess he hurt some of those kids pretty bad."

"Yeah! He broke Billy Wannaman's nose! They had to take him to the hospital."

Coal frowned. He had been happy putting this part of his day far in the back of his mind. "Yeah, I heard that too."

"I'm glad!" said Virgil from the back seat. "That guy's a jerk."

The girls nodded in full agreement. "Yeah, he had it coming to him, I'm sure," Cynthia said. "My dad couldn't stand Billy."

Nodding, Coal let out a sigh. "I figured it was like that. Unfortunately, Slugger's an adult, and that kid's underage. So this town's going to make it into a huge deal, no matter whether that kid deserved it or not. In fact, the second something like this happens, the kid usually turns out to be the biggest angel around."

The girls nodded their wise agreement.

"Will Slugger have to go to jail?" asked Virgil.

"I hope not, buddy. But he might have to do some community service, and I'll bet he ends up paying some fines—and maybe the medical expenses for your 'Billy' friend too."

"He's not *my* friend!" Virgil averred.

"I know. I was being facetious. Hey, let's all forget about this now, okay? I was hoping you guys might like to take a little side-trip with me somewhere." Of course he didn't tell them yet what he had in mind.

On the way over to Wally's, he saw Karen Richardson walking toward the restaurant in a too-thin coat, and he pulled over at the curb, just ahead of her, and rolled down his window.

As she neared the car, he leaned out. "Hey, Karen!"

"Hi, Coal!"

"You headed to work?"

"Yep."

"Well, hop in. We're headed there too."

In reality, it was one of the warmer days they had seen in a while. It had started out at thirty-five degrees and gotten all the way up to forty-one now, and any residual snow from the last few weak storms was gone, even from the most shadowy yard.

"It's not far," pointed out Karen.

"Too bad. I'm the sheriff, and I'm ordering you to get in here," Coal commanded with a grin.

So Karen got in, and they stopped in front of Wally's and all trooped into the restaurant together.

When Coal told them they were having a donut and cocoa, Katie's eyes got big. "Are you sure? Grandma's gonna tell you you ruined our appetites."

That made Coal laugh. "Like the every-day cookie maker would know anything about that!"

That made them all laugh, even the reserved Virgil. When Karen came back with cups and started making their cocoa, she looked over at Cynthia. "How are you doing?"

"I'm good." Cynthia smiled, but Coal could see sadness behind her eyes. It reminded him that he needed to take the girls to Idaho Falls again for another visit with Doctor Pearson. All their recent traumatic events weren't simply going to go away because they tried to ignore them.

Katie piped up to tell Coal they had been studying a neat story in school from mythology, and then she volunteered to tell him and the others about the Titan, Prometheus, stealing fire, and about Pandora's infamous box. When she finished with her brief version, Coal said, "Hey, when I bring Slugger home tonight, you should tell him that story. I think he'd like to hear it."

It was a thought not contemplated to its potential completion, but Coal didn't think far enough ahead to consider that.

*   *   *

Coal dropped the kids off at home later, then returned to finish up things in the office and check in briefly with late-working prosecutor Mike Fica to see how the Medina case was proceeding.

He stopped back in the cellblock afterward to look over the sullen Angel Medina and Ray. He couldn't tell if Angel was looking at him because of his black glasses, so he turned all his attention to Ray.

"You need anything?"

"Freedom," said Ray with a chuckle.

"I wish you'd thought of that before." Coal found himself stupidly feeling sorry for Ray almost every day. The man had certainly done bad things, but Coal couldn't help thinking of how Ray had tried everything to keep Moby Hargis from taking the rap for the killing of his father. No matter what else they said about Ray, a man that cared so much about a poor retarded kid who should have meant nothing to him couldn't be all bad.

Ray sighed. "Yeah, buddy. Me too."

Coal cleared his throat. "Last chance. Burger? A magazine? Anything?"

Ray shook his head. "Thanks anyway. I think I'll just sit here and contemplate my life tonight."

"All right. One thing before I go, though: I wish you wouldn't call me 'buddy'."

Coal measured Folger's into the coffee maker and filled the pot with water, hoping if somebody else made coffee in the morning they would get the hint. He was tired of coffee that looked and tasted like discolored tea.

Before going for his hat and coat, he leafed through the mail, picking up one envelope that had a hand-written name in the return address spot, and his own name written out as well, in fairly nice handwriting. In some ways he almost thought it could be feminine, but the name, Grant Fairbourne, was decidedly masculine, and there was something about the bold strokes in the name that set the writer apart as a person of some self-confidence.

Slicing the envelope open with his truck key, Coal fished the three-page contents out and looked at the cover page. Just like the outside of the envelope, the introductory letter was hand-written from this Grant Fairbourne, introducing himself to Coal as one who had read of his search for an emergency deputy and said he was originally from Challis and looking to get back to God's country from where he worked now, over in Caldwell, on the far west side of the state.

Fairbourne was smart enough to leave his phone number, both with his address on the letter, and in the resume that made up the other two pages of the envelope's contents.

Putting everything back in the envelope and folding it in half, Coal tucked it away in his shirt pocket. It would bear further research. And heaven knew he needed a good new deputy, at least until they found out more about Todd's recovery status.

A glance at the clock dragged Coal out of his seat with the rest of the mail left sitting on his desk. It was six o'clock, and time to pick up Slugger from work.

Slugger was in good spirits when Coal arrived at the store, and all the way home he went on about his good experiences at work, and of how kind of a gentleman Joe Taylor was, which corroborated what Coal already knew of his friend.

All in all, Slugger's report of his day, after the school bus incident, was good enough to put a smile on Coal's face, and a warmth in his heart. It even helped him forget for a while the mood in which he had left the house that morning.

As he was opening the front door, his mother met him. She gave Slugger a huge smile and squeezed his arm. "Hi, Slugger. I hope you had a nice day." He said something back to her, but she had already turned her attention to Coal. The look in her eyes told her son their conversation had remained on her mind all morning as it had on his.

Shutting the door after Slugger went in, Connie stepped onto the porch with Coal. "Hey, Son. I want to apologize for this morning. I really was just worried about you."

Coal smiled. "I know, Mom. I've been thinking about it all day too. Thanks for always trying to keep me safe."

Tears came into her eyes as he hugged her tight, then pulled away and gave her a kiss on the cheek. "I love you, Mom."

"I love you too, buddy. It sure is good to have you home."

After supper that evening, when the boys got up to watch *Happy Days* on TV, Slugger took another huge helping of mashed potatoes and gravy and grinned at Connie.

"Ma'am, I swear I never had no better mashed taters than this. What you put in 'em, some sugar?"

Connie laughed. "Well, Slugger, you would sure giggle if I told you the secret."

Slugger sighed and took a great big spoonful. "I don't mind a good giggle, ma'am."

"All right. You guessed right: sugar."

"Excuse me?"

"Sugar. Powdered sugar. Just a little, though—to take away any bitter edge. And some whipped cream too."

Slugger looked at Coal, as if trying to confirm what his mother was saying, and Coal shook his head and rolled his eyes. "Don't question her, buddy. This woman is the queen of sugar."

Slugger laughed, almost choking on his potatoes. He had a contagious laugh, and Coal and Connie couldn't help joining in.

Finally, Slugger caught his breath, giving a big shake of his head and grinning. "Well, you was right about the giggle. I never heard o' no sugar in taters, ma'am. I can't wait t' tell my mama 'bout this."

When Slugger was cleaning up his plate, and it was obvious he would soon ask to be excused, Katie looked at Coal, as if for the go-ahead. He gave her a slight nod and a wink, and she turned to Slugger.

"Hey, Slugger? You want to hear a story we've been learning

about in school?"

Slugger looked at her and gave her a big, warm smile. "Well, shore I do, Miss Katie. Please."

So Katie began, in her most animated storytelling voice, to line out the myth of the Titan Prometheus and how he stole fire to give to man, against the wishes of Zeus. Zeus took revenge on Prometheus by giving his brother Epimetheus a woman named Pandora, who was modeled after the beautiful Aphrodite and whom Epimetheus couldn't resist even though Prometheus warned him not to accept any gifts from the gods. Zeus gave Pandora a box, with the warning that she was never to open it and could only hold onto it for safekeeping.

Katie said, "It wasn't really a box, though, like they always call it. It was a big jar they would store things in like wine, or oil, or wheat. But this time Zeus filled it full of a lot of really bad things, like death, sickness, greed ... um ... envy, hatred, pain, disease, hunger, poverty, and war." She stopped here, having extended all ten fingers while she counted. She looked over at Coal. "Is that all?"

Coal laughed and held up both hands. "Hey, Sis, this is your story! Don't get *me* involved." That made everyone else laugh.

Katie grinned sheepishly and turned back to Slugger. "Okay, so that was almost everything. But Pandora was really curious, because Zeus made her that way on purpose, and she finally had to look in the jar. She opened it up, and all that horrible stuff came out and went into the world. She slammed the lid down as fast as she could, but the only thing left in the jar was hope." She looked at Coal as she said that. By the look of her eyes she felt that was by far the most important of the things in the jar. "After that, men only had hope to hold onto to survive all the other bad things Pandora let out of the box.

"Now," she went on, "when somebody talks about Pandora's Box, it means something that shouldn't be messed with because it might start something bad."

Slugger sat there nodding as she finished the story. He was staring at the vase of fake sunflowers in the center of the table, taking the tale in and obviously pondering it deeply.

When he realized all of a sudden that Katie was done, he looked up at her. "Tarnation, Miss Katie. That was some story. I don't know why I never heard that before, not in my school."

"Did you like it?"

"Boy, I shore did. A lot."

That gave Katie a huge smile. "Do you want to hear more? I have other ones, and we're going to be learning some more of them in school."

"Let's let Slugger rest up and ponder on that one for now, sweetheart," Connie said. "I think he's had a long day at his new job."

"You shore got that right, ma'am. A good day, though." He swiveled his eyes back over to Katie, his lips pursed, deep in thought. "Hope, huh? Well, that's good they still got hope, I reckon. We'd be nowhere without that. I wonder if them gods ever put love and kindness on the earth, if it wasn't in that box."

Long after the children were all gone to bed, Slugger was leafing through a book he had pulled off the shelf while Coal and Connie bored themselves watching *Police Story*.

"Hey, Sarge, look at this," Slugger said suddenly. Coal looked over at his friend, who was holding his book up with the pages open. A photograph of a large white bird with a gracefully curved neck took up an entire page.

"Egret," Coal said.

"Yes sir," Slugger agreed, pulling the book back down to himself and staring at it. "Ain't he a perty thing? Mama always loved them things when we'd see 'em in the bayou. And sometimes they'd fly right over our house. 'Great egret', says here." He sat there silent for a while, obviously lost in thought, perhaps in memories. "We would drive down t' the swamps sometimes," he went on, validating Coal's surmise. "We'd see them things, and Mama an' Papa, they'd make a great big deal about 'em. You know, they must be three feet tall, them birds. And they got them long yellow beaks and skinny black legs. Necks like a graceful snake.

"I remember Papa sayin' how beautiful an' pure they looked with all them white feathers. Huh." He shook his head and started to thumb through the pages again. He probably didn't know it, but he had drawn Coal's attention enough that he was still watching him.

Slugger stopped turning pages again. "Ha!" he exclaimed. "Here's another bird we used to see. Says it's called ... an ... hinga?"

"Yeah, anhinga," Coal confirmed. "I've seen pictures of them."

"Yeah, yeah. But Papa called it a snake bird. He never liked 'em. Strange, huh?" He looked up at Coal.

"What do you mean strange?"

"Well, Mama an' Papa, they was always talkin' about white things, and buyin' white things. They loved that great egret, but they thought that black snake bird was ugly. How come you s'pose that'd be? It's almost like they was ashamed t' be black, an' shamed of anything else that was black too."

Coal didn't know what to say. Slugger had a lot of thoughts to work through, and Coal didn't know that he could help with a single one of them.

When Coal and Connie turned off the TV and went to bed, Slugger was still sitting up looking through his *Giant Golden Book of Birds*. It seemed he had found something that touched his soul.

CHAPTER TWENTY-SIX

Wednesday, January 17

Feeling the blood flowing hot and strong through his body after a good chest and back workout and a hot shower, Coal dressed and then went out to feed the horses for Connie, who had overslept and was running late getting breakfast for the kids so they could eat before the bus came. To his surprise, he found Slugger already outside, sitting on a chair out in the barn with his coat wrapped tight around him.

"Morning, buddy. What in the world are you doing out here in the cold?"

"Mornin', Sarge. Oh, just sittin'. Maybe I better get used to the cold if I'm gonna be stayin' here long, right?"

Coal smiled. "Good thinking." He went over and dragged a new bale of hay off a stack in one of the stalls and threw it over by Slugger. "As long as you're trying to be a country boy, you should use that for your seat. Put it up against the wall and it'll be even more comfortable than that chair."

Slugger grinned and got up, pushing the hay bale the rest of the way to the wall and sitting back down as Coal took another one off the stack and started outside with it.

"Hey, Sarge?"

Coal stopped, still holding the bale, and turned partway around. "Yeah?"

"What's that sound? Is that a crow?"

Coal cocked his head and listened for a moment. Soon, there came the rattly voice of a raven chattering somewhere nearby. With the hay bale still dangling from his fingers by the twine, he stepped out of the barn farther and looked around, spying the huge black bird up on top of the weather vane on the barn.

"Come see for yourself, buddy. It's a raven."

Slugger came out of the barn and raised his eyes as Coal continued on out to where the horses waited at the edge of the corral and dropped the hay, drawing out his pocketknife. He cut the twine and threw three flakes out to Cody, then three more to Bolt. He turned as he pocketed the knife to see Slugger standing there staring up at the weather vane. The raven still perched there seemed to be as interested in Slugger as the man was in the bird. As it turned its head, keeping an eye on him, its deep black feathers shimmered violet and green in a stray beam of sunlight.

All of a sudden it took flight and sailed upward, circling like a small version of a turkey vulture until it was high above. Strange behavior for a raven, Coal thought. It hung on the air currents for several seconds, then tipped its tail and sailed away toward a grove of trees.

When the bird was gone, Slugger shook his head and looked over at Coal. "Man, that was cool! Now that's a perty bird, Sarge. Real perty. You see that color when it turned its head? It was shore enough black, but there's a lot more to that bird than just black."

"Sure is."

As they drove toward town later after the bus had carried the older children off to school, they saw two more of the big black birds, flying seemingly without effort over the highway toward the Lemhi foothills.

Slugger hurriedly rolled down his window just in time to hear the gargling call from above. He grinned and looked at Coal. "I don't know, man. There's just somethin' about that bird. You see how graceful they're flyin'?"

Coal nodded.

Slugger sank back against the seat, and after a few minutes of contemplative silence he said, "You know, I wonder why Mama and Papa never cared about no black-colored birds like crows an' the like. Even them snake birds. They were neat to look at too.

"You know, Sarge, I was readin' in that book o' yores last night about them ravens. They say that's one o' the smartest animals in the world—even smarter than a dog. You ever hear that?"

Coal nodded. "Yeah, I've heard that." He thought about how ravens made their living, raiding the nests of other birds and eating their eggs or even their young, but he didn't want to ruin Slugger's reverie by bringing up ugly facts like that.

Slugger nodded thoughtfully. "Man, Sarge. Now that's the kinda bird I'd like t' be—with that big, deep voice, flyin' high, black as the night, an' knowin' no shame in it."

After dropping Slugger off at the hardware store, Coal sat in his office and sipped the strongest black coffee he could turn out. Folger's wasn't the greatest coffee ever made, but if you doubled up on the grounds even it could almost taste like real java. He had brought in a little mustard-yellow refrigerator that he set on the long table by the coffee maker, and from it he drew one of several bottles of fresh milk, downing almost four cups of it to wash down the coffee. He had a feeling it would be a good day.

The prisoners were fed, and soon Coal had to start going through the yearly budget which K.T. Batterton had left him. He wasn't sure yet what he had to work with. He hadn't had much time to look at it. But he wasn't ready even yet.

Before getting wrapped up in a chore that made him almost sick to think about, since he and numbers had never been friends, he pulled out the envelope from the job applicant, Grant Fairbourne, which he had forgotten all about in the joy of spending last evening with his family.

Going through the man's resume, he found himself impressed.

As Grant had said, he was from Challis, where he had spent time in his teens as a hunting and fishing guide. He had some good references to show for it, both from his employer and from some of his clients. Fairbourne had next spent two years in Monterrey, Mexico, on a proselytizing mission for his church, and he had that two years to thank for the fluent Spanish he still spoke. He had come home to start work as a jailer for Bannock County, moved to the position of deputy on the road after just six months, and then gone on to be a police patrolman in Caldwell, and then to detective in homicide and robbery investigations.

Now thirty-three years of age, Fairbourne, who according to his resume stood six feet tall and weighed in at a respectable one hundred ninety pounds, was well-versed in interview and interrogation techniques, self-defense tactics, and was a firearms instructor with a specialty in handguns.

All in all, Fairbourne seemed a little too good to be true for someone who sought employment in a Podunk place like Salmon, and someone Coal needed to snatch up fast if he was going to get a good person on the road here. He called the number Fairbourne had left him and got ten rings and no answer. He would try again later.

Since that phone call wasn't procrastination enough, he called Annie Price's number, and to his surprise she picked up. "Hi, woman! I thought you'd be at work."

Oh, come on. I do have a life—sometimes! What do I owe the pleasure of this early morning call to?

Coal glanced over at the clock. "Oh, crap. Sorry. Did you work late?"

I did. But it's okay. I'd take your call any time, she replied with a laugh.

He wasn't foolish enough to remind her that she probably wouldn't have taken a call from him the last night he was with her.

"I was just checking on you," he admitted. "Everything all

right?"

Yes. Coal, I'm still so embarrassed about Monday night. Can we please pretend that never happened? I don't know what came over me. If I take you to dinner and a movie will you stop asking about it?

Coal froze. Dinner and a movie. His mind scrambled ahead. Had he made any plans? With Slugger? Connie? The kids? Anyone else? He couldn't think of anything, and he had been putting Annie off for so long now. There was no reason not to, was there? Maura was dating Jordan now, and they had agreed that seeing other people was fine. It was time.

"Dinner and a movie would be great, Annie."

There was a long silence on the phone. Finally, Annie's voice came on again: *Wait. Did you just tell me yes?*

He smiled. "I think I might have."

I think I'm going to faint. Hey. Is this Coal Savage?

Coal grinned. "Funny."

Coal! the woman went on. *Wow. Okay, now I feel like an idiot. I almost don't even know what to do. I think I had finally come to the conclusion you'd never say yes.*

"Well, don't fall and knock yourself out," said Coal. "I'll pick you up after I take Slugger home tonight. Is that all right? Probably five-thirty or six?"

Wow. Wow! Gee, Coal. Yes. Yes! Any time you get here would be fine. I'm so excited I can't think.

He laughed. "All right, take it easy. You're going to give me a complex."

He hung up the phone feeling content. It wasn't every day he did something that made someone so happy so easily. Happy wasn't even the word for what Annie had sounded like—ecstatic fit better. But there was another call he needed to make that wasn't going to be quite so joyful. However, he had to do it.

He dialed Maura's number from memory and got a busy signal.

Five minutes later, he dialed it again. Still busy. He tried McPherson's and got Florin Beller himself, the owner.

"Hello, Mr. Beller. Coal Savage here."

Hello, Coal. How can I be of assistance?

"Well, say, is Maura working today?"

Yes. She'll be in at nine.

Coal looked up at the clock. It was eight-thirty. "Sounds good. I'll try her back. Thanks."

He hung up and thought of Kathy. The thought made him laugh at himself. His mother would accuse him of going through all the phone numbers in his little black book.

"Well, hell," he said aloud. *Why not?* He dialed the ranch. Predictably, there was no answer. He doubted there were many mornings when he could find her inside. That was a big ranch for a woman alone to handle, and she must be working ten hour days or longer.

Looking down at the folder that contained his year's budget and all the notes leading up to its creation, Coal sighed. There were a hundred things he could probably come up with, somewhat pleasant, or at least mundane things, but all things that would keep him from having to think of the budget. However, he couldn't justify putting it off any longer.

So he got in the truck and drove out to Kathy's.

Before he even reached her house, he saw movement out in one of the holding pens, and there was Kathy, sitting up high on a blue roan Larry had bought for her several years ago and pushing a knot of cattle from the one pen into another. These were the twenty or so head of fat two-year-old steers Larry and Kathy always kept on the ranch during the winter to supply local butcher shops and grocery stores throughout that part of the state and into Montana.

Coal drove on in, and without asking, he caught up his favorite horse of the MacAtees, a big grulla quarter horse, as far as Coal knew the only registered quarter horse Larry had ever kept on the place. He saddled it up and rode out to meet Kathy.

The woman about fell out of her saddle when she saw him coming. When she recognized him, she whipped off her hat and slapped the leg of her tight Wranglers. "Well, I'll be danged! Coal Savage, coming to help the common folk." She laughed, and it made her deep brown eyes sparkle.

She already had the steers handled, and from horseback she rode over and closed the gate. She lived by the old rule about how a cowboy never does anything he can't do from a horse, figuring it applied to cow*girls* as well.

She turned and trotted over to Coal, a wide grin wanting to break her face in half. She was wearing a brown Carhartt coat, a sky-blue bandanna wrapped tight around her throat, and rosy cheeks and chin that rendered her eyes magical somehow.

"Well, hey there, cowgirl." Coal doffed his hat to her and put it back on his head. "I guess I'm a little slow saddling up."

"I guess you are. You come all this way out here to herd cows?"

He laughed. "Actually, I came all this way out here to dodge going over my budget."

"Then I shouldn't ruin your plans. Let's go for a ride. You warm enough?"

He searched Kathy's eyes and thought back on the times they had ridden these Lemhi foothills, he and Laura, Larry and Kathy.

"I'm warm enough now," he said like a fool.

*   *   *

Coal spent an enjoyable three hours riding the now winter-gray hills with Kathy MacAtee, then sat in the house listening to John Denver and Glen Campbell records and sipping coffee before his errant sense of responsibility drove him back to town. He felt re-freshed. Renewed. His butt was just sore enough to remind him how much he missed having a horse beneath him. But best of all was the memory of how he had made Kathy MacAtee smile.

As he pulled onto 28, he said out loud, "I'm trying, Larry." Sometimes it felt good to speak his friend's name out loud.

When Coal got back to town, smelling of leather and horse, he pulled in at the high school and looked at his watch. Well, this was as good a time as any.

He went in and spoke with the principal about the incident with the school bus full of black students. The principal agreed that it would be a great idea to have an assembly addressing the whole incident, and they set it for the following day.

Once he left the school, he drove almost all the way up Main, then pulled in against traffic and parked in front of McPherson's, going in to find Maura. She was in the back with a lady customer, so he waited. It didn't take long for her customer to realize someone important was waiting on Maura, so she politely excused herself and wandered off.

Maura sauntered over in a wild-looking pink shirt and light-colored jeans, her favorite Luccheses on her feet. When she got close to him, she raised an eyebrow. "You've been outside."

After digesting that statement for a moment, Coal laughed, putting a hand up to his still wind-blown cheek and feeling the ice in it. "That obvious, huh?"

"Hey! I'm a country girl. I can see when somebody's been out in the weather. Florin said you called."

"Yep."

She looked back and forth at his eyes. "And ... ?"

"Just checking up on you."

"Oh yeah? Is this the sheriff talking, or the cowboy?"

"Haha. Maybe both." He wanted to know about Jordan and how their dates were going. So he didn't ask. And she probably *wanted* him to know, too—so she didn't tell him.

"You coming to collect the rent then? Or tie me on the train tracks, or ... Come on, cowboy—throw me a bone. What's up?"

The closest thing he had heard himself come to a giggle in a while escaped him. Ignoring the Snidely Whiplash reference to tying her on the train tracks, he said, "Collect the rent? Shoot, if we collected half the rent we could get from all the people who stayed at our house we'd never have to work again. No, actually, I remember what we talked about a while back, and I've been meaning to ask you about it." He didn't elaborate.

She gave a little shrug and glanced around the store before looking back at him with a puzzled look and a shake of her head. "You got me. We've talked about a lot of things. Do you mean about watching me undress?" She gave him a wink.

He tried to smile. It didn't work. Here he went. This could go bad fast. "No, about your boys. And your ex."

All the teasing and fun fled from her face like birds before a wildfire. "Oh. Okay."

"Is anything changed?"

"The boys are coming in two weeks—unless something changes."

His face brightened. He tried to read behind her mask and see some kind of happy spark. "Hey! That's good!"

She lifted a shoulder and let it fall. "Yeah. Kind of."

"What's wrong?"

"He said I'd better enjoy it. When the paperwork goes through next month I won't be seeing them again until they turn eighteen."

Coal stared at her, his face gone hard in spite of himself. "What are you talking about? He can't take your kids."

"That's what I said. He said 'watch me'."

"I'm going to make some phone calls."

"Coal ..." She held up her hands, palm out. "Just ..." She dropped them again to her sides. "Just ... don't. It's not worth it. He's got a lot of money from whatever Nyle TrueBear does for money, and he's got high-up friends. You're not going to do any good. You might even make things worse."

"How could it be worse? So you just give up your boys without a fight?"

She stared at him, her eyes trying to be hard, but filling up with tears. Flexing her jaws, she said, "Yeah, well, I've been giving up things since I was thirteen. Why stop now?"

"Maura—"

"Hey, I'm sorry, but I'd better get back to work."

She couldn't meet his eyes. She started to turn away, and he wanted to reach out and catch her arm. Instead, he let her walk away. He had done enough already. Making her come to tears at work wasn't something he had had any intention of doing.

Turning around, he walked out past Florin Beller and another employee with only a nod of his head and stepped back out into the gray morning with the knowledge that he had just ruined Maura's day. He seemed to do that a lot.

CHAPTER TWENTY-SEVEN

Friday, January 19

Coal sipped Folgers and longed for a cup of real coffee. The budget itself, along with K.T.'s vast and complicated notes, his lists of wants versus needs, sprawled out in front of him, nearly overpowering the desk.

One of the things he had wanted and didn't get was a new pickup. Coal smiled grimly. Coal's own severance pay had gotten that, and other than gasoline the county hadn't paid a dime for it yet beyond having the radio installed. But next year he was going to see if he could do something about that. He wasn't that into providing things at his own expense for a county government that had a lot more money at their fingertips than he did.

Coal sat and looked over the figure for the price of gas, then tallied up all the gas receipts so far that fiscal year on his fancy little Texas Instruments calculator. The department seemed to be running about normal in that category.

Boring. Man, was this boring.

He looked outside at the parking lot and thought about his date with Annie two nights ago. Other than the fact that he had a hard time getting his mind off Maura and her dilemma, it had been a great time. He could still feel and taste the sensuous kiss she left him with before he could get off her porch—not that he had tried to stop her. He also thought about Kathy and the horse ride. That Mrs. MacAtee was quite a horsewoman. She looked every bit as good wearing Western clothes as Maura did, and that hat of hers ... Somehow that old, dusty, sweat-stained thing stirred his cowboy heart.

Damn budgets! He looked back down at the papers and thought he should probably drive down past Northfork and check on the river road. After all, winter could be hard enough to roll some pretty big rocks down on the road, and folks had been known to be stuck in there for days before the county could get big machinery down there to help them out.

Yeah, and they have this thing called a telephone, buddy, he reminded himself. *People tend to get on it and make calls when they have rocks on the road. Or they get their own tractors and move them themselves. Keep your mind on your job.*

Taking a deep breath, he looked at the clock. Ah, saved by an appointment! It was only twenty minutes until he had to talk to the students of Salmon High. Normally, dealing with a bunch of teenagers was near last on his list of favorite things to do, but in lieu of working on the budget, it would be welcome. After that, he would come back and work for another hour or so, then go to lunch. And then the budget could sit until he got another burst of energy—or responsibility. Whatever one wanted to call it.

Driving over to the high school, Coal went in and met with the principal. He lined out the gist of what he wanted to say and the mood in which he would present it, then went to the stage in the auditorium to wait.

Immediately after the bell rang, students began to trickle into the big, dark room. The ones who were responsible, good kids were usually pretty obvious, as they came in earliest, without dilly-dallying around in the hallways. He was proud to spot Cynthia and Katie coming in among the early ones and sitting toward the front. Once there were a few hundred students gathered, and a general uproar through the hall that, in spite of the sound-absorbing quality of the cloth seats, was starting to make Coal's ears ring, the principal came up. He spoke for a minute, managing to quiet the crowd of ravenous beasts who were being forced to listen to the sheriff before being released to lunch. This was going to be stiff competition.

Coal got up and looked over the crowd. He had managed somehow to pick out Billy Wannaman, one of the big reasons for this assembly, who sat far to the back. Even back there his swollen nose and the ugly purple across the middle of his face made it plain who he was. Besides, he had the homely, smug face of his father.

"For those of you who don't know me, like your principal told you, I'm Sheriff Savage. Coal Savage. I'll tell you all right off that I don't normally stand on ceremony. Once we get to know each other, if we end up on a friendly basis, I really don't mind if you call me Coal, as long as you don't mind me calling you by your first name too. On the other hand, if we *don't* end up on a friendly basis, we're probably both going to call each other things that neither of us wants to hear."

After a pause, a ripple of laughter started through the crowd. Coal smirked. It was a start. But then he wasn't up here to be a comedian.

"So you all pretty much know why I'm here, and I'm going to make it short. I understand you'll be released early for lunch if I don't talk too long.

"I got to see something in this town Tuesday that disappointed me quite a bit. And I hope most of you were disappointed too. I thought better of the people of Salmon, and especially the students of this school. Now just so you know, I'm sure most of you had nothing to do with what happened. It was just a handful of people. But a handful is a handful too many.

"In case by some miracle you haven't already heard, there was a busload of black students here from out of town for a sporting event. They showed up, and some of our students decided it would be a good idea to greet them by throwing rocks at the bus. It *wasn't* a good idea. So a friend of mine, a black man from Louisiana, stepped in, and I guess you know the rest. My friend's name is Slugger, and he won the name honestly. He likes to fight. But I've never seen him on the side of wrong. Apparently he hurt some students. Broke one boy's nose. Now I'm the sheriff of Lemhi County, and I'm not supposed to say things like this, but from everything I hear that boy had it coming, and maybe more."

For several seconds, after the hum that rose up in the room died down, he let that sink in. He wondered what the principal thought of his statement.

"You heard me right. If I had been in Slugger's place, quite honestly, I might have done the same thing. But the law says he can't. And now he's in trouble. He's in trouble because some of the students in this school think it's okay to hate other people because of the color of their skin. He's in trouble because apparently my hometown hasn't been teaching their children how to treat other people.

"Let me tell you a story real quick. I fought in the Vietnam War. I was a guard at a prison over there, and it was one of the roughest places I've ever seen. No, scratch that—it was *the* roughest place I've ever seen. Hands down. We had a riot in August of 1968, and it got real ugly. Most of the prisoners were black Americans. They just went haywire.

"But you know who was backing me? My right hand man? The guy who stood by me and stayed cooler and more calm than anyone else in the middle of that riot? My friend Slugger. Yeah. He was in Nam with me. He was a soldier. And over there in the military people didn't notice the color of skin so much. We noticed the color of a uniform. We were brothers. It didn't matter how we looked on the outside. Everybody bleeds the same. We found that out over there way more times than any of us wanted to.

"I told you I wouldn't hold you here long, and I'll keep my word. I just want to have all of you ask yourselves a question: Who am I? Who am I really? Is my spirit any different from a black man's spirit, or a Mexican's, or a Chinaman's? Is it different from *anyone's* spirit? Last time I read God put us all down here to learn to get along, and he never said we only have to get along with people who have the same skin color as we do. He said to love your neighbor as yourself. Got it? Your neighbor. He didn't say 'love your white neighbor as yourself'. He said your neighbor.

"There's a lot of white guys who came back from Vietnam alive only because there were black guys who saved their lives. Or Indians. Or Mexicans. Japanese. We were brothers over there. I don't care what color you are, guys. Everybody just wants to be accepted and understood. That's all those black kids on that bus would have asked for. They came out here to Salmon hoping to have a friendly competition, but really having no idea what they were getting into. But look at the story they're taking home with them. Pretty sad, if you ask me.

"That's it, guys. That's all. Just think about it. Treat other people right, no matter what their skin color is. Do it for the right reasons, not just because I'm going to slam your head against a wall if you don't. Thanks for listening."

He was walking away when the auditorium erupted in applause. Now it was time to meet with young Billy Wannaman in person.

At noon, after the fun time spent with Billy Wannaman at Salmon High school, Coal went over to Lemhi Lumber and found Slugger in the back, cutting a board for someone. After the customer left, Coal asked, "You about ready for some lunch?"

Slugger grinned. "My stomach feels like my throat's been cut." He let out a belly laugh. "Ain't that what you used to say, Sarge?"

Coal returned the laugh. "Good memory, buddy. Yeah, I think I did say something along those lines."

After clearing lunch with Joe Taylor, they went over to the Salmon River Coffee Shop. Tammy Hawley gave them her big grin when they came in. The place got a little quieter than normal, but a majority of the regulars in Salmon had gotten used to seeing Slugger around by now. Some of them obviously didn't like having him come in, but they had learned to keep their thoughts to themselves. They had also learned that he frequented places all around town, so if they were going to boycott every restaurant that allowed him in, they might end up fishing in the river for their lunch before long.

"Hi, Slugger," Tammy greeted him.

"Howdy, Miss Tammy. You shore look good."

Slugger didn't catch the man sitting in the booth behind him grumbling something about how a man his color shouldn't be telling a white woman how good she looked. But Coal heard clearly enough. It was rancher Phil Harringer. For a moment, he contemplated getting up and going somewhere else to eat.

"Hi, Coal. How are you?"

"Great, Tammy."

She stared at him for a few seconds. "So you going to ask me how *I* am?"

"Oh. Yeah, Tammy, how are you?"

"Wonderful! I met a man."

Coal laughed. He knew this man she was talking about must be something special, but he wasn't going to tumble that easily. "I've met lots of those. Some of them I was sorry I met."

"Oh, stop it!" She waved him off. "No, really. I met this guy, new to town—a diesel mechanic. He moved up on the Bar from Burley. His name is Doug Pfeifer."

"Oh yeah?"

"Yeah. He likes to lift weights too, just like you. I think you'd really like him."

"Huh. Wow, Tammy, that's great. Good for you." He was genuinely happy for her. Tammy had been alone for years now, and it was baffling. She was one of the prettiest ladies in town, and always so friendly and full of life. No accounting for taste, he guessed. "I'd like to meet this Doug guy. I mean, I can't just let you date any old guy."

Tammy giggled. "You're so funny, Coal. Okay. What are you two having?"

She took their orders down and left, and Coal and Slugger sat there relaxing for a minute or two. Phil Harringer was sitting with two other diners, and Coal could hear their conversation growing louder and louder by the minute. He started to realize they must be trying to get a rise out of him or Slugger, or both, and since they weren't taking the bait, the trio had decided to ramp it up.

"Well, I don't care," Harringer said with calculated loudness. "I never did trust no nigger, and he's just as much nigger as any of the rest of them."

Coal saw Slugger's face when the words registered on him, but he didn't have time to stop him from getting up and turning around to face the other booth.

"What was that you said?" Looking down, Slugger faced the three men, his hands slowly starting to curl into fists at his sides.

Harringer stared up at him and blinked. "This is a private conversation, buck."

Slugger took a step closer, but now Coal was at his shoulder. "Hey, buddy. Easy does it. Don't let these idiots mess up your day. They're just mud ducks, quacking away."

Phil Harringer considered himself a big, bad fellow, a powerful man in this valley when it came to politics. But he was eying Slugger closely, and he was smart enough not to step up out of his booth. He shifted his eyes to Coal.

"Listen, Tin Star, I'm not done with you yet. This is a private conversation, and you aren't invited. We're talking about Bill Cosby, in case you'd like to know." One of the other men snickered.

Coal nodded. "Oh. Convenient. Good for you, Harringer. Hey—so how're those trees of yours doing anyway?"

Harringer's eyes hardened. It took him a while to think of any retort. "I don't know, Sheriff. Those trees remind me a lot of you ... dead. I think they just don't know it yet."

Tammy came walking over, looking nervously from Harringer's booth to Coal and Slugger. It was obvious she had heard most of the conversation, if not all of it. "Hey, you two. I just found another table on the other side of the restaurant I think you'd like better than eating right here."

Slugger's eyes didn't budge from Phil Harringer. "Thank you, Miss Tammy. But I like this here booth jus' fine."

"No, really that's a lot nicer table over there." The look in her eyes was pleading. She put her fingers gently on his arm. "Come on. I'll show you."

"Come on, Slugger," Coal prodded. "The air around here smells like tree killer anyway. I think I'd prefer the other side. And since I'm buying ..."

Slugger raised his chin, looking down his nose at Harringer while he ignored his two nameless cronies. Coal was still behind Slugger and couldn't see what was in his face, but Harringer had to have seen something in his eyes. He had stopped thinking of cutting remarks to make, and a huge hint of caution had come into his expression that Coal had never been witness to before.

Although it took Slugger a while to calm back down, they enjoyed a good meal of chicken fried steak and potatoes on the other side of the restaurant. Toward the end of the meal, Slugger indicated his steak with a couple of stabs toward it with his fork. "Man, Sarge, this is really good stuff. This is a great place to eat. Thanks again."

"I'm glad you like it. Yeah, they do a good job. Five stars, remember."

When Tammy came around with their check, Coal touched her

elbow. "Are those loud mouths gone yet?"

She nodded. "They are. I'm so sorry about that, you two. I can't stand that man. I wish someone would shut his big fat mouth."

"Wow! Tammy! I've never heard you talk like that before."

She grinned a little sheepishly. "Sorry. He just makes me so mad."

"Nothing to apologize for. I was just playing with you. I totally agree. Don't worry—he'll get his."

Coal and Slugger got up and went to pay at the front. Jay Castillo was the one at the register. "Hey. Tammy told me about Harringer. I'm thinking of telling him he's not welcome in here anymore."

"You wouldn't have any argument from me. What if he makes you lose business, though?"

"You think he will?"

"Naw. I doubt he has any friends. I don't know who those guys were with him, but if they were really friends, they don't mean much anyway. But it's your choice. I'll still keep coming in."

"I will too," put in Slugger. "That was some real good eatin', sir."

"Thanks. We pride ourselves on serving good food."

Coal picked up the two lunches Jay's crew had prepared, took Slugger back to work, then went back to the jail to feed the Medina brothers. Neither of them even got off their bunks to get their food, and Coal left without speaking to them.

It was four-forty-three when a call came in that a car had slid off the river road into the river after trying to pass another car on a curve and nearly hitting an oncoming mining truck. Coal had Flo call Jordan at home, although it was his day off, and then he got in the truck and headed downriver.

He wouldn't be there to pick Slugger up after work.

Leaving Slugger to do something Slugger should not have chosen to do.

But Slugger always had to live up to his name.

CHAPTER TWENTY-EIGHT

Coal was at least wise enough to have the foresight to radio in to Nadine, the relief dispatcher, and have her call Connie at home to see if she could go in and pick Slugger up at work. Unfortunately, the report came back that Dr. Darger, the vet, was out at the house checking on the status of their horse, Cody, and the nail he had stepped on the day of the big showdown with the Medina brothers. So Connie's trip to town would be delayed.

It was a full two hours before the big tow truck came and left, hauling the once nice white '69 Pontiac Bonneville convertible, now a months-long restoration job waiting to happen, out of the river and back toward Andy's Auto Body.

As a courtesy, Coal gave a ride back to Salmon to the very shaken young couple—the driver who couldn't see too well around curves in winding highways, and his wife, who currently seemed to consider him on a scale of popularity with dog diarrhea. It ended up being another thrill for them riding with Coal once the radio started crackling and the call came over: There was a fight at the Owl Club. And, Nadine made sure to add, *It's possible your friend might be involved.*

Of course he might. Coal clenched his jaws to keep from swearing in front of the already upset young couple.

He pushed the pickup as hard as it would go, and luckily by the time the call had come they were mostly on the straightaway, and well away from the river. Even so, both the young man and the wife who currently deplored him had white knuckles by the time

Coal veered off 91 and made the hard left onto Main Street on most of two tires.

He told them they were going to have to disembark just shy of the Owl Club bar, and for some reason neither of them tried to argue, although they had another mile to go before they would be home.

Coal screeched the truck tires in slamming on his brakes almost to the infamous Owl Club. He took only enough time to turn it off and grab the keys, and he paid no attention to whatever his passengers were doing. They were on their own now.

A crowd was milling at the front of the Owl Club, most of them still directing their attention to the front door, which one brave soul was holding open.

Coal yelled a few feet before reaching the first person to clear the way for him, and bewildered faces turned to look at him, then parted like the Red Sea.

Inside the bar, there was a reasonable amount of yelling and name-calling, but the physical part of the fight was at a stand-still. As usual, Slugger Janx was still standing, with half of a broken pool cue in his hand and a barbaric, bellicose look in his eyes as he whirled around to keep an eye on those who by their looks were wishing they had the guts to wade into him. Bob Wilson and Officer Tim Lacey were in the room, but it looked like they were a little buffaloed. It was some twenty brawlers to their two.

"Hold it!" Coal growled a curse word he didn't normally use to draw the attention of the brawlers, including three or four that were hanging back and nursing various bruised and possibly broken parts of their bodies. He recognized none of them, but with all the mine and logging activity around that was no surprise.

"Everyone back off!"

Red Levine, the bartender, yelled out his own reinforcement of Coal's command: "He said back off, Chuck! Not 'leave'!" Looking over, Coal saw one of the men trying to slink toward the back of the room.

The man froze. His eyes swung to Coal. "You heard him ... *Chuck.* You move and this whole thing becomes all about you."

Bob eased over to Coal. "It's good to see you, Coal. I think we could get these other guys under control. But your buddy, that's a different story."

Coal nodded. "I know. Once he's got war in his eyes, that's pretty much that." He turned back to the mob. "All of you except Slugger, get over against the wall!" He wanted to join Slugger in manhandling a few of these bar patrons. If he knew Slugger, it wasn't him who had started this row.

With Bob Wilson and Lacey on one side, Coal on the other, perhaps the gang of brawlers felt safe from Slugger, and they sidled over to the indicated wall. The whole time, they kept their eyes on Slugger, not on Coal or the other officers.

Coal stepped closer to Slugger. "Hey, buddy. It's me. Stand down. At ease."

Slugger turned wild eyes to stare at him. The whites of his eyes, in the shadows, seemed even pinker than normal—almost red. "That's an order, soldier. Give me that stick."

Slugger's eyes blinked rapidly. Coal knew it was the soldier talk that was slowly reaching him.

"At ease, soldier. Stand down," repeated Coal. "Stand down now."

A grimace came across Slugger's bloodied face, where Coal could see at least one cut, just beneath his left eye, and possibly a torn right ear, although in the shadows he wasn't sure.

Slugger stepped closer. His breathing was slowly returning to normal. "What you want I should do with this stick, Sarge?"

"Hand it over to me. Nice and easy."

Slugger slowly extended the stick, his impromptu club. As Coal reached out for it, he saw that the end was shaking violently. The vibrations were so strong they even seemed to rattle his own hand as he accepted the offering from Slugger and let it fall to his own side.

"What happened, soldier?" Coal asked, feeling safer remaining for the moment in army non-com mode.

Slugger's upper lip curled, and he sliced a look toward the shadowed crowd standing mesmerized with their backs against the wall. He forced his gaze back to Coal, blinking furiously. "They ... They come at me. They called me a nigger. Then one of 'em spit on me. I ... Sarge, I come unhinged."

Coal almost allowed himself a grim smile. Slugger always came unhinged, it seemed. "Okay, buddy. It's all right. Why don't you go over there and take a stool?"

Still shaking, eyes wild, Slugger backed toward the bar. With his left hand, he fumbled around behind him until he found a swiveling stool, then pulled himself up onto it. Both of his hands flopped down between his legs. He was coming down off a high, and his body was only now beginning to realize it: Slugger was spent.

Coal turned to where Bob and Lacey were standing in front of the other faction in the fight—all twelve of them, Coal ticked off quickly in his head.

Facing the brawlers, Coal stood wide-legged, hooking his left thumb behind his belt. The bloody club hung at his right thigh.

Coal scanned the brawlers, his jaw set. He felt his lip wanting to twitch, and he fought it. What he wanted was to go forward with what Slugger had started, but of course he couldn't.

He spoke to the side. "Bob, it's your town. What do you want to do?"

"I want to start citing a bunch of numbskulls," Bob replied without hesitation. "But I doubt half of them would ever show up."

Tim Lacey spoke for the first time, and Coal instantly wondered if he realized how much his words would gall the white crowd. "I think it's kind of funny, myself, how one Negro was able to clean the clocks of all these white boys. Judging by some of you, I'm wondering if you already haven't paid the price of the party."

Coal looked over three of the men, who were seated at a table because apparently they could no longer stand, two who were lying stretched out on the floor close by as if dead, and the standing crowd who, to the man, looked as if they had been in a stampede of bison.

Coal jabbed the broken cue at the face of the biggest man, who wore a black beard as thick as a bear hide. "You. What started this fight?"

The man hesitated too long.

"Can you hear?" Coal growled.

The man tried to collect his manhood. He knew the eyes of all his cohorts were on him. "He pulled a knife on me."

Coal almost swore. "A knife? You're seriously telling me he pulled a knife on you?"

Confusion came over the man's face, perhaps from alcohol, perhaps because he had a moment of wondering if Coal had a way of knowing he was lying. Then his face hardened in resolve. "Yeah, he pulled a knife. Like I said."

"Do all you people take a class called 'Fight Excuses 101'?" Coal couldn't keep the derision out of his voice. He was aware of several pairs of eyes bounding around from one to another—the expressions of men either thinking they had missed something at the beginning of the ruckus, or who were wondering how black beard was going to back up his knife story.

"What's your name?"

"Ross," the man replied. "Evans."

"Where do you live, Evans?"

"Panther Creek."

"At Cobalt?"

"Yeah."

"Miner?"

Evans nodded.

Coal swiveled his eyes over to the man next to him. "What's his name?"

Looking confused, the man said, "Ross Evans. Like he said."

Coal nodded. It was hard to believe he was going through almost the exact same scenario he had at the last bar fight Slugger was in. They were reenacting a bad play.

"All right, Evans. You say this man pulled a knife on you?"

"Yeah."

"Where is it?"

Evans froze. Seconds ticked by like ponderous drum beats in Coal's ears. There *was* no knife.

"Here it is." The voice had come from a man who was standing back behind a couple of men to Coal's far left.

"Who said that?"

"Me."

"Step out here, *Me.*"

The man came out, all wrinkled one hundred forty-five pounds of him, with huge ears apparently designed to pick up faraway sounds in front of him.

"Who are you?"

"Dick Cohan."

"Dick, huh?" Coal was pretty sure he had a smirk on his face. "Okay. Well, Dick, why don't you take that knife by the blade and walk over here to me."

With his hand shaking almost as bad as Slugger's had been, the man slunk forward, holding the haft of a knife out in front of him. Its handle appeared to be real stag horn.

Coal reached his left hand out and took the knife. "That's a nice-looking knife ... *Dick.* You say this man pulled that on your friend Ross here, huh?"

The man nodded hard enough Coal thought his head might drop off his scrawny neck. "Yes sir. Yeah, he did."

"All right. Go back to the wall." As Cohan was turning, Coal could see a thick leather sheath on his right hip, beneath a green army-issue coat. And just like the time before he would have bet money that sheath no longer had a knife in it. Déjà vu.

Coal backed toward Slugger. He had eyed every one of the brawlers pretty closely, and every one of them bore marks from Slugger's fury. In spite of their twelve to one, in fact, Slugger appeared amazingly to have gotten the least of the damage of anyone here.

"Well, Bob, it looks like Slugger pulled a knife on Evans, there. So I guess that's aggravated assault. I'm going to have to run him in."

Bob looked over at Coal. Bob had low-hung eyebrows and almost black eyes, and the two factors gave him the perpetual appearance of looking a little mad about something. It was only someone who knew him as well as Coal did who would have recognized the humorous little smirk on his face.

"I guess so. You want any help?"

"No. I've got it." Coal turned to the other brawlers. "Well, boys, it looks like you're all free to go." He looked at the two men who had now sat up on the floor and the three who remained sitting at the table. "I guess Bob will call an ambulance for you gents."

The walking wounded looked around at one another. Dick Cohan looked a little disconcerted—maybe even disappointed. But he turned with the others, and they all shuffled outside.

Coal turned to barkeep Red Levine. "Any damages, Red?"

Levine glanced around the room, then looked over at Slugger. Finally, his eyes returned to Coal. "Hey, Sheriff, I don't know what you're going to do from here, and I really didn't see the start of the whole fight—but I'm pretty sure this guy didn't pull a knife on them."

Coal nodded and allowed himself a mischievous smile. "Well, thanks, Red. It seems like this year's alibi is to claim somebody pulled a knife. Come on, Slugger. There's sure to be some men waiting outside, so it looks like I'm driving you up to the jail this time."

Slugger gave his friend an incredulous look, but he didn't fight. Coal guessed he was still full of adrenalin, since by his expression it was clear he had no clue what Coal was doing.

He walked toward the door as Coal told Bob and Tim Lacey so long, glanced over at the wounded, then followed the black man out. On the sidewalk, mostly across the street, Coal recognized clusters of men from the fight.

He took handcuffs from his back pocket and leaned close to Slugger's back, speaking softly. "I'll take these off in a minute, Slugger. But for now, put your hands behind your back. Yeah, we're doing *this* again."

CHAPTER TWENTY-NINE

With so many pairs of inquisitive eyes watching them, Coal took a look around to make sure the couple who gave their Pontiac a bath in the Salmon weren't still hanging around in hopes of finishing their ride home, and then he spun the pickup around on Main and drove up to the courthouse.

He didn't wait until they got down in the jail to make Slugger turn around, and he unlocked the handcuffs and slid them off. "Better?" he asked Slugger when he turned around massaging his wrists.

Slugger chuckled. "Considerable. Man, Sarge, I'm sorry."

The apology took Coal aback, and he stared at his friend. "I haven't even given you a talking to yet."

Slugger grinned. "No sir."

"So what really happened down there, buddy?"

"Just like I told you. I was tryin' t' do my best—'til they spit on me."

Coal bunched his jaw muscles. "Well, damnit, Slugger, I almost hate to even say anything, but I guess I'm going to have to. I'm afraid I would have done the same thing. Oh! Hang on a second." He held up a finger to signal Slugger to wait and opened the passenger door, reaching in to where he had slid the knife, a high quality Schrade, into the glove box. "I almost forgot—you better get a sheath for this. That's a nice blade, buddy."

Slugger looked down at the knife, then back up at Coal, confused. "But Sarge, you know that really ain't my knife. They're lyin' again."

"Sure it is, Slugger. All those men swore to it, and it's their word against yours. Besides, I guess you earned it." He winked.

Slugger gave out with a laugh. "Okay, man. I guess it is mine after all."

"I guess it is. Maybe I read you wrong. I think maybe you keep going downtown to build up your knife collection."

Slugger grinned, obviously embarrassed. "I won't do it no more. I'm stayin' home from now on."

"Good to hear. Hey—you want to go inside for a little bit?"

Slugger shrugged. "Sure, I guess. I'd like to see the inside of a jail where the cops ain't crooks."

Inside, Coal told Slugger to sit down and relax, then went and got him a tall glass of water from the fountain in back, looking in on the Medinas. Coming back out into the office, he handed the glass to him. "Drink this down, buddy. Then tell me something. I know you already said you're not doing it anymore, but all joking aside, what were you thinking anyway? What made you think it would turn out okay if you went into that place?"

Slugger took a long drink of water, then wiped his mouth. "What you talkin' about, Sarge?"

"Come on. The bar. Why'd you go in there? What did you think was going to happen?"

Slugger stared his old friend down. "Hey, Sarge. Listen. I don't like bein' the one that's always causin' you headaches around here. I know you got troubles enough without me bein' here. But what about *my* rights? Huh? When do I decide I got the right to go where anybody else does, get me a drink, play me some Eight Ball? At what point you suggest I can stop worryin' about what might happen everywhere I go and start tryin' to have a real life of my own?"

Coal sat still, aching inside. He studied Slugger's eyes, which earnestly looked back at him. He wasn't sure how to respond. Slugger was right. The world was taking away his rights to do anything he wanted. His rights to enjoy himself and entertain himself like any other man. The world was treating him like he was something less, and it was time for it to stop. But it wasn't going to. At least it wasn't going to any time soon. So did Slugger keep walking into situations he knew he would have to fight his way out of, just to prove he had the same rights as any other man? Or did he spend his life cowering in a hole?

"Brother, I wish I had an answer for that. I sure wish I did."

Slugger almost smiled. His eyes got moist. "You know what hits me in the guts, Sarge?"

"What's that?"

"You callin' me brother. No white man in the States never called me brother in my life."

"You *are* my brother. Brothers in arms. You would have died for me in Nam, Slugger, and I'd still die for you."

"Thanks, Sarge." He smiled when Coal clapped him on the knee. "So what am I gon' do now? Do I sit at your place the rest o' my life, cowerin' like a dog that's been beat its whole life? Go back an' forth 'tween there an' the hardware store? Maybe the eatin' place—but only if yore with me? What am I gonna do? Sarge, I'm lost."

Coal wondered if he wasn't getting more emotional as he got older. Right now, he felt like he could cry for his friend. He had no answers for him. No answer but to wish the world were a different place, and that all men were truly one color.

"I can't tell you, Slugger. I don't know. I'm honestly starting to wonder if I know anything about the world anymore—and about people."

Saturday, January 20

Coal knew he should have called first, but he didn't. Instead, after getting up early to feed the horses and hammering out a grueling arm and shoulder workout, he showered, got dressed in brand-new Wranglers and one of the new shirts he had recently been forced into buying at McPherson's, and drove over to Maura's.

If Jordan Peterson was there this early in the morning, it would tell Coal everything he needed to know. But that was the thing: He *had* to know.

Without realizing it, an eighth of a mile from Maura's, with the eastern sky a pale, yellowing gray, Coal was holding his breath. He caught himself sitting up taller in the pickup seat, as if that would give him a view of Maura's yard any sooner.

Taking a deep breath, he forced himself to calm down. And then, there it was: nothing. Beautiful, wonderful nothing. Maura's yard was vastly empty except for her beautiful, hideous International Travelette. Jordan had not stayed the night.

Pushing away the guilt he felt for checking up on Maura, even after they had decided together that it was all right to be with other people, he pulled into her yard. Shades of gray bathed everything, but today all those shades of gray seemed fresh and beautiful. He could hear the heelers barking inside the house as he went out and threw flakes of hay to Maura's eager-looking horses, then went back to the truck.

His heart was pounding as he sat down in the cab and slammed the door, letting the heater lull him. But even with the motor purring and the heat blowing on him, his heart continued to race. He cursed himself for a fool. What was he, fifteen years old again? And was he some kind of spy? He should be ashamed of himself.

But he wasn't.

Finally, he couldn't take it anymore. He turned off the engine and got out, shutting the door as quietly as he could. Going up on the porch, he tried the doorknob, and it was unlocked. He opened it just enough to let Chewy and Dart get his scent, then let them outside. After giving them both as much attention as he could bear to use the time for, he pushed the door open again and eased inside, ready to hear a shotgun rack. The dogs took off playing in the yard and tending to their important business while Coal stood at the entrance to Maura's living room and thought back on the night he had scared the dickens out of Annie. In the past, he had always gotten a kick out of putting a good scare into someone, but he remembered too well the guns Maura carried in her pickup, and it was only sensible to assume she brought them into her room with her at night. Scaring a woman like Maura might be downright deadly.

Coal sat down and pulled his boots off, then crept to the fridge and opened it. Unlike Annie's fridge, this one was well-stocked, with bacon, beef, eggs—some of them already boiled—and half a roasted chicken covered in tinfoil. He sat there toying with the idea of making Maura breakfast in bed, although his original intention was to ask her to go to breakfast with him.

At last, still undecided, he went down the hall, to the room at the end he remembered being Maura's bedroom. The door was open wide.

He chuckled to himself. How was this woman so deaf? If his dogs had been carrying on like Chewy and Dart were, he would have been up with a loaded pistol. If someone were walking around his house, creaking his old floors, he would have made sure they sang out or that they dropped on their face on the floor and started giving good reasons for being in his house. But no, Maura slept on.

Well, it was time to see how good this woman scared. At this point, he figured he could get all the way to her bed and dive on top of her before she could grab a gun. If she was the type to get terrified at a practical joke like this, well, he had the rest of their lives for apologies.

Taking a deep breath, he edged around the corner. Then he stopped. Maura's bed had been carefully made, every wrinkle smoothed out of it as good as any raw recruit's bed he had ever seen at boot camp.

But there was no Maura.

CHAPTER THIRTY

After letting Chewy and Dart back in the house, Coal sat in the GMC for half an hour without starting it. It wasn't much over twenty-six degrees, and a brisk wind was pushing against the truck—a rarity lately in the valley—so even though the sun had made an appearance, and the sky was blue, it was still cold. Coal, however, could not feel it.

With his head resting against the back window, he contemplated his life. His guts told him one thing: If it hadn't been for Laura, and the way she died, he would have been with Maura. He thought a lot of Kathy and Annie both, but with Maura there had been some kind of connection he had with no one else. Even now that it was gone, it was hard to fathom its absence.

When he finally started the truck, his first thought was to drive into Salmon and go by Jordan Peterson's house. Maura had to be there. Where else *could* she be? But there were two big problems: One, Maura's truck was here, so Jordan would have had to pick her up, and from outside the house there would be no way to know if she was in there or not. Two, he really didn't want to know. At least now he could continue pretending things were not as they appeared to be.

The notion crossed his mind of sitting down the street from Jordan's, as long as it took, to see if when his deputy left his house Maura was with him. But again, he didn't want to know—he told himself.

In the end, he pulled out of Maura's yard and drove back home. When he got there, Connie was pouring batter into a black cast iron pan for an umpteenth pancake, and the kids were all still gathered around the table, but looked to be slowing down.

The chorus of greetings from the table somehow managed to reach Coal, and they and the fawning of the dogs lifted his spirits a little. But not tremendously.

As Coal passed the table, he had to do a double take. He looked down at the grinning face of Slugger Janx, his teeth starkly white against the dark of his skin.

"Mornin', Sarge! Would you look at what I got here?"

Coal was already looking. He couldn't believe what he was seeing. Sissy Miley was sitting there on Slugger's lap, a big smile on her face as she chewed on an over-sized chunk of home-smoked bacon.

"Well, if that doesn't beat all." Coal dropped a hand on Slugger's shoulder. Then he gave a soft pat to Sissy's cheek, making her smile even bigger. "Good morning, sweet little girl. Slugger, it looks like you've got a bit of the black magic in you—no pun intended." He laughed after realizing what the comment had sounded like.

Connie turned from the stove to look at Coal, a bit of motherly concern in her eyes. She, of all the people in the room, was seeing through his happy façade, and he could feel it reach him like a warm summer wind. When he came over to her, she reached over and gave him a hug with one arm. "Well, that was quick. That wasn't much chance for a visit."

Normally, Coal would not have wanted to talk. This time, for some reason he did. "She wasn't home."

"Oh." Connie turned and pretended the pancake batter was still in dire need of whipping until Coal finally let out a laugh.

"What?"

"You taught me a long time ago that too much stirring makes the pancakes stiff. Stop that. You're making me nervous."

Connie's expression went into a mix of half smile-half frown.

"Oh, aren't you the smartie? So ... Where do you think she is, Son?"

"I wouldn't have the faintest idea. You know what? Let's not worry about it. I'm hungry for some cake and pig—and chicken seeds." He grinned after using the almost forgotten nickname his father had used when referring to eggs, a simple joke which used to amuse the three Savage boys beyond any reason.

For once, Connie obeyed his wishes and didn't say anything more as she filled his two plates (he couldn't stand syrup from the pancakes getting onto his eggs and bacon). Coal sat in silence at the table, the dogs waiting by the living room stove as he ate, and all the rest but Katie gone to watch Saturday morning cartoons—*Scooby Doo,* to be exact, if he was hearing correctly.

"Dad? You okay?"

Coal looked over at Katie, and in a rush of emotion reached out and gave her hand a squeeze. "Sure, sweetheart, I'm fine. Thank you."

"Okay." She stood up and seemed about to go join the others, but she paused behind him and gave his neck a big hug. He patted her hand. Suddenly, there must have been a lump of chicken seed in his throat, because he wasn't able to speak. Katie could, though. She whispered close to his ear, "Daddy, I love you."

And then, leaving him no room even to embarrass himself, she waltzed on in to the living room.

The plan for the day had been for the whole family to pack up and drive to Idaho Falls, walk the grounds of the LDS temple, stroll along the banks of the Snake River, where the falls this time of year should be incredible, have dinner at some fancy restaurant, and then return home after dark. Connie had borrowed a big, black fourteen-seater van from a family friend for the occasion.

The whole day would be a fantastic time for family together-ness, rejuvenation, and getting reacquainted, but one of the high-lights for Coal had been his intention of having Maura

PlentyWounds along. Oh well. Another time, perhaps. He still had every expectation of enjoying the day, because he wouldn't have a police radio to bring him any bad news from Lemhi County, and he was simply going to enjoy the heck out of his little family while they were all still in one piece.

And then the phone rang.

Coal was just standing up, having dropped his napkin on the table, and his next plan was to clear the dishes and take them to the sink, where he would stand with Connie and do the drying, while she washed. He fondly remembered that ritual from his childhood, when his brothers were generally doing something in town or out in the country shooting guns or making mischief.

"I'll get it, Mom," he said, pretending there was no feeling of dread in his chest. In fact, what if it was Maura, calling to offer some perfectly good excuse for why she wasn't at home and asking him if he was the one who had fed her dogs and the horses?

Feeling a little lighter at that thought, in spite of a worried expectation that it would be something not nearly so pleasant, he answered the phone.

Good morning, Sheriff! Er—I mean Coal! Hey, this is Mike Fica.

"Oh, hey, Mike," Coal replied, now recognizing the county prosecutor's pleasantly unique voice.

How is everything going? How's the family?

Coal wanted to chuckle. As far as he knew, Fica didn't know any of his family, but he never failed to ask about them and make sure they were okay, and he would never settle for any answer as simple as "fine."

So they took a few minutes in conversation about Connie and the children, including Cynthia and Sissy, while Coal stood there waiting for a bomb to drop. This had to be something about Slugger Janx. There was a catch to this seemingly friendly Saturday morning phone call, and he was pretty sure he knew it.

He hoped somebody would believe him if he told them this was the first time he was wrong.

So, hey, Coal, I've been having a hard time sleeping these past couple nights, and something hit me this morning.

Here it came. "What's that, Mike?"

Well, it's about the Medina brothers.

Coal's thought train had shot off on a sidetrack so fast he nearly fell off the back of the caboose. Slugger Janx wasn't even on this train!

"Oh. What about them?"

Well, you tell me what you think, Coal, but give it some thought, all right? I've been looking over all the files on these guys, from down in Vegas, and ... Okay, let me cut to the chase. It looks like especially Angel has been pretty heavily involved with the mafia down there, right? And since Rey is his brother, anyone would reasonably assume that Angel would have shared a lot of inside information with him, wouldn't he?

"Sure, I suppose so."

Okay. So ... Coal, maybe I'm just getting paranoid as I get older, but ... Don't you think these guys could be in real danger if you keep them here in your jail?

It was like a tennis racket smashed Coal upside his head. *Danger!* Of course Fica was right! He had a known member of the mafia in his jail, and his brother who had been in very close contact with him, at least since leaving Vegas, and assumedly in Vegas as well. There was no way on Earth the mob was simply going to sit by and leave those two up here in Idaho rotting in a jail cell until they decided to give themselves a break by turning state's evidence against the big fish in Vegas. No way.

A cold feeling had encompassed Coal from head to foot. It wasn't just the Medinas who were in danger ...

"You're right, Mike. My heck, you're right. I never even thought of it." And that fact embarrassed him, as four years with the FBI should have taught him better. "And if they're in danger, so am I and all my deputies."

Uh-huh. And maybe your family too. I think you need to move them to some other jail. Don't you?

"I agree. Mike, I think you might just have saved me an awful lot of trouble. Once again, I owe you."

When he hung up the phone, it took about five seconds to put two and two together and realize the entire nature of this Idaho Falls journey was about to change.

With a big sigh, he dialed the operator and asked her to put him through to the Idaho Falls Police Department.

CHAPTER THIRTY-ONE

When Coal pulled the van up at the back of the courthouse, in front of the jail door, he turned and looked back at the kids. All of them but Sissy, who was seated on Connie's lap, had staked out their territory in the back of the van.

"All right, guys. I'm really sorry about this, but it can't be helped. So just remember the drill. You can speak to them if they act like they want to talk, but otherwise, just keep to yourselves and let them do their thing back there. I know it's all kind of awkward, but we're going to have to make it work."

He went into the jail, finding it chilly and empty. Victor Yancey hadn't even worked last night, so a night jailer was nonexistent. And Jordan didn't come on until two or three—pretty much when he decided to show up, as long as it was around those two times and he stayed his full ten or more. Right now, Coal didn't even want to think about Jordan.

He got the keys and went back into the cell block, and this time, unlike usual, both the Medinas sat up on their cots. Angel didn't look at him, or if he did Coal couldn't tell because of the glasses. But his head was tipped toward the floor, and he massaged the back of his neck, under his impressive mop of hair.

Ray, on the other hand, blinked a couple of times and tried to smile at Coal. "What's new, boss?"

"We're moving."

"Now, what?" Ray jumped up off the cot. "What do you mean 'moving'?"

"Exactly that. I'm taking you to the big house," he said with a smirk. "At least as big as Idaho Falls has. We're changing jails."

Angel's face shot toward Ray, and Coal saw his jaw harden. "What's the deal? What's wrong with here, Coal? We kind of prefer this."

"You'll prefer there, Ray—when your boys from Vegas show up."

Ray and Angel exchanged glances. When Ray spoke again it was in a more subdued voice. "Oh, yeah, right. Like they'd be coming up here." Even as good an actor as Coal knew Ray to be, something didn't ring true about his voice. Coal studied his face for a few more seconds, trying to read him. Finally, he gave up.

"All right, come on. You first, Ray. The whole works—cuffs and leg irons, and then we'll connect them together."

Ray's expression had grown dark. He didn't say a word. Coal's guts told him Mike Fica had made his phone call at just the right time. The Medinas knew something he didn't.

He was able to truss Ray up in cuffs and leg irons easily enough, and he chained him momentarily to his open cell door, then went to open Angel's cell.

Angel remained seated on his cot. "Get up, Medina."

Angel looked up. His eyes were likely sullen. But all Coal could see was those big fly eyes that were the lenses of his glasses.

"I'm stayin' right here."

"Like hell you are."

"I got a shattered hand, and a hole in my leg, gringo, but I'd like to see the army that's gonna make me get up an' leave this jail."

This whole time, Ray stood silent. There was a part of Coal, way deep inside, that hoped, maybe for old times' sake, Ray would speak up on his behalf and try to persuade his brother to come easy. But he guessed blood was thicker than water, after all.

With a loud sigh bordering on a groan, Coal stepped out into the hall and removed his hat, setting it gently on the floor, crown down. Then he walked back into the cell and up to Angel Medina.

He reached with his right hand for Angel's left wrist, his legs purposely offset to protect his groin. Angel struck at Coal's jaw with his right fist, the one that wore a cast, and was hard. But Coal's jaw was no longer there.

Coal had openly invited Angel's move. In fact, he had high hopes for it. He dodged his head to the right and struck down Angel's incoming fist with his left hand, came up a little taller at the same time that he whirled to his left and sliced Angel once on the left side of his neck with the knife edge of his right hand, then once on the very top of his head with the heel of the left.

Angel pitched sideways off his cot and melted into the concrete floor like a dummy made of tar.

Ray started rattling his chain against the bars by yanking hard on it. "What the hell! Coal! You killed him!"

Coal stood away from Angel Medina and swept the hair back off his forehead. He didn't bother to look at Ray when he replied. "He might wish he was dead, but all he's going to have is one whale of a headache."

Leaning down, he calmly applied the ankle cuffs, then wrangled both of Angel's arms up behind him and shackled his wrists, last of all hooking a chain between the handcuff chain and the longer one between his feet. He purposely made Angel's linking chain a little shorter than normal.

As he walked out of Angel's cell, he leaned down and picked his hat up off the floor, rocking it gently down over his hair. With a bit of a smirk he couldn't contain, as he walked past Ray he said, "You might as well hang out in here for a while and I'll go let our van driver know there's going to be a little delay while we wait for your brother to come around."

*   *   *

On the way out of town, Connie, who was now at the wheel so Coal could move fast if he needed to deal with one or the other of the Medinas, said, "Hey, I didn't notice the ambulance at the hospital on our way up the hill. Did you?"

Coal glanced back toward Steele Memorial to see that the Lemhi County Quick Response ambulance was indeed parked outside. "No, I didn't notice."

Connie kept driving for a minute, then said, "Do you suppose Maura might have been out on a call?"

"Nice thought, Ma, but she only has the Travelette, and it was parked at her house."

"Oh. Okay."

Connie was wise enough to stop bringing it up, but Coal's mind wasn't. He began tossing hopeful scenarios around in his head, and it took Sissy, who was seated on his lap, to make him stop.

Without an obvious thing leading up to it, she picked up his right hand and took his thumb in her little hand. "Is that one?"

Coal stared down at her. His mind was churning, trying to find some frame of reference for what the girl had said. Finally, he said what any wise child psychologist might have: "Huh?"

Sissy looked up at him earnestly, then wiggled his thumb again, as if to say, "Coal, stay focused!" Again, in clear English, she said, "Is that one? Number one?"

A laugh of glee escaped Coal. "Yes. Yes, Sissy, that *is* one."

She took his index finger then. "Is that two?"

Coal looked over at Connie, who shrugged, both with her shoulders and with her eyebrows.

"It is. How do you know that, Sissy? Did your uncle teach you to count?"

"No." She turned and pointed to the seat behind Coal. "Slugger bin teachin' me."

Coal whirled around and looked at his friend. "What's this?"

Slugger grinned. "Oh, yeah. Sometimes when I got a little time I ain't usin' I been teachin' her some numbers. Nothin' fancy."

Coal felt two things at once: Proud of his friend for thinking of such a thing, and Sissy for learning it, and ashamed of himself and his own family, who had apparently never thought of doing such a thing.

Nodding thoughtfully, Coal looked over at Connie. "Mom? What have you been teaching Sissy to do?"

His mom gave out with an indignant grunt. "Well, to be a little lady, for one. And to feed the dogs."

Coal grinned. But he still felt shame that his friend had to come all the way up from Louisiana before Sissy even learned her numbers. That was something he was going to make sure changed in the Savage residence.

For the next thirty miles, the children picked songs and sang them, too often at the tops of their lungs. Wyatt was the most exuberant singer of all, especially when it came to "I've Been Workin' on the Railroad" and "My Grandfather's Clock."

Finally, a loud groan erupted from far in the back. "Hey! Make them stop already. Judas priest! My head already hurts bad enough." It was Angel Medina, and one of the rare times Coal had heard his voice since his incarceration.

"Angel." Coal spoke just loudly enough for him to hear. "If you don't shut your trap, I'll come back there and put you back to sleep. These kids are getting ready for opera school. I know you wouldn't try to take that away from them."

They pulled up to the Bonneville County jail in Idaho Falls an hour and a half later, and Coal got Ray out of the van and on his feet. Then he called Slugger over. "Hey, give me a hand with this one, would you?"

"Hey!" Angel growled loudly. "You get him away from me, man! I ain't havin' no nigger put his stinkin' hands on me."

Coal reacted badly. And without thought. He was standing over the prone form of Angel Medina, who lay on top of his cuffed wrists, with his legs still chained, and he had one foot on the Mexican's throat, bearing down. He heard the deep voice behind him.

"Well, you must be Sheriff Savage."

CHAPTER THIRTY-TWO

Coal looked up to see a man in a very nicely cleaned and pressed deputy sheriff's uniform, no gun belt on, but a badge on his chest, looking at him with one corner of his mouth slightly bent upward.

Coal straightened up so he was now looking five inches down to meet the man's eyes. He decided it might look better if he stood off Angel Medina's throat, so he acted on the thought.

"Umm ... Yeah. Coal Savage. And you are ... ?"

"Lieutenant Brawver. Vern, if you'd rather."

"Oh, yeah, you're the—"

"Yeah, I'm the one you spoke to."

Coal sighed, feeling sheepish, and walked over to stab his hand out toward Brawver. The man shook it, then tilted his head to look past Coal.

"So if don't need the prisoner any longer as a door mat, you wanna bring him inside?"

Clearing his throat, Coal said, "Oh, yeah. We had a little issue when I was about to take him out. I guess he didn't like my partner touching him." Coal indicated Slugger with a jerk of his thumb.

Brawver looked over at Slugger. "Hello." Slugger, unsmiling, introduced himself.

"Good to meet you," said Brawver. "Well, let's get everyone in out of the cold, shall we?" By now, the twins had disembarked from the van and stood side by side staring up at Brawver, who still hadn't smiled.

"Holy! You got a whole van full. You start your criminals out a little young up in that country, don't you?"

Coal met his eyes and searched them. They both laughed at the same time that Coal realized Lieutenant Brawver was just a regular guy after all. He introduced the twins, who bravely shook hands when the Lieutenant offered, and then Brawver continued on over to the van, looked inside the door the boys had left open, and made the acquaintance of the women of the family.

The Bonneville County jail was a lot bigger, of course, than the one in Salmon. Much more crowded too. The whole family made themselves at home in the lobby while Coal, Brawver, and a jailer the size of a VW Beetle went on with the Medinas.

As they walked the prisoners down the long corridor in the cellblock, Coal wondered if any of these inmates had a clue as to the caliber of man who was stepping into their midst. A lot of the men in here were Mexican as well, along with a few Indians. There was a scattering of white guys, most of them looking pretty strung out.

Brawver led Coal and the prisoners all the way to the last cell, with the big, quiet jailer riding drag on the herd. When Brawver stopped, the jailer walked around him, unsnapped a saucer-sized ring of keys off a keeper on his belt, and unlocked the cell door, pulling it wide.

The Medinas trooped inside and sat down on cold iron cots. Brawver studied Angel's leg and hand, but he chose to hold his silence for now.

Coal looked at Ray for a while. Ray looked back.

"Well? I guess this is it, huh, buddy?" Ray said.

"Remember, that 'buddy' thing went away."

"Oh. Yeah. Well, old habits ... You know."

Coal nodded.

"Do we stay here now for the trial too?" Ray asked. "Parting ways for good?"

"No, I'm sure I'll see you again. The murder and grand theft auto—oh, and kidnapping. That was all in Lemhi County. They'll get their piece of you."

Ray took a deep breath. "Okay. Then I guess we'll see you."

"I guess you will."

Coal turned and walked back down the hall with Brawver and the jailer, hating himself inside for the little part of him that somehow couldn't stop caring what happened to Ray Christian.

When they got to the lobby, Lieutenant Brawver said, "So ... let me take a wild guess. Besides the bruised neck on that big fella, are you responsible for the leg and hand thing too?"

"Uhh, yeah. I guess I am."

"Remind me to stay on a friendly basis with you," said Brawver, and he reached out and shook Coal's hand.

After leaving the lieutenant with instructions about the care of Angel's injuries, Coal took Slugger and the family, and they all went back out and piled into the van. At last, they were about to start the enjoyable part of their trip.

Coal drove first over to the west side of the Snake River. It was still fairly full, and now and then a chunk of ice would come floating along it. Geese and ducks wandered the shores as if they were the real owners of the river—which Coal guessed they rightfully were.

Katie said, "Dad! Canadian geese!"

Coal smiled and squeezed her shoulder. "They're beautiful, aren't they? Oh—and they're just *Canada* geese, not Canadian."

"Oh yeah." She looked sheepish.

Coal didn't know why he cared what his kids called the geese, except that he was carrying on a tradition started by his father, when he was only three or four. Old Prince would have taken him to task if he would have called some poor creature by a wrong name.

They strolled along the shore, Coal carrying Sissy, who was understandably afraid of the geese, which weren't too much shorter than she was.

They came to a point directly across the water from the huge, shining white Latter Day Saint temple, and Slugger stood with his lips parted and stared at it. It looked like a gargantuan wedding cake, set daintily down in the middle of a beautifully landscaped yard—although right now the landscape was dormant.

"What *is* that thing, Sarge?" Slugger asked.

"That's the Mormon temple."

"The Mormons? I heard o' them. Scary, huh?"

Coal laughed. "Probably most of what you've heard isn't true. They're just like you, buddy."

"What do they do inside there?"

"A lot of things. Church members get married in there. And they take care of a lot of other ceremonies." That was a door Coal didn't feel like opening just then.

Slugger shook his head. "Well, man. That's really somethin', huh? I never seen nothin' like that."

As they finished their walk along the Snake, Slugger played with the geese and ducks a little, wishing out loud that he had some bread or grain to give them. He enjoyed the slowly moving river. But most of all, he could not keep his attention away from that temple for long.

When Coal drove the van over there next, Slugger stood staring up at it. Even as the others started to drift away, he seemed to be nailed in place.

Coal stopped at his side. "What do you think, Slugger?"

Slugger shook his head again. "I bet I c'd be safe in a place like that. You think?"

"I bet you could, buddy. I bet you could."

Slugger looked over at Coal, and a big, warm smile lit his face. "I'm shore happy bein' up here with you an' yore family, Sarge. Man, I shore am."

Returning his smile, Coal said, "We're happy having you, my friend."

Slowly starting to nod his head, deep thoughts came into the black man's eyes. "We really are friends—ain't we, Sarge?"

"Of course."

"I mean, you didn't bring me all this way up here for nothin', right?"

"No. Why would I do that?"

"So ... You must really think I'm worth somethin' then. Some little bit."

Coal turned fully to face his friend. Slugger wasn't one to get into deep conversations like this. He had been doing a lot of thinking. "I think you're worth a lot. You sure are to me and my family. And God."

Coal didn't even know where that last comment came from. But he wasn't sorry he had added it. He himself might have forgotten God a lot of times, but God had never forgotten him—or Slugger.

Coal noticed suddenly that Slugger's eyes had gone moist. "You're a good man, Slugger. I've never been more proud to call anyone my friend."

CHAPTER THIRTY-THREE

It was a silent ride back to Savage Lane, most of it in the dark. Silent, that is, in respect to anyone in the van talking. Everyone had pretty much worn themselves out, except for Coal and Slugger, who drove and rode, respectively, and stared in quiet contemplation out the windows as the humming highway and the darkness rolled by.

The van had FM radio in it, and even a tape player and a box of tapes, so there was no lack of sound. When the radio stations all finally died, they listened all the way through *Chicago V* and Pink Floyd's *Obscured by Clouds* album before Coal had to switch over to the music of his roots. They finished out the trip listening to The Sons of the Pioneers sing *Legends of the West*.

For some time Coal had believed Slugger was asleep like everyone else in the van. He had long since traded seats with Connie so she could hold Sissy in the back, and his head was lolled over to the right, his breathing even.

"Sarge, you really think there's a place like that?"

Slugger's voice made Coal jerk in his seat and almost swear. He looked over at his friend, whose head was still turned the other way.

"What's that, buddy?"

"This song, Sarge. The song yore playin'."

Coal had been listening to the music for the last several songs only as background. Truth be told, he was barely able to stay awake himself, so he had stopped singing along quietly to the music. Now he tuned in. The song was called "Me and My Burro," and it talked about the singer meeting up with an old miner who told him he was on his "last long ride," and he was heading up to heaven—to the "Promised Land."

"You think there's such a place like that, where everyone is free, like it says in the song?"

Coal drew a deep breath, blinking his eyes to clear his vision. "Yeah, Slugger. Yeah, I do. Things will be a lot different up there than here. This is just kind of like ... Well, in a way, it's sort of like a prison. Or a war. Maybe a proving ground. I don't know what you want to call this life. But yeah, I guess proving ground is probably best. We show what we're made of, and then we move on to where things are peaceful and everybody's happy with each other."

Slugger was silent for a long time. They passed the dark and lonely looking Lemhi Store. He finally sat up straight in his seat, stared out the windshield for a while, and then, looking down at the hands folded in his lap, he said, "I'd shore like t' find a place like that."

*   *   *

Coal didn't know how his mother had managed to convince him it would be good for him to go to church with the family every Sunday, but somehow she had. He stumbled out of bed after a much too-long nap the next afternoon, seeing that everyone else seemed pretty fresh, compared to him. After all, everyone but Slugger had had at least two to three extra hours of sleep on the trip home the night before.

He stumbled into the bathroom, scratched off the dark chocolate brown of his whiskers, then got in the shower and stood there like a zombie while the water ran down him. Finally, he managed to get upstairs and put on his ugly black wool suit and a black tie, ending up looking like an undertaker by the time he was done.

They all piled in the van and headed up the road under a gray afternoon sky. When they got close to Maura's, Coal could feel Connie looking over at him. But he had no intention of stopping.

"Coal!"

He swore as they passed Maura's place.

"What?"

"You stop and go back. Maura's expecting us."

"What? Since when?"

"Since I called her this morning."

Coal pulled over to the roadside, such as it was, and let a couple of cars pass. Then he started the dangerous process of backing down the highway the one hundred feet to Maura's. Dangerous it was, but not as dangerous as continuing on to church without Maura.

He had almost made it to where he could crank the wheel and turn into her property before he said, "Mom, why did you have to call her?"

"Son. You stop acting like a brat. I wanted her to come. That's all. Her feelings would have been hurt if I didn't ask her. I think she likes it."

"Yeah, well, I guess after Friday night she probably ought to go in there and do some repenting anyway," he grumbled to himself.

"What was that?"

"Nothing," Coal said as he turned and drove into Maura's yard.

"You know something, Coal," Connie said, tight-lipped. "I heard you. And you should be ashamed of yourself. Who are you to judge someone else? You don't even have any facts."

Coal nodded, making sure his eyes didn't contact hers, which at the moment would have caused him serious burns—or worse. "Yeah, whatever. Okay. Drop it, all right? I'm sorry."

Connie grunted. She knew him well enough to know he was only sorry he had let her hear him say it.

They sat in front of the porch for ten or fifteen seconds. No one opened a door of the van, and Maura's door stayed shut as well.

"Coal." Connie's voice was low and hard. She was holding

back right now, but she wouldn't hold back later.

"What?" he snapped.

"You get out of this van and go knock on her door. You know what? I'm pretty disgusted with you right now."

And here they went again. Coal Savage, ex-Marine, ex-army prison guard, ex-FBI agent, sheriff of Lemhi County, Idaho, forty-two years old, and his mother was still keeping his man parts in her hip pocket.

With an exaggerated sigh, he threw the van in park, left it running, and got out. Before he could reach the steps, the front door opened, and Maura stepped out. She was wearing a beautiful red dress he had never seen before, with red satin trim on the bottom and a wild sprinkling of white flowers. She looked stunning.

"Good afternoon, Coal. I hear you had quite an adventure yesterday," she said as she came down the steps.

He blinked, trying to think of something to say. "Yeah, I assume you did too."

"What?"

"Nothing."

She went silent, and he opened the van door for her, then forced himself not to shut it on her foot as she got in.

Fortunately, the rest of the drive to church was short. Coal had to listen to his mother make a fool of herself making small talk while Maura pretended his demeanor hadn't hurt her feelings. He was only glad his mother still had the sense not to ask Maura where she had spent Friday night.

In church, Coal was forced into his usual place next to Maura. He tried to keep at least a few inches between them, but his maddening family shoved her from one side and him from the other until they were tightly pressed together.

When they started to sing "Nearer My God to Thee," Coal's heart melted. With the sultry voice of an angel tunneling straight into his ear, and singing about getting nearer to God, how was he supposed to stay angry? All that was left him was the deep hurt of being pushed aside—and that was his own foolish fault.

Somebody was up speaking about obedience, and then the congregation sang a song titled, "Master the Tempest is Raging," and he marveled at the sound of Maura's voice once more, performing this deep, powerful piece that swung so easily, and swiftly, between fearsome drama and overarching peace. The next speaker regaled them with all the ways to overcome temptation. By the end of the speaking, and during the singing of the peaceful "Jesus, the Very Thought of Thee," Coal was breathing a sigh of relief that no one had gotten up to speak out against profanity. The whole place would surely have come down on Coal during that one.

With the "amen" after the prayer, everyone started gathering their belongings and their families to make the mass exodus out of the chapel into an even deeper gray day than what they had left behind walking into the chapel.

Outside, the children all crowded around Coal and Maura to wait for Connie to come out. The twins were running around the parking lot, tempting fate and testing to see if God really did take care of children and fools—both of which fit his boys right then. The girls were talking, and Virgil was doing his best to imitate a tree—silent and strong.

"I hope I don't embarrass you, but you sure look nice today."

Maura's eyes snapped up to Coal's. "Wow. Thank you. Embarrass me? Shock me, maybe."

He chuckled. "Sorry. You're saying I don't give you too many compliments, huh?"

"Where'd you ever get that idea?"

"Maybe because my mother is constantly telling me that."

"Oh. I see, so I'm a test case? You're trying to see if you can turn over a new leaf?"

He rolled his eyes. "I might turn *you* over—my knee."

Maura's eyes went wide. "Ah-ho! I'd love to see you try that one! You obviously have never been in a cat fight."

"I've broken some of them up."

"Not the same thing."

"Okay, I'll give you that. Hey, how did me telling you how good you look turn into talking about cat fights anyway?"

"You think about it."

He laughed. "So I don't suppose you'd think about coming over for dinner. Or maybe you already have plans."

"I do."

"Oh. Okay. Sorry."

Connie walked up. "Are we all ready?"

Coal nodded. "Yeah, as long as the twins haven't been squished."

Connie berated him as they walked toward the van. "Coal, you of all people should know better. That isn't even funny! Wyatt! Morgan! Coal, look at them. That's dangerous."

"Oh! Dangerous, huh? You used to send me out with the double-bit ax to split firewood when I was eight years old, Mom. That thing was taller than me! You're one to talk about danger."

"You're still here, aren't you?" she countered.

"Uh-huh. And so are they," he said as the twins came running up.

Amid a little more banter, they made their way to the van and headed home. As they were nearing Maura's, Coal slowed down to make the turn.

"What are you doing?" asked Connie.

"Uhh ..." He looked down at the steering wheel, over at Maura's house, then at his mom, affecting a bewildered look. "What does it look like I'm doing? Isn't this Maura's?"

"Yes, but Maura's coming for dinner, honey."

"What?" Now stopped at the turn-off, Coal whipped around to stare at Maura. "You told me you already had plans."

"Oh, well you didn't ask me what they were."

"Oh my hell."

"Coal! It's the Sabbath!" Connie slapped his arm.

"I didn't know cussing was allowed the rest of the week."

"Stop it. Now drive home."

Coal took a deep breath, holding back a grin. "All right, Miss sealed lips, are the dogs okay? Everything set here?"

"Yep. I took care of it all before you got me."

With a bittersweet feeling inside, thinking about what his cold feet may have cost him in the long run with Maura, Coal waited for a couple of cars to pass, then pulled back out on the road and headed for Savage Lane.

They were having Maura for dinner (Coal had to hold back a laugh at the faintly cannibalistic images that phrase called up) and Deputy Jordan Peterson wasn't. A small comfort, but right now he would have to take whatever comforting thoughts he could find.

CHAPTER THIRTY-FOUR

When they got home, Coal had to look twice to prove to himself that the sixty-four Chevy was gone. He looked over at Connie. "Where's the old truck?"

His mother looked around in obvious surprise. "Umm ... Well, I don't know. I thought it was right there."

"So did I."

As if called up by their thoughts, Coal saw movement from the corner of his eye, out on the road toward the highway. Glancing that way, he saw the old pickup coming their way. "That's interesting," Coal said.

He continued on to park the van, then jumped out and met the old blue truck turning into the yard. It didn't take much looking to catch a sheepish look on the face of the driver, Slugger.

The black man got out after parking the pickup where it had been earlier, and he turned to face Coal. "Hey, Sarge. Sorry, I really needed a soda, so I borrowed the truck. I hope that's okay."

"I guess you didn't get your soda, did you?"

"What's that?"

"It's Sunday. No stores open in this neck of the woods."

Slugger laughed sheepishly. "No, you're right. I didn't get my soda. Just a pointless drive around town. But at least I got out. I hope it's okay about me takin' the truck, though."

Coal shrugged and gave his friend a grin. "Well, sure. It's not like you could ask permission. And I know how bad some cravings can be."

"Thanks," said Slugger.

Together, they all tramped into the house.

An hour or so later, everyone sat around the big table in the no man's land sprawled out between the end of the long bar dividing the kitchen and dining room and the carpet marking the beginning of the living room. Ten people, ranging in age from Connie's ancient-ness to little Sissy's innocence, ten people who had somehow become a family. Coal had to laugh inwardly when he realized how much that sounded like the opening song for *The Brady Bunch.*

The spread of food, and the aroma of it, made Coal feel almost satisfied just looking it over, on one hand. On the other hand, it made him feel like he hadn't eaten in days. Connie was always good at setting a nice table with lots of delicious food, but Coal felt like she had gone out of her way in preparing this dinner—maybe even a little over the top—and of course the reason for her to do that would be seated ominously close to his left arm. Today, he both loved and hated knowing that.

Two days earlier, Connie had concocted a fabulous beef stew, the best Coal had eaten in weeks, including Kathy MacAtee's. She had intentionally made enough for Napoleon's army so she would have enough left over to make the three huge, steaming beef pot pies that squatted tauntingly down the centerline of the table now. But that wasn't quite enough for Connie. No, she had to go and make plump, golden baking powder biscuits that could almost have been used as spare tires, and she had set out a bowl of her locally famous homemade strawberry-rhubarb jam, along with jelly made from wild Oregon grapes. Of course she had her poisonous margarine sitting there, and the lovely fresh butter Coal always picked up at the dairy because he would rather flush his head down the toilet than put his mother's Blue Bonnet on anything that had a chance of ending up in his mouth. Contrary to what the TV always told him, everything really did not "taste better with Bluebonnet on it".

To appease the health-conscious, Connie had also boiled up a bunch of broccoli, and Coal dished up a bowl of that first and downed it right away, knowing if he didn't, by the time he was finished with half a pie the broccoli was going to look and taste about as appetizing as fishy river mud.

It was about that time when Murphy and his ridiculous law stepped in.

Both dogs started raising Cain at the window, and the noise startled Coal, which was quite an accomplishment since he wasn't normally the jumpy type.

Coal leaped up, knocking his chair backward and catching it just shy of hitting the floor. Slugger was up too, along with Maura, Connie, and most of the children.

It was a brisk walk of two seconds to be standing at the picture window looking out at the yard and Lemhi Road, and Coal was in time to watch a vehicle come to a stop in the yard.

"Oh, hell. Now what?"

It was a car he knew well. It belonged to Bigfoot Monahan.

As the entire family, even Sissy, congregated at the window, with the lace curtains still drawn, they watched the giant of a man unfurl from the driver's seat. It surprised Coal to see the passenger door come open as well, depositing both Bev Monahan and their son Butch on the ground beside the car.

With nervous looks on both their faces, woman and boy moved around in front of the car, where they joined their patriarch and took on the relative appearance of white-skinned pygmies. Bev folded her arms protectively around her son's shoulders from behind, and for several seconds the three of them simply stared at the front of the house.

"Coal, what do you think is going on?" asked Connie. "I sure don't like the looks of that man."

Coal didn't reply directly to the last comment. He had seen two completely different sides of Paul Monahan. But he found it impossible to read the man's face right now. With no obvious sign of emotion on it, his countenance fell back to the natural look of a man who wanted to crush anything in his path and had the ability to do it.

"I have no idea, Mom," Coal said. "But I'd better go find out."

"Hey, Sarge," Slugger cut in. "Man, I gotta tell you somethin'."

He spoke in a tone of voice that put an alarm in Coal's head, and the look on his friend's face made it worse. As he saw the Monahan family moving with purpose toward the house out the corner of his eye, he stared at Slugger. "Oh no, buddy. What is it?"

"Well, I didn't think it was important t' tell you, but when I was drivin' into town I come upon a broke-down car in the road. I stopped to help 'cause they were right there in the lane."

"Okay ..." Coal felt leery.

Slugger indicated outside with a nod of his head. "Well, it was a different car than that, but that woman an' the boy was in it, with some older woman drivin'."

Coal almost didn't dare wait for whatever came next because Monahan had reached the bottom step up to the front door. "What happened, Slugger? Are we in for a fight?"

Bewildered, Slugger shrugged. "I don't know, Sarge. I mean, they acted kinda scared of me, but I changed their tire for 'em, 'cause they didn't have no jack, an' the older woman even thanked me an' tried t' give me some money."

A knock on the door set Dobe barking even louder until Coal said his name firmly, whereupon he stopped and went into a bold pose, with his back legs poised to shoot him forward if need be. There was no time to hear any more of Slugger's story.

With the whole family crowded up behind him, Coal reached out to open the door. Monahan had already opened the screen door, and it was resting against his back.

Much to Coal's relief, now that Monahan was up close the look in his eyes wasn't threatening. If anything, it almost looked nervous.

"Hello, Paul. What do we owe your visit to? How'd you find the place?" He immediately realized he was crowding the big man with too many questions, but the second one was the one that really had him concerned.

"Easy to ask around," replied Monahan in that deep, bear-like voice. Then he paused, as if he had forgotten why he came or suddenly didn't have the social tools to come out and say it.

"Do you want to bring your family in out of the cold for a minute?"

Monahan looked confused. His eyes flickered. Coal saw the man's tongue run across the inside of his lower lip. "Well ... I wouldn't— You mean that'd be all right?"

Inside, Coal's feeling of high alert had died almost completely down. He wasn't sure why Monahan was here, but he was sure of one thing: It wasn't to start any kind of war.

"You bet. Come on in." He told Virgil to move the dogs back, and then the whole clan backed away from the door as Monahan turned and put out a big arm, as if opening a door to invite his family inside.

Young Butch came up the steps with Bev clutching his shoulders. The woman gave Coal a shy smile as they stepped across the threshold. Monahan ducked his head a little to follow behind them, and as Coal shut the door the big man rested his hands on his wife's shoulders, giving the three of them the look of a family standing for a portrait.

"So what can we do for you folks?" asked Coal.

"Well sir ..." The big man's eyes swiveled over to find Slugger, and on his face they settled. "I reckon we really came t' see him."

"Hello, sir," said Slugger in response. "How are you doin'?"

Monahan nodded. Coal sensed nothing in the big man more than embarrassment bordering on a strange fear. He seemed to be in a situation that was completely foreign to him.

"Good. I, uh ... That is, my woman tells me they had a flat tire on the way back from town with our neighbor lady."

"Yes sir." Slugger's eyes slipped down to the faces of the woman and the boy, and he nodded. "Howdy, ma'am. Son. Nice t' see you again."

Bev gave her shy smile. The boy, unsure how to act, looked up at his father.

Monahan shifted his big feet, still gripping his wife's shoulders, perhaps a little too tight. "Well, I'm not good at stuff like this, understand. But I figgered we should come over t' ... I guess t' pay our respects an' thank ya for helpin' out. There was other cars that had drove on past 'fore you came by."

Slugger gave a tentative smile, knowing all eyes were on him now. "No problem. I was happy t' help. I couldn't see leavin' nobody stranded out there like that, an' bein' in danger o' gettin' run into."

Coal had no idea how anyone else in the room felt, but as for him, there was a huge feeling of warmth inside. This was not the kind of meeting he would have expected with Bigfoot Monahan.

"I don't know if the sheriff told you 'bout how I grew up," blurted out Monahan, breaking the silence with a burst that seemed to have taken all his strength. "Well, it don't matter. We didn't mean t' disrupt your family things, but ... Ya know, just wanted t' say thanks for stoppin'."

It shocked Coal to see Monahan's right hand leave his wife's shoulder and thrust out toward Slugger, but by the way it came out he had been trying to work up to it for a while.

Slugger's glance sliced over to Coal as if seeking guidance. Then he took a step forward, eagerly taking the big paw, offered in peace. Monahan gave the hand a good squeeze and a pump. He nodded his head, then stood there obviously hoping for a way to smoothly escape an encounter that had taken about all he had.

"Good day t' you folks," he said, glancing about at the faces of the rest of them.

With a big smile, Connie said, "Good day to you too, Mr. Monahan. It was good to see you. Come over any time."

Coal almost laughed, but only inside. Bigfoot Monahan had
come here offering an olive branch. It was vintage Connie Savage
to take it with both hands.

After the Monahans had driven away, there was only one topic
of conversation in the room for quite a while: all things Monahan.
Coal didn't say much himself. He simply sat listening to the different viewpoints, basked in the light in the faces of his family and
friends, and wondered at the strange and often surprising world in
which he lived.

Eventually, everyone settled down to eating in earnest. Slugger
couldn't stop complimenting Connie on the wonderful pie and biscuits, and he commented that maybe he really had stumbled into
some kind of paradise, or "Promised Land," as it had talked about
in the Sons of the Pioneers song.

"I declare, Miz Connie, I couldn't get much closer t' heaven
than bein' here with you folks."

"You are so welcome here, Slugger," Connie said with a warm
smile. "I imagine you miss your family, but we're happy you've
come to be a part of ours."

Slugger looked at her, nodding. He looked like he wanted to
say something, but his eyes moistened up, and he dropped his
glance to his plate, where he was moving former beef stew around
among perfect golden flakes of crust. Coal saw his friend swallow—one of those swallows a man really has to fight for because
his throat is so tight.

At last, he looked back up, and he scanned the table's occu-
pants, reaching out with his left hand to give Morgan a little
knuckle dig in the ribs, then match him giggle for giggle.

"I, uh ..." Slugger paused. He looked over at Coal for strength,
but that seemed to render him even more emotional. He took a big
breath. He looked around again. He was unable to push out the

tears swimming in his eyes, so he stopped trying. "I shore want to tell all o' you how much it's meant to me bein' up here with y'all. Yore right, ma'am—I shore do miss my folks, an' Baby, that grinnin' little brother o' mine. But I gotta say I never felt more t' home than I do when I'm here in this house. Y'all give me a kind o' hope I had stopped believin' was still in this world."

Maura reached out without warning and gave Coal's leg a squeeze under the table. She must have seen the emotion come into his eyes to match his friend's. The same ailment had overcome Connie, but she smiled at Slugger through her tears. "That is about the sweetest thing anyone has ever told me, Slugger. Thank you."

Slugger could only nod. He dropped his eyes once more to the forkful of food he had been building for the past minute or so and shoveled it into his mouth.

Coal had just done the same, taking a huge mouthful of pie in, when Wyatt turned to Maura, who sat to his right, and opened his innocent, untrained five-year-old mouth.

"Maura, where did you go in the morning yesterday? We were gonna take you to the city with us."

Over all Coal's years, he had had quite a number of interesting things come out of his nostrils. Besides the obvious unmentionables that originated in there, he had launched fun liquids such as pop, milk, and of course mundane everyday water, as well as the occasional chewed-up carrots, and once even a whole kernel of corn. But right then it was all he could do not to run an experiment on beef pot pie.

After managing to swallow his mouth-too-full of food, he glared at his plate and wished Maura wasn't between him and Wyatt, so he could give him a good hard kick under the table.

"Oh!" Maura looked down at Wyatt. "That would have been fun!" Of course she didn't elaborate, and his innocent question was left hanging out on a tender branch, waiting to be plucked.

It must have seemed overly ripe, because it tempted little

Morgan too much not to do the plucking.

"Yeah, Maura—where were you? Daddy went to find you."

Coal couldn't think clearly how many times he had ever sworn at the twins. He sincerely hoped it wasn't often. But he was pretty sure that in his head at that moment he used up about five years' worth. The last phrase went something along the lines of, *You couple of little—* And that was when the brilliant plan struck him to excuse himself and head for the bathroom. But he couldn't. When Maura looked across the table at Morgan, the supposedly innocent little fiend, and began to reply, something froze Coal in place. Here it was: the moment they had all been waiting for. And how was Maura going to squirm out of this one?

"I don't know if I should talk about it right here at the dinner table, sweetheart."

Ha! Coal frowned, bringing a hand up to scrub at his chin. *Way to skate out of it, girl.*

"But to answer your question—" Coal cringed and looked over at Connie "—I got a call on the ambulance around six o'clock. There was a wreck down by Lone Pine."

Coal and Connie's eyes were still locked together. Both of their faces went blank for a moment, but then Coal frowned. Maura's truck had been in her yard the whole time! Who was she kidding?

"Oh, hey, Coal!" Maura turned to him and barely missed catching the look with which he was spearing his mother. "That reminds me: I couldn't get Ebenezer started yesterday morning. He was cold as a fish. So I had to have Ronnie Davis pick me up in the ambulance when he came by on his way toward Lone Pine. Do you think you could help me pull that dumb thing in to Ken's again?"

Coal discovered that he had some kind of back up voice that stepped up to the plate for him and replied to Maura. That had to be the case because his normal self could not have spoken any words through the thickness of the egg all over his face. "Uh, yeah, sure. We'll do that. Excuse me for a minute, will you?"

His chair almost tipped over again as he got up to walk down the hallway to the bathroom, listening to the momentary dead silence resonating from the table behind him. He shut the bathroom door to block out the world, then stood in front of the sink, staring into the suddenly all-too-clear mirror at a blithering idiot.

Eventually, Coal had to come out of the bathroom and face his mother. He was pretty sure none of the kids or Slugger had any clue the terrible things he had been thinking about Maura, so he was fine with them. It was that death-stare from his mom that made him want to go up to bed without telling anyone good night. But eventually, he had to face the music.

Mother Nature's fortunate timing saved Coal from too much of an uncomfortable evening, for as he flushed the toilet that didn't need flushing, washed hands that didn't need washing—except perhaps to wash away whatever he could of his guilt—and started back down the hall, he heard excited voices, and as he came into sight he saw everyone in the house gathered at the front window.

"Look, Daddy! It's snowing!" came the excited cry of Katie Leigh.

And sure enough, it was a winter wonderland outside, with huge goose feathers twirling down out of heaven in apparent zero-wind conditions. The beauty of the scene punched Coal right in the heart, for in the gathering blue dusk the Christmas lights under the eaves were a-glow, and as the snowflakes tumbled gentle and fragile past them, they each had their moment of catching color from whatever light they had floated nearest to, and the visual effect was the shrapnel of a shattered rainbow whirling to the ground.

Connie had plugged in the lights on the Christmas tree as well, which she was attempting to make last clear until February—her yearly tradition—and the family was lit in a dim array of color from both sides, as if their clothing were absorbing the shards of that very same rainbow.

Maura whirled to find Coal, her eyes sparkling in the light. For that magic moment in time he was able to forget all his guilt, to wash it away in the outpouring of joy and love he read in Maura's eyes. He guessed he wasn't walking fast enough, for she came and met him halfway across the living room floor, snatching his hand and dragging him back to the picture window, where it was standing room only. Even Shadow and Dobe had crowded up and put their paws on the windowsill to see what the fuss was all about, and Virgil had knelt down and had his arm around Dobe's chest— bosom buddies who had truly discovered each other in the last short while.

"Coal ..." Maura's voice was nearly a whisper, as quiet as if they were back in church. "Look at that. Finally, huh?"

Coal smiled through the emotion welling up inside him. He let go of her hand and put his arm around her, drawing her tight against him. With his other hand, trying to go unnoticed, he jerked a thumb toward Slugger so Maura would look over at him. His buddy's eyes could not have been more full of child-like delight if he had been twenty years younger on Christmas morning. His lips were parted, and his eyes scanned the moving picture outside the window as if he could catch every snowflake, as if he could draw their magic in and hold onto it forever.

The twins were first to start clamoring about going outside, and after all these weeks of nothing in the snow department to speak of, Coal wasn't going to be the one to disappoint them. Before he knew it, everyone had caught the spirit, even Connie, and there was a mass gathering of warm coats and boots, and then a race to put them all on and see who could make the first tracks in the snow.

If Coal's heart could have gotten any warmer, it was when he saw Sissy turn to Slugger, who was the closest person to her, and put up her little arms. Slugger picked her up and hugged her, then looked over at Coal and grinned. He was the first one out the door; he didn't even bother donning a coat.

There was no traffic on Savage Lane or Lemhi Road on this

peaceful night of winter nights, so the whole family took to the road, letting the dogs run out ahead and frolic in the whiteness, now and then turning to look back and make sure their family was following, or to look skyward in wonder at the snowflakes coming down to gather on their fur.

Half an hour later, they were coming back toward the house, and Connie said, "Hey. I think everyone should stop. Would you look at that?"

And there, like a Christmas postcard through the down feathers that filled the night, the colored lights shone out from the eaves, seeming somehow magnified to be much larger than they had ever managed to be without the moisture in the air.

Still holding Sissy, Slugger walked close to Coal. "Man. That's somethin'. I never seen snow before, Sarge. Just in pictures."

"So I guess your life's complete."

Slugger grinned. "I guess it is. Thanks for bringin' me here, man." And then, with a surge of emotion, he said, "I really got me a family. And a home."

CHAPTER THIRTY-FIVE

A little later, when everyone else had gone inside to try and concentrate on *Mutual of Omaha's Wild Kingdom,* although their attention was drawn time and time again back to the picture window,
Coal drove Maura to her house to feed her animals.

Maura put two dishes of food and a bucket of water on the
porch for the dogs, although they chose to stay with her and Coal
as they threw flakes of hay out in the trampled snow to the impa-
tiently stomping Sarah, Hilly, and Brusher, and big, domineering
Homer.

"Isn't this night magical, Coal?" Maura said, dusting the hay
off her gloves by slapping them together.

He nodded. "Yeah. But I have to tell you something."

She turned and searched his eyes. "Ohhh-kay. You look pretty
serious."

"Yeah."

"Is it that bad?"

"Maybe. I feel pretty stupid."

"Well, sometimes you are, so it's okay." She grinned, but he
had a hard time smiling back at her. "Okay. Now I don't know if
I'm ready to hear this. Should I go put my pocket knife somewhere
else?"

That made him laugh, but not in too jolly of a manner. "I hope
you won't need it."

He then went on to tell her how he and Connie had planned out
Saturday, to include her in the family trip to Idaho Falls. How he
had come here in hopes of either making her breakfast or taking

her into town to a fancy meal, depending upon what their moods called for after she got over his early morning surprise. And then he told her of his shock at finding Ebenezer parked in the yard, and her bed made, but no sign of her anywhere.

That was as far as he got before he faltered. He could imagine what conclusions she would be coming to now, and he knew he had to continue, but he wanted to go on about as much as he wanted Homer to rear up and kick him in the face.

Maura nodded. "So ... Okay. Okay. Coal, why are you telling me this? Any of it? You could have just kept quiet."

"Yeah, I know. That's just not me. I owe you an apology. Whether you knew about it or not."

"I understand. So there's more. I can tell that. And I think I'm understanding now why you seemed so distant when you came to get me for church."

"Yeah."

She searched his eyes. The brightness of the snow, which had put down a little over an inch but now had nearly come to a stop, gave enough light to see her face by—which was both good and bad.

"And when you didn't find me, you thought ..."

Here was the place where ugly gray gremlins rose up inside his body and twisted his intestines into bowlines and figure eights, with a few nice fisherman's knots thrown in.

"I thought you spent the night at Jordan's."

She stared at him, her expression unchanging. He tried to keep her eyes in his, although he felt two inches tall.

Maura let out a long sigh. She folded her arms across her chest. "Okay. All right. Hey, I'm going inside for a few minutes. I'll be back, okay? I promise. I've just—" She stopped there, motioned with her hands in front of her as if patting the heads of two invisible children, turned, and went up her steps and into the house.

Coal stood in the new-fallen snow listening to the contented sound of the horses munching hay and Chewy and Dart eating their food on the porch. Of all the sounds in the world, he could hardly think of anything that gave him more comfort. But right now it did nothing. In fact, with all six of them going at the same time, and no two of them in sync with each other, the high-speed, mixed-up sound reminded him of how his heart sounded and felt right now.

It seemed a full hour, when in reality it was probably more like ten minutes, before Coal saw Maura's front door open again, and the yellow light shed a warm glow out into the snow before she shut it off, letting the dogs back inside.

By the determination in Maura's walk, Coal surmised that she had worked up a lot of gumption inside the house, and she was coming at him now like a freight train—only a little more deadly looking.

She stopped in front of him, shoving her hands down into her coat pockets. "Okay. Coal, I want to talk. I hope you'll let me ask you some pretty direct questions. I don't want to hurt your feel-ings, and you don't even have to answer if you don't feel like it. But ... Well, I guess I would probably have to assume the answers if you don't."

No matter what she asked him, his guts couldn't feel any more turmoil than they did now. It was time, as they said, to fish or cut bait.

"All right."

"All right," she echoed him. "Have you slept with Annie Price?"

Had he been at least a little bit relaxed, he would have an-swered yes, because he had, indeed, *slept* with Annie, but of course not in the way Maura meant. However, that idea never crossed his mind until later.

Instead, his answer was an adamant, "No!"

Her eyes mined for the truth in his. She nodded, drawing her shoulders up by her ears and blowing a fine cloud of steam out through pursed lips. He expected her to speak, but ten seconds went by, and she didn't. To him, that meant she wasn't convinced.

"I guess you've heard something."

She had dropped her shoulders but now brought them up even higher. "Yes. This is a really small town, you know. I'm told you've spent at least two nights with her."

Coal's first instinct was to swear, to curse the blabbing mouths that didn't have enough of their own business to tend to keep them from tending to someone else's. "That part's true."

Her mouth came open, then clamped shut. A few more moments passed. "It is?"

"It is."

"And you didn't sleep with her?"

"No."

Inside her coat pockets, Maura drew her hands closer together, an involuntary way of protecting herself from a man and whatever lies he was concocting for her.

"What kind of man does that?"

"Does what?"

"Spends a whole night with a woman that looks like Annie but doesn't do anything?"

All of the snide, off-color things he could have said instantly got thrown in the fire. His relationship with Maura had always involved a lot of teasing back and forth, but this was not the time for that.

"A man who has no clue what he wants in life, I guess."

"Coal. Listen to me. You have every right to be happy. To be satisfied. You're a man, and you're not a very old one. I'm sure you're still full of ... Well, whatever it is that men like you are full of. Testosterone or whatever. If you sleep with someone, we already decided we don't belong to each other, and I can't say one thing about it."

"Okay."

"Okay." She was the human echo tonight. "So what about Kathy MacAtee?"

This time a surge of humor rose up inside him. This really was the fifth degree. But he caught himself short of laughing.

"I haven't slept with Kathy either. She's my best friend's wife."

"Widow," corrected Maura.

"It's the same thing."

"Not even close."

He shrugged. "What do you want me to say? I haven't slept with anyone, Maura. Not a soul. Not since Laura died, and not even for a long time before that. Not even in my dreams."

Tears Coal was pretty sure Maura hadn't expected filled her eyes. She hurriedly blinked them away. "Me either."

"I'm not ready to get past what happened with Laura," Coal volunteered. He didn't expect to say it. It was as if someone else had voiced the words.

She nodded. Her chin started to quiver, but she looked away for a few seconds, fought it, and won. Looking back at him, she shrugged again but this time dropped her shoulders back down on the instant. "I guess I can't ask you to spend the night with me then."

Stunned silence filled the void between them. "Can I let you know when I ever get there?" he finally managed to say.

"That's fair. More than fair."

"I'm sorry I thought the worst about you and Jordan. I hope you can forgive me."

"I've been thinking you slept with Annie, and maybe Kathy too. How could I not forgive you, Coal?"

He shrugged and gave a little shake of his head. He felt suddenly almost giddy, with the relief that filled him to overflowing.

"Do you want to spend the night at our house?"

"I have to work tomorrow," she said in an apologetic voice.

"What time?"

"Nine."

"And you're getting to town how? Riding one of the horses?"

She laughed. "Well ... Could you take me?"

"Only if you come stay with us."

"What about the animals?"

"How many times have you left them overnight? Quit with the excuses or I'll just throw you over my shoulder and take you."

She laughed, pushing her hands deeper in her pockets as she straightened her arms.

"Okay. I won't take that challenge this time. But ... Coal, can I at least have a hug?" He caved to that request in a millisecond. "Coal?" she said into his coat.

"Yeah?"

"I want to tell you I feel happier than I've been in a long time. Thank you."

Before leaving Maura's, Coal called Connie to warn her that Maura was coming for the night, and Connie, even knowing she was going to be sharing her bed again, didn't skip a beat. *I was hoping you'd be that smart, Son. Good for you. We'll be waiting.*

He hung up and turned to Maura. She looked so incredible and vulnerable that he took her in his arms again. He held her so long Chewy and Dart started to get nervous and began prancing around them whining.

Maura giggled. "I guess it's time to go."

*   *   *

Late in the night, Coal woke without any idea of why, and he instantly thought of the snow. He crept downstairs and went to stand in front of the window and look out at the beautiful pale new world.

"Hey, Sarge." The voice from the dark made Coal whip around.

"What the hell are you doing up?"

Slugger chuckled. "I got thinkin' 'bout the snow."

"That makes two of us."

"Shore is perty. Seems like it covers up a lot o' evil stuff in the world an' makes it all looker brighter an' pertier, even if underneath it's dark and mean."

Slugger struggled off the new couch and came over by Coal, who was pondering that last statement.

"Yeah, buddy, I guess it does that. I never thought about it that way."

"An' it's white," Slugger said. "Whole time I was little I was taught that things that was white was good, an' dark things was bad. But yore family don't treat me that way. They treat me like I'm same as them."

"You are the same as they are, Slugger. You just need to find your way in the world."

Looking out at the white wonderland, Slugger slowly began to nod, and a little smile crept onto his face. "Yeah. That's true, Sarge. Yeah! I think I'm finally gonna be able to do that—all because o' you an' yore family."

CHAPTER THIRTY-SIX

Monday, January 22

The next morning, Coal and Maura rose early and got ready for work. Coal had told Maura he had something to show her before she went to work, so she called Florin Beller and asked if it would be all right if she ended up a few minutes late. To Coal's delight, the kind store owner had told her, *By all means.*

The cab of the pickup was quiet but for the hum of the road and the overworked heater fan. As a brilliant sun kissed the tops of the mountains, Coal drove out along the river toward Northfork, then made the turn there toward Montana. Sipping on hot cocoa from a thermos, they went all the way to the top of Lost Trail Pass without his giving Maura a hint what he was up to.

Just before crossing into Montana, he turned around and parked as near the road edge as he could. The sun was blinding on all the vast whiteness that blanketed the ever-receding peaks and frosted the boughs of the conifer trees. With his sunglasses on, and his heaviest coat, with two shirts under it, Coal got out and reached back to take Maura's hand, now covered in a homemade mitten. The slamming of the truck door sounded like coupling train cars in the icy universe of the vast forest.

They climbed up on the pile of snow the county plows had pushed up high on the road edge. With the end of last night's snow-fall, the temperature had plummeted, and up here in the high coun-try it couldn't have been above ten below zero. It made Coal's nostrils stick together when he breathed through his nose.

Still holding Maura's hand, he looked down at her. "What do you think?"

"Oh, wow, Coal. Just ... Wow. This is incredible. Doesn't it make you feel like there's nothing but peace in the whole world?"

"Yeah. It kind of does."

Letting go of her hand, he put his arm around her and drew her close. He felt her arm close around his back. Then he told her what Slugger had said the night before, about the white snow representing goodness and covering up all of the ugly black darkness beneath.

She stood contemplating that. "Wow. Coal, that makes me want to cry."

"Yeah. It's pretty sad. I can only imagine what that kid's been through before I knew him. And it still keeps going."

"It makes me ache for him."

"I know. I thought it would be different up here. Away from the war-protestors and the prejudice back home. But it didn't turn out much different in Salmon—except for the war-protestor part."

"I'm glad he at least doesn't have to fight that up here."

"But it's not enough. I don't know how to make his life right, even in Lemhi Valley."

"No, Coal. No, don't think that way. I've watched him light up the last few times I've been around him. I think he's going to be okay. Don't you?"

"Well, I hope so. I hope you're right."

"You know what I want?"

"What's that?"

"Next time it snows, I'd like to come up here earlier with you to watch the sun come up."

He laughed. "That was my idea today, actually. I didn't know you had to put on a gallon of makeup."

"Oh, you can stop it." She rammed him playfully with her hip.

"It's either you wait for me or you spend the morning with a troll."

"Right. Don't forget, I've seen you without makeup before. Still never saw anything resembling a troll."

"Gargoyle, troll—what's the difference?" She giggled.

"What I saw was Sleeping Beauty, so I guess beauty really is in the eye of the beholder."

"I thought you weren't trying to get me in bed. You keep talking like that and you're going to have trouble."

He laughed and squeezed her tighter. "All right, funny girl. I guess it's time to get you to work. You obviously need to have your hands occupied to keep your mind out of the gutter."

*   *   *

The radio reception never was very good in this country, due to all the high mountains around. But as they were coming down off the pass, after passing Gibbonsville but before coming to the fork in the road at North Fork, the radio began to crackle, and they could hear a woman's voice.

Coal had grown to hate the sound of both the phone and the police radio, and he had to fight to hold back a word he didn't want Maura to hear after their peaceful, wonderful morning.

He picked up the mic, held it near his mouth for a second waiting for anything further, then keyed it. "Is there traffic for the sheriff's department?"

More crackling on the radio. That started working Coal's insides into knots again, but it wasn't only that. He had been having a bad feeling all morning, and the broken radio traffic only magnified it.

At North Fork, Coal made the corner in a civilized manner but then threw caution to the wind and depressed the gas pedal farther than he knew he should.

Maura was sitting right next to him, and he felt her hand drop on his leg and squeeze it.

"Coal ..."

He looked down at the speedometer. "Sorry. Sorry, I'll slow down." He knew Maura was remembering that far-too-recent day when the two of them had gone chasing after the red Buick driven by Bud Miley until they saw it fly off the road and into the river.

The radio crackled again, but this time a voice calling the sheriff was clearer. It was Flo.

"This is the sheriff. Go ahead, Flo."

Sheriff, where are you? He told her, and she came back on. *I want you to be careful, but you need to get here as soon as you can. Have you heard the police traffic?*

Coal let out a fast, hard sigh and filled his lungs again. He didn't want to respond, because that would make Flo speak again, and she was going to say something he didn't want to hear.

Steeling himself, he depressed the mic. "No, we're just getting back in radio range. What's happening?"

It's not good. It's about your friend ... again.

"Flo. Is he all right?"

Sheriff ... I don't think so, not this time.

Maura let out one of the words Coal had been avoiding. She looked up at him, but they were going around a tight corner, and he had to let his peripheral vision handle her. "Coal, I'm so sorry."

He just nodded. He could think of nothing to say.

When they got past all the tight spots on the river road, Coal gunned it again, glad that Maura had kept him in check, yet scared to death of being too late for whatever lay ahead.

He got back on the radio and called dispatch. "Where am I going, Flo?"

Start down at the hardware store, if the police are still there.

"Is Slugger there?" He didn't really care who heard the name go across the air.

No sir, he's gone. No one knows where. Sheriff ... Do you want this all over the air?

He wasn't feeling the slightest bit official this morning. "I don't care. I don't have time to stop and make a call."

There was a fight at the lumber store ... And a stabbing.

The sound that escaped Coal came to his own ears as a mix between sigh and moan as he dropped the mic and put his hand to his forehead, massaging it and shoving his hat back on his head. Maura was furiously rubbing his thigh, but he could hardly even feel her hand. A stabbing! After all the false charges of pulling a knife, now there had really been a stabbing? The thought made Coal sick.

He heard Maura's words: "He'll be all right, Coal. Just keep holding onto hope. He'll be all right. He'll be all right."

Her chant of hope would echo in his head for days to come.

CHAPTER THIRTY-SEVEN

As Coal roared past the Shady Nook, he got back on the radio and practically yelled into it without even trying to raise Flo beforehand. "Flo! Anything new?" No answer in ten seconds. "Flo!"

Sorry, Sheriff, I was away from my radio. No, nothing new.

He switched over to the city police frequency. "Any police unit on the Lemhi Lumber call, respond. This is the sheriff."

Coal! The voice of Bob Wilson. *Hey, this is pretty bad. Your friend's gone, nobody can find where. I'm out on the road toward Challis, but I'm turning around. Meet me at the lumber store.*

Coal flew up to Lemhi Lumber and looked at Maura. When he realized he had driven right past McPherson's, the curse word that had been leaping back and forth on the tip of his tongue finally found an opening and exploded into the cab, bouncing around like a herd of ricochets.

"Hey, sorry! I forgot about work."

"It's okay. I'm going to try and call in."

"No, don't."

She grabbed his arm as he threw open the door and tried to jump out. He turned and looked at her. "What?"

"I want to stay with you, Coal. Please."

He had no time for arguments that involved bullheaded females. "Okay. All right, come on."

He jumped out, and she followed him into the store. He could hear her boot heels clicking in a near run before he realized how fast he was walking.

Joe Taylor almost ran from his office. "Coal! Judas, buddy!

Oh, hell!" He looked over at Maura and reddened. "Sorry, Miss."

Maura only shook her head in reply.

A long and too-familiar yellow snake caught Coal's eye, suspended a few feet above the floor to his left. Looking that way, he saw the yellow tape that indicated a crime scene, warning onlookers away. There was blood splattered around, even up on some boxed merchandise a couple or three feet off the floor. He realized suddenly that he had walked over other drops that led to the door.

"Joe! What happened? Where's Slugger?"

Taylor shook his head. "Man, I have no idea. It all happened so fast. I didn't even see it start."

"Did anybody else?"

"Yeah. Hey, Leo, can you come over here for a minute?"

Coal was shocked to see Leo Erickson, the aging rancher who had been like a father to his friend K.T., hobble around a corner.

"Leo saw it all," said Joe, obviously agitated and still a little shaky.

"Coal! Hey, son. Is that Negro fella a friend of yours? That's what they told me."

"He is, Leo. I brought him up here. What happened?"

"Shoot, Coal. That guy's all-out crazy. I never saw anything like it."

Leo was quite shaken as well. "Take a deep breath, my friend. I need you to tell me what you saw."

"Well, there were two guys in here, and your friend was helping them, but one of 'em spilled his coffee, I think. Now that part I didn't see."

"Okay, okay. Then what?"

"Well, both of 'em started yelling at your friend, calling him a klutz. One of 'em—I think it was the one that didn't spill his coffee—he started acting like it was all pretty funny, and he said something about how if your friend would have stayed down on the plantation picking cotton he'd be a lot safer."

Coal cringed. "Ah hell. Okay. Then what?"

"Well, that Negro fellow, he started getting pretty worked up. You know, real feisty."

"Yeah. I know."

"And he threw some insult back at those two, something about their mothers being bred to dogs or something. And he told them they could just carry their own stuff out. Well, then those two really got carried away and started shoving at your friend."

Coal could see it now. "And then Slugger pulled a knife on them, didn't he?"

"No sir! No, sir, he didn't. That was later. And it wasn't those two."

Joe Taylor was standing there looking agitated. He started to cut in, then stopped himself. "You go on, Leo. It's your story, pardner. You tell it."

Leo turned his eyes once more to Coal. "Well, it looked like to me your friend decided in the middle of everything that he didn't want a fight. It was like he just got hold of his temper and decided to get away. He tried to walk off, and they started to follow him. And then ..." Leo's eyes suddenly filled with rage, and so did his voice. "And then that damn Phil Harringer and two of his friends came in. You know him, Coal. He's the guy that put K. T. out of his job."

Coal nodded. The mere mention of Harringer's name had already turned up his level of anger. "Yeah, Leo. Yeah, I know him. Go ahead."

"Okay. Well, that's when it all really happened. I saw Joe coming in from outside, but by then it was too late. That Harringer started pushing your friend back against a shelf and told him he'd better not ever dare to raise his hand to a white man, and if he ever did then he would see what the law had to say about it. And he said something about how many people he knew and how if your friend didn't learn his place he'd be out of this valley."

Joe Taylor couldn't hold back any longer. His words exploded out of him. "Coal, I swear that knife came out of nowhere. I had no idea he was even carrying. It was just all of a sudden in his hand. I was telling Harringer and his buddies to get out of the store, and before you know it Slugger up and put that knife in him."

If Coal hadn't been wearing his heavy boots, he might have jumped straight off the floor. "Wait, Joe! *What?* Slugger stabbed *Phil Harringer?*"

"Yeah, man—right in the guts, and in the leg. Right here." He pointed at his upper thigh.

Coal put a lot of feeling into his double decker of swear words. Rubbing a hand down his face, which he knew must have gone completely white, he said, "Did he ... Is Harringer ... ?" He couldn't quite voice his thought.

"No! No, Ronnie Davis an' Jay Castillo came and got him and ran him down to Steele. They had him bound up pretty good, and when he went out on the stretcher he was yelling and screaming something fierce. He was far from dead. But man, that boy got him good!"

Coal looked over again and scanned the blood. On a flat surface, it always seemed like there was far more than there really was.

"Where'd he go, Joe? Leo?" He stabbed his eyes back and forth between them. "Where'd Slugger run off to?"

"Hell, buddy, I don't know," Taylor said. "The cops have been combing the whole town looking. It sounds like he just went up into thin air."

Coal swore again and almost turned into Maura. Her face was as white as a cloud, her arms folded across her chest. She searched Coal's eyes, but she didn't speak.

"Joe, do you think he'll come back here?"

"Ha! Hell no! Coal, that boy was running like a greyhound when he lit out of here. He's not coming back here ever. That much

I'll lay money on."

"Which way did you see him running?"

"Toward the river."

Coal nodded and turned back again to see Bob Wilson standing there behind Maura.

"Hi, Coal. Let's talk outside."

Coal and Maura followed Bob outside, and they stopped on the sidewalk. "We've covered every street in town, and the roads at least three miles out—the main ones, anyway."

"Last time he hid in a vacant building."

"Sure. Well, if he did that, he could be anywhere."

"Did he have time to grab his coat?"

Bob nodded. "Joe says he was already wearing it when the trouble started. He'd been hauling stuff outside for customers, and this cold was really sapping him."

"Yeah, I doubt he'll ever get used to this. He's only ever been in Louisiana and Nam."

Bob gave another nod. "Well, at this point I guess we can only keep driving around and stopping people to ask if they saw anything. Maybe start hitting some of the businesses and a few houses farther out."

"Yeah. Yeah, you're right. You got anyone else out?"

"Everybody else. All of the city badges, and then your boy Jordan came in too. Oh—and say, there's some officer from somewhere over by Boise. He came by to talk to you, and when this hit he jumped in on it. So we've got six guys—and now you."

"Joe said he ran toward the river, but we came in from that way—all the way from the pass. We never saw him."

"Yeah, and I think Jordan drove that stretch too."

"What about the Bar? Anybody go up there?"

"The chief did, but he said the cold's keeping everybody in, and he never really talked to anyone."

"All right. I'm going up there first. Me and Maura," he

corrected when he looked over to see her standing there hanging on every word.

They jumped back in the pickup and headed up Courthouse Drive onto the Bar. Cruising the neighborhood, Coal was seeking out empty-looking places, especially ones with sheds or garages that looked accessible even to someone without a key.

He had flagged down several cars and asked their drivers if they had seen Slugger, with no luck. The first pedestrian he spotted was an older gentleman in a wool hat with the earflaps held down by a strap under his chin. He was on his way down Fulton walking a dog.

Coal pulled over and jumped out, leaning across his hood. "Excuse me. I'm looking for a black man who might have come up here, wearing a heavy brown coat."

"Oh, yes sir! Is he a robber or somethin'?"

Coal started. "You saw him?"

"Yes, I did! What'd he do?"

"Nothing. Can you please tell me where you saw him?"

"Over there." The old man pointed toward the southwest. Coal turned to follow his finger, and he felt his face pale. The only thing that direction was the Salmon River. But it was flowing along beneath white cliffs that had to be several hundred feet high at the least.

"What was he doing?"

"Beats me. Just marchin' along, sorta. Looked real wore out. And suspicious."

"What do you mean 'suspicious'?"

"Well, he looked at me when he seen me in my yard, an' then he just made a hard left and went off that way like he just plain didn't want to be near people."

"You say you were in your yard?"

"Yes sir."

"And you saw him across the street?"

"That's right."

"What's your house number?"

"Seven-oh-one Fulton."

"How long ago did you see him?"

"Half hour? Maybe?"

"Thanks." Coal felt his heart pounding. He turned and scanned the sagebrush flats. A hundred yards away a herd of deer was grazing, and now and then one or two of them would lift their heads and perk their ears his way.

That was a lazy, relaxed herd of deer, feeding in lush, cured winter grass. But even with good forage, they were alert enough not to let Coal near them. His guess was that no one had gone past that herd of deer. They would have run.

With a sick feeling growing in his stomach, he got back in the truck and drove to seven hundred and one Fulton Street and looked to the south. The sagebrush there began to slope away. Toward the river. There was nowhere else to go—either past that herd of wary deer, or back toward town.

He turned to Maura. "You want to stay in the truck?"

"No. I want to be with you."

"This could turn ugly."

"I want to be with you."

Coal ducked his head. "All right then. Come on."

He walked across the street and into the new snow on the other side of Fulton. It took two minutes to find the fresh boot tracks—*big* tracks—heading due southeast, right toward the Salmon River.

CHAPTER THIRTY-EIGHT

Coal started walking too fast. It was easy because the snow was fresh, and there was only one set of prints besides those belonging to the deer, one dog, and a lone coyote. Those prints belonged to Slugger Janx, war hero.

Maura broke into a run, which Coal only knew because he could hear the sound of sagebrush crackling. She came alongside him and grabbed his arm, turning him partway around. "Coal, don't you think we should call for backup?"

He stared at her. "No. Not this time. Slugger's my responsibility."

"You don't know what state of mind he's in now. Coal, you've got to be extra careful."

"I've got it, Maura. If you're scared, you might want to go back to the truck."

The look she gave him back was filled with hurt, and he couldn't even apologize. To avoid facing it, he turned and started on, stepping in Slugger's tracks where he could, although Slugger was out-pacing him. Somewhere important to go.

The slope of the land and the sudden look of open air not very far ahead, and then hazy distance beyond, told Coal he had to be coming close to the cliffs. Because he could see no one around, he had a gut-wrenching feeling he might already be too late.

Coal heard a cry that seemed to explode over the tops of the sagebrush, crackling in the still, frosty air.

He whirled to see Slugger standing in stunted sage, ahead of him and Maura, but some one hundred yards to the west—upriver.

"Sarge, don't you come no closer t' me!"

It was too far away to make out the man's facial expression, but he was standing with both fists clenched at his sides. Coal couldn't see it, but he was guessing the knife was in Slugger's hand.

"Hey, buddy!" Coal called out. "What are you doing up here? You're gonna freeze your butt off." He took a few steps nearer.

"Get away, Sarge! I told you, don't come near me."

Coal turned and looked at Maura. "I really don't know if you should be here."

Maura's eyes were pleading. "I don't want you up here alone."

He shook his head. "I won't be alone. One of my brothers is here with me."

She gave him a sad smile and a little shake of her head. "But he's not in his right mind."

"You've got to go, Maura. Please."

"You're not my boss, and I'm not going to obey you. I hope you can forgive me later."

He swallowed hard and tried to stare her down. At last, he frowned. Turning, he started forward, now at a much slower pace. Nearly two inches of snow had fallen the night before, on a somewhat temperate evening, for January. It had fallen soft and a little wet, and when the temperature plummeted to where it sat now, not much over five degrees, it had turned to a hard crust. It sounded loud across the flat.

"Sargent Savage! Sir! You gotta listen to me, man! I don't want you comin' over here. Can't you see?"

Coal raised placating hands. "I came to bring you home, soldier. Stand down."

"I ain't standin' down! No! No, *sir!* I know what I done. I killed that man."

"You're wrong, buddy. You didn't kill him. You stabbed him pretty good, but he isn't dead. And he's not going to die."

Coal was within fifty yards now, and although his pace had slowed he was still moving forward. He could see the desperation in Slugger's face.

Forty yards. Still moving forward. Slugger gave out with a sob. "It don't matter, Sarge. They gon' put me in a cage. I ain't never goin' in no cage again. I know what happens in them cages."

For Coal to try and deny that Slugger would do jail time would be an outright lie. He was sure he had never lied to his friend, and he wouldn't start now. Slugger would be put on trial, most likely for aggravated battery or even attempted murder, and with his record they were going to put him in the prison in Boise. The writing was carved in the wall. Slugger had finally gone too far.

But without telling Slugger a lie, there was one thing Coal *could* guarantee: "You know that kind of thing won't happen to you in my jail. Come on. Come with me. We're brothers—remember? Brothers in arms."

Fifty feet away now. Coal could see the whites of Slugger's eyes. He couldn't be sure, because his friend's feet were still in the low brush, but he thought he was within only five or ten feet of the cliff's edge.

Slugger stood there for a long time pondering what Coal had said. Finally, a sad smile came to his face. "Yeah, Sarge. Yore right. You *are* my brother—more than any other man. I know that. But it ain't gon' help this time. Nothin' gonna help."

Coal took five more steps, and Slugger took two steps closer to the cliff.

"Hey! What are you doing, buddy? Get away from there! You know how far that is to the bottom?"

"Far enough, I reckon."

"Slugger. You don't know what you're doing. Come on back with us. See, I've got Maura with me. She's worried about you too. Come on back and be with the family. We can figure this out together."

Slugger stood still. He could have been a statue, for all his lack of movement against the windless horizon. Coal stepped closer. Fifteen easy steps. Twenty feet away. Slugger stepped closer to the cliff, and now Coal could see the edge himself. It looked so abrupt. So final.

"Hey, you know what?"

"What?"

"I haven't smoked a cigarette in a long time. But I'm kind of in the mood right now. How about you?"

Slugger thought for a moment, then nodded. "Yeah. Yeah, Sarge, that sure does sound good. You got cigs on you?"

"No, not here. Come with me to the store. We'll get some. Whatever brand you like."

Slugger frowned. "Naw. Naw, I don't need one that bad—only if you got 'em with you."

Coal's heart was racing, and the feeling almost made him nauseous. He could actually hear his pulse whipping against his eardrums. "Well, then how about this: You and I will stay right here. Don't you move an inch. And Maura will take the truck to town and get a pack and bring it back here. What kind do you want? Marlboros? That's 'where the flavor is', you know."

Coal's use of that slogan made Slugger laugh. "Naw, Sarge, that's okay. I guess I don't want no smokes. Thanks for the offer, though. Hey, man, I'm tired. I'm real tired, y' know?"

"Me too. We both need to go rest up. I'll take you back to the house for a while."

"No, I'm just tired o' this country. It don't want no part o' me, and y' know what? I guess I don't want no part of it neither."

"You'll feel better in the morning. I promise."

"No, I won't. Sarge, you know that story yore Miss Katie told me that night? The story about that there box that was really a jar? An' that perty gal that was s'posed t' keep it an' never open it, but then she did, an' all that bad stuff got out in the world?"

Coal nodded. "Yeah. Pandora's box."

"Yeah! Yeah!" For just one moment, Slugger seemed almost happy, pleased to have the woman's name recalled to him. "Pandora's box."

"What about it?"

"Well, what do you think you'd feel like if you opened up that box, an' all that bad stuff escaped, but you just knowed hope was gon' be in there, an' you was holdin' onto that hope? But when you looked down in there the box was all empty. Turned out that hope you was lookin' for wasn't in that box after all. All that bad stuff in the world, ever'where you turned, but you didn't have no hope you'd ever get out of it."

Coal allowed himself to think about it too long, and the thought was heart-wrenching. "Yeah, buddy. I guess that would be pretty bad."

"Yeah. Well, Sarge, I think I musta opened that box. I looked in it, and y' know what? There ain't no hope."

"There's always hope, buddy."

Slugger gave a sad smile. "Okay, but I think we all got our own Pandora box. We know what's in our box we was given. You seen hope in yores, but I seen an empty hole."

"Don't talk like that, Slugger. I promise you things will look better tomorrow."

Coal had worked his way now to within six feet of Slugger.

"You better stop right there, Sarge. Hey. You know what I been thinkin' on?"

"What's that?" Coal stayed where his friend had ordered him to. He was too close for screw-ups.

"I was thinkin' that in all these years I been callin' you Sarge. I never did call you by yore name."

It hit Coal that this was true. "I guess not."

"Well, I ain't in no army no more, Sarge. You care if I call you by yore name? I'd like t' hear what it sounds like when I say it."

Coal smiled. "You bet. That'd be fine with me."

"Coal. Coal." A little grin came to Slugger's face. "Man. Now that sounds real good. Coal."

Coal gave him a nod. "You know what, brother? You're right. Sounds pretty good to me too."

"I like it when you call me brother ... Coal. You know, you an' me, we been through a awful lot."

"We sure have."

"I ain't never said it to a man before—fact, I guess I never said it maybe t' nobody before, an' maybe it's gonna sound a little queer or somethin', but ..."

Slugger paused for too long, so Coal asked, "What, buddy? What's that?"

"I just kinda like t' tell you, I love you, my brother. Not in no queer way. Just like a brother." Slugger averted his eyes. The words had obviously embarrassed him.

"I don't say that much either, buddy. But I love you too." Coal glanced over and saw tears rolling down Maura's cheeks. She made no attempt to wipe them off.

Slugger followed Coal's eyes to the woman. "Hey there, Miss Maura! Don't you cry now. That makes me sad t' see. You got a good man here." He turned and looked down. From where he was, he could surely see the river, sparkling hundreds of feet below.

"Sarge—I mean Coal—you tell my mama and papa goodbye for me, will you? I'm sorry, brother, but I really gotta go now."

Coal's eyes flew wide, and he surged forward, reaching out his hand. Slugger turned and spread his arms, leaping over the side of the cliff in the graceful swan dive Coal had taught him, years ago near the city of Long Binh, South Vietnam, in the dirty Dong Nai River. Like a raven, but without wings, he plummeted toward the rolling waters of the River of No Return.

The only sound was the echoey cry of a raven, floating on the frigid air on the wings Slugger Janx needed so badly.

Coal stood frozen on the cliff's edge. Maura had slumped to her knees a little behind him in the crusted snow, her mouth wide-open and her eyes full of tears of shock.

Slugger Janx was making his way to the Promised Land, where brother loved brother, and there was no chasm between white and black.

THE END

Look next for ***BOOK 5: THUNDERBIRD***

Author's note

Oh how I wish this book were complete fiction. That all mankind truly loved each other and that we had not learned hatred for other races on which to build a story like this. But, as sure as the sun rises and sets, unreasoning hatred and prejudice are here in our world, unfortunately to stay. And of this hatred and prejudice was born the idea and the plot for this book

I don't have any big, earth-shattering thing to talk about in this author note. I will just tell you that, if you were wondering, I wrote this from the heart, from my wishes for a more loving, accepting world. The places in Louisiana are all real, right down to the descriptions of the courthouse, the Bayou LaFourche, and everything else. The smells, the sounds, and the political and racial atmosphere of the 1970's.

I am told that the hatred by citizens of this country for returning Vietnam War veterans ran as high as sixty percent in some areas, and of course in the south the prejudice and hatred of black people by whites is legend. It was a double-barrel shotgun for returning vets of color. Insurmountable prejudice at its most extreme. Slugger Janx is a fictional character, but representative of so many real vets who were came home to face this kind of hatred, when so many had felt like they would come home heroes, as had soldiers in wars of the past.

Yes, I wish this story was simple fiction, but it is not. For many, this kind of life was reality, and there was nowhere for them to turn. They were not wanted in Vietnam, and they were not wanted in the United States, and in time they really were forced to wonder: Was there any country where they could truly belong?

For those of you who picked up on and tried to stick with the little stories within the book that may have seemed to die away, never fear. I keep careful track of my sub-plots. You will read in future novels of Maura's fight to keep her sons, and of Annie's plight to hang onto her sanity. And we are not finished by any means with Kathy MacAtee. You will not be left hanging, so "hang" in there.

A special thanks to my cover model, whom I will introduce only as Jackson because I cannot pronounce nor write his real Nigerian name, and because Jackson is the name with which he introduced himself to me on a warm evening as he strolled the city of Pocatello and I walked my rounds on duty.

About the Author

Kirby Frank Jonas was born in 1965 in Bozeman, Montana. His earliest memories are of living seven miles outside of town in a wide crack in the mountains known as Bear Canyon. At that time it was a remote and lonely place, but a place where a boy with an imagination could grow and nurture his mind, body and soul.

From Montana, the Jonas family moved almost as far across the country as they could go, to Broad Run, Virginia, to a place that, although not as deep in the timbered mountains as Bear Canyon was every bit as remote—Roland Farm. Once again, young Jonas spent his time mostly alone, or with his older brother, if he was not in school. Jonas learned to hike with his mother, fish with his father, and to dodge an unruly horse.

Jonas moved to Shelley, Idaho, in 1971, and from that time forth, with the exception of a few sojourns elsewhere, he became an Idahoan. Jonas attended all twelve years of school in Shelley, graduating in 1983. In the sixth grade, he penned his first novel, *The Tumbleweed,* and in high school he wrote his second, *The Vigilante.* It was also during this time that he first became acquainted with Salmon, Idaho, staying toward the end of the road at the Golden Boulder Orchard and taking his first steps to manhood.

Jonas has lived in six cities in France, in Mesa, Arizona, and explored the United States extensively. He has fought fires for the Bureau of Land Management in five western states and carried a gun on his hip in three different jobs.

In 1987, Jonas met his wife-to-be, Debbie Chatterton, and in 1989 took her to the altar. Over some rough and rocky roads they have traveled, and across some raging rivers that have at times threatened to draw them under, but they survived, and with four beautiful children to show for it: Cheyenne, Jacob, Clay and Matthew.

Jonas has been employed as a Wells Fargo armored guard, a wildland firefighter, a security guard for California Plant Protection and Inter-Con, and police officer. He is now retired after almost twenty-four years of proud employment as a municipal firefighter for the city of Pocatello, Idaho, and works full-time job as a private security officer guarding the federal courthouse under contract with the security company Paragon.

One of Jonas's greatest joys in life is watching his second son, Clay, become a recognized writer of much talent in his own chosen field, that of fantasy and science fiction, with his current series *The Descendants of Light*. There is no greater compliment a son could give to his father than to follow in his footsteps.

Books by Kirby Jonas

Season of the Vigilante, Book One: The Bloody Season
Season of the Vigilante, Book Two: Season's End
The Dansing Star
Legend of the Tumbleweed
Lady Winchester
The Devil's Blood (combination of the *Season of the Vigilante*
novels)
The Devil's Blood (The Trilogy)
    Season of Doom
    The Bloody Season
    Season's End
The Secret of Two Hawks
Knight of the Ribbons
Drygulch to Destiny
Samuel's Angel
The Night of My Hanging (and other Short Stories)
Russet
Rusted Fence and Broken Cowboys (Poetry collection 1)
Lying in Wait to Lie in Rhyme (Poetry collection 2)
Windfall
Tenn Rhoades to Hell
A Final Song for Grace
Jinx: A Novel of the Great Depression

High Warning series
A Wilder Heart
The Wilder Legend
Wild and Blue

Savage Law series
Law of the Lemhi, Part 1
Law of the Lemhi, Part 2
River of Death
Lockdown for Lockwood
Like a Man Without a Country
Thunderbird
Savage Alliance
Dark Badger
Morgan Rose
Bar None
The Old Broken Heart
Woman of the River

Gray Eagle series
The Fledgling
Flight of the Fledgling
Wings on the Wind
Death of an Eagle

The Badlands series
Yaqui Gold (co-author Clint Walker)
Canyon of the Haunted Shadows (co-author Clint Walker)

Legends West series
Disciples of the Wind (co-author Jamie Jonas)
Reapers of the Wind (co-author Jamie Jonas)

Lehi's Dream series
Nephi Was My Friend
The Faith of a Man
A Land Called Bountiful

Books on audio tape

The Dansing Star, narrated by James Drury, *"The Virginian"*
Death of an Eagle, narrated by James Drury
Legend of the Tumbleweed, narrated by James Drury
Lady Winchester, narrated by James Drury
Yaqui Gold, narrated by Gene Engene
The Secret of Two Hawks, narrated by Kevin Foley
Knight of the Ribbons, narrated by Rusty Nelson
Drygulch to Destiny, narrated by Kirby Jonas

To order autographed books, go to www.kirbyfjonas.com or write to:

Howling Wolf Publishing
1611 City Creek Road
Pocatello ID 83204

Or send email to: pocatellocowboy@gmail.com